About the Author

Debra's a Yorkshire lass through and through, whose passion from an early age was to cycle and walk in the beautiful Yorkshire countryside. In her late teens, she fell in love with the Lake District, especially the Langdale Valley, and hopes that one day she'll be able to live there.

Of course, coming from Halifax and living across the road from the Rowntree Mackintosh factory (now Nestlé), Debra was destined to have a sweet tooth. Cycles and walks always involved chocolate of some sort, a Yorkie Bar, Toffee Crisp, or a couple of Quality Street chocolates, but Debra's also quite partial to Cadbury's Dairy Milk.

In the late 1990s, Debra moved from Yorkshire to Scotland. Life continued to include walking, cycling, and chocolate, but in 2005, along came Scotsman Jim, who fell in love with Debra's gentle Yorkshire accent, and they became Mr and Mrs.

Debra still lives in Scotland with her husband and their Border Collie, eating chocolate, walking, and cycling, but she continues to take regular trips down to Yorkshire to see her children and grandchildren.

Debra still dreams of living in the Lake District.

Books by Debra Murphy

The Magical Tearoom on the Hill

Beatrix The Time Travelling Collie

Beatrix

The Time Travelling Collie

Debra Murphy

Published in 2023 by Lawers Publishing

This Edition Published in 2024

ISBN Paperback: 978-1-8382830-8-7
ISBN Ebook: 978-1-8382830-4-9
ISBN Audiobook: 978-1-8382830-6-3

A CIP catalogue copy of this book can be found in the British Library.

Illustrations by Jessica Leech at The Ricketty Desk

Photographs and images copyright Debra Murphy
Typesetting and design by Debra Murphy

For further information about this book, please contact the author at:
https://mothermurphys.co.uk/

For Derek,

This book is dedicated to Beatrix,
a very special Border Collie, and my best friend,
who inspired me to tell her story.

Enjoy these magical tales,

[illegible]

x

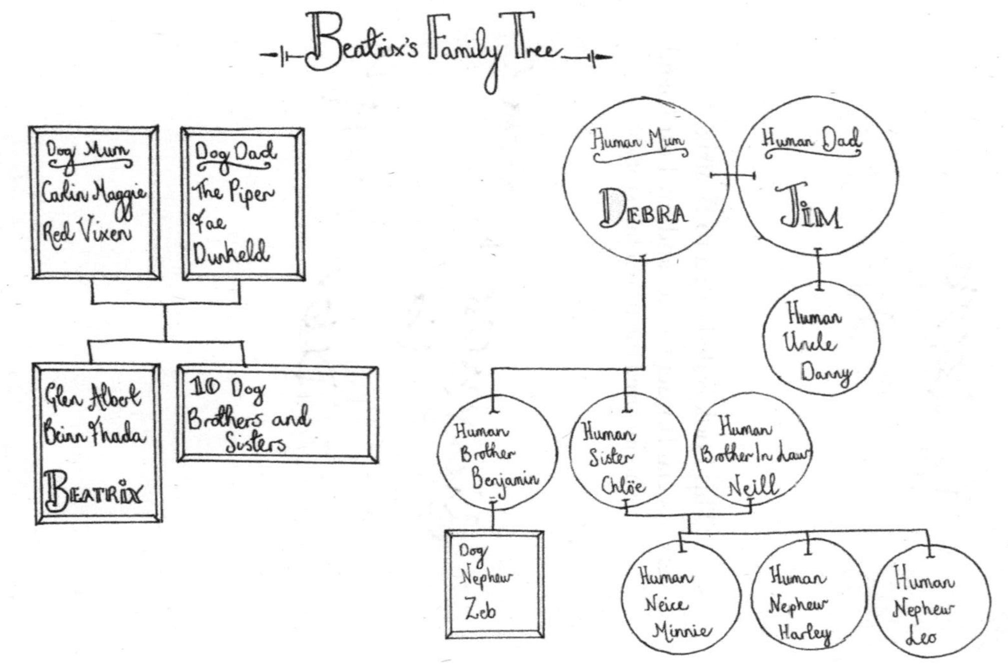
Beatrix's Family Tree
Dog Mum
Calin Maggie
Red Vixen
Dog Dad
The Piper
fae
Dunkeld
Glen Albert
Beinn Fhada
BEATRIX
10 Dog
Brothers and
Sisters
Human Mum
DEBRA
Human Dad
JIM
Human
Uncle
Danny
Human
Brother
Benjamin
Human
Sister
Chlöe
Human
Brother In Law
Neill
Dog
Nephew
Zeb
Human
Neice
Minnie
Human
Nephew
Harley
Human
Nephew
Leo

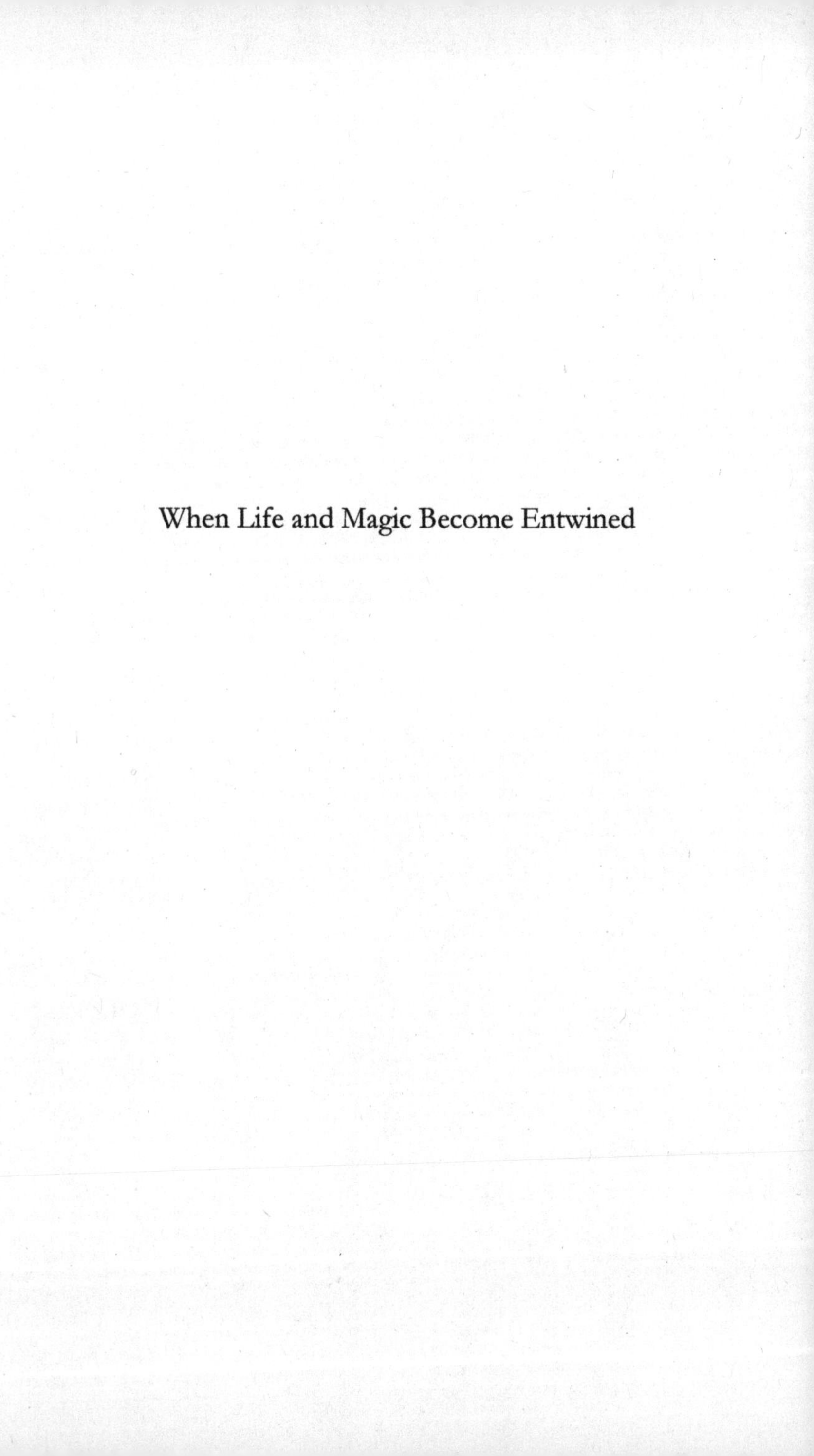

When Life and Magic Become Entwined

Part 1
Becoming Beatrix

Prologue

Then, just as I was about to catch my tail,
Mummy sprang over to me, knocking me to the floor
"Stop, Beinn Fhada," she yelled.
"Don't you dare do that. Not yet."

In the small town of Kirkintilloch, nestled below the Campsie Fells, a Yorkshire-born girl was recovering from surgery. Unable to walk to the end of her street, she felt her life was slowly slipping away, and feared she would never again feel energised enough to go cycling and walking the hills she loved. But somewhere deep within her tired, weary mind, a gentle, quiet voice whispered,

"The dog is waiting for you, and you will smile once more with her."

Here are some stories of an incredibly special Border Collie who began her life as Beinn Fhada, or to give her full name, Glenalbert Beinn Fhada. As she left her farmhouse and dog family to start a new life with Debra and Jim, she became Beatrix, the human dog.

From the beginning, strange coincidences make this story magical. Once Debra had stopped ignoring and began to listen to the quiet voice in her head, she could visualise a black and white Border Collie, a female and one she would call Beatrix, after the author, Beatrix Potter.

Debra had always been in awe of Beatrix Potter and the wonderful children's stories she wrote.

Beinn Fhada, the puppy, was born on a farm in Dalguise, just north of Dunkeld in Scotland. Was it by coincidence that Beatrix Potter stayed at Dalguise House every year with her family from the age of four, in the same village where Beinn Fhada was born?

Then there's the equally odd fact that this little black and white Collie's kennel club name was that of a Munro, Beinn Fhada. Debra was an outdoor girl, who loved being on the hills and had already started to tackle the more accessible Scottish Munro mountains.

What follows is the tale of a tiny black-and-white bundle of fluff, who turned out to be Debra's lifesaver, in more ways than you could ever imagine. She grew up alongside Debra, walking slowly beside her as Debra recovered physically and mentally. She snuggled up to Debra when she was weary, showering her with unconditional love, and they quickly became best friends. Soul mates even.

Together they had many adventures, and Debra knew that this was an extraordinarily special dog, who it would seem had convinced herself she was a human.

These stories are a combination of memories from Beatrix and Debra. Beatrix tells the stories, and Debra always does the typing as Beatrix couldn't get her paws to work the tiny keys on the laptop. Perhaps one day, somebody will create a bark recognition software package for other dogs to tell their stories.

As Debra began to write down and read out the tales of their adventures, some scary, some funny, and some downright frightening, Beatrix re-told the stories to Debra from her memories, which were often very different tales.

Beatrix also revealed some of the mystical secret adventures she had when she regularly left the comfort of the home she shared with her humans.

Get comfortable and read more about this fantastic dog.

Chapter 1

Dalguise, Perthshire

27 January 2013

The snow was deep in the valley, the bitter north wind howling fiercely around the farmyard. There is no prettier place than the Highlands of Scotland in the middle of a snowstorm, but it's not for the faint-hearted.

In the large, but well-sheltered barn across from the farmhouse, a large male Border Collie, The Piper Fae Dunkeld, was pacing the floor as his partner, Carlin Maggie Red Vixen, weathered the storm and endured, without complaint, a long, slow labour. Over the next few hours, he watched with pride, admiration and love as the tired mother safely delivered eleven perfect Border Collie puppies.

Let's begin this magical story by peeping into the first few hours of the story through the eyes of that one little female puppy.

"What's happening? I was so warm and cosy where I was. Now I've been forced out into the cold. So many strange smells. I can't get my eyes to open. And the cold. It's so cold. It's all so frightening. Where are you, Mummy?"

I was one of eleven puppies born that night during a wild snowstorm. I wasn't the largest, but nowhere near the smallest; I was the only girl in the litter. Over the next few weeks, my brothers and I all settled into a routine. Each day we discovered new talents. Gradually we were all able to see, a great relief! And it was lovely to see Mummy, after only being able to smell her for what seemed ages. But the most fantastic thing to happen when I was about three weeks old was that my ears started working. Things were a bit muffled at first, but slowly it was as if somebody had washed my ears out, and all the grit that was stopping them from working, had dissolved. Now I can hear anything. Sometimes it's great to hear all the different sounds, but other times it's pretty frightening, like if it's thundering outside or the farmer is using his noisy machinery. Just as it was wonderful to be able to see Mummy for the first time, it was fantastic to be able to hear her voice. She has a lovely, gentle voice, and I could listen to her all day.

Once we'd all gained sight and hearing, we quickly found our feet and spent our days and nights running around the barn, playing tig, fighting, sleeping and, of course, snuggling up to Mummy to get lots of milk and cuddles.

I was in awe of Mummy. The way she controlled all eleven of us was terrific, but most of all, I could feel the all-encompassing love she gave, equally and freely, to us all.

I was often the butt of my brothers' jokes. They laughed at me for wanting to join in with their games, telling me I was just a girl. But I showed them. I was the only one able to jump up to the high beams in the barn and could weave in and out of my brothers far too quickly for them to catch me.

Our ever-tolerant mummy would watch over our games and only interfere if things got out of hand, or too rough. Sometimes one of the boys would nip my ankles a bit too hard, even making them bleed on occasions. Quick as a flash, Mummy was in amongst them, letting the boys know they were out of order and showing me how to keep my wounds clean. But there was no mollycoddling. It was like Mummy wanted to make us strong and capable of looking after ourselves.

There was one incident that both confused and frightened me, involving a discussion I never forgot. One day I felt a little bored, and the boys didn't want me to play with them. I thought I'd make up my own game and I would chase my tail to amuse myself. I was enjoying it and getting up quite a speed as I started to spin around, making the straw on the barn floor fly all around me. I was having great fun, and even the boys had stopped their games to watch me.

Then, just as I was about to catch my tail, Mummy sprang over to me, knocking me to the floor.

"Stop, Beinn Fhada," she yelled. "Don't you dare do that. Not yet."

To say I was taken by surprise is an understatement. I couldn't understand it as I'd seen the boys doing this so many times, and Mummy had watched them all, allowing them to make a mess and smiling when they yelped as they nipped their tails.

"But why, Mummy? Why can the boys chase their tails, and you won't let me?" I asked.

Mummy sat beside me, allowing me to snuggle up to her and began to explain.

"You don't know this, but you're an incredibly special Border Collie. You mustn't chase your tail until you're older. In the future, everything will become clearer, and you'll know exactly when the time is right for you to chase and catch your tail."

"I don't understand it, Mummy. Tell me why," I begged.

"I can't. It's just how it is. It was the same for me, and now it's the same for you. You will know when that day has arrived. You will also know when the time is right for you to talk of this with another chosen Border Collie puppy," Mummy said, smiling at me. "But you must promise me you'll never talk of this conversation with your brothers or anyone else."

And in that very moment, I understood, and felt Mummy's immense love for me, and thought my heart would burst.

As you can imagine, I thought about this conversation many times over the years, but kept my promise to Mummy never to discuss it with anyone else.

Over the next few weeks, Mummy would sit all her puppies down after dinner and teach us how to clean ourselves. She showed us how to keep our bits of white fur looking pure white.

"You know, children," laughed Mummy. "This skill is something humans can never do with their clothes, despite all their expensive soap powders and automatic washing machines."

She explained how well-mannered puppies don't go to the toilet near their food or their sleeping areas, (gross!) and that we must always respect and help each other.

Looking serious, Mummy told us, "Remember, children, one of the most useful things you must learn in the human world is to give your head a little tilt and look at humans out of the side of your eyes."

We all tried this, and I must admit, we did look cute. Mummy smiled, telling us that the silly humans can't resist this look, and that it will get us just about everything we want, and may even get us out of trouble.

Mummy told us many tales about humans and how they need the help of dogs. Sometimes they need help to control their silly sheep, but often it's the humans who really need the support themselves.

She taught us about love, loyalty, and trust, and how we have to give these things with all our hearts, and then humans would learn to return the same love, loyalty and trust.

What was clear from these lessons was that Mummy was enormously proud to be a Border Collie, and made sure that we understood just how special we were.

"Children, some dogs talk all day and all night long. They never stop. It's so rude and so annoying. Humans don't like dogs who talk all the time. It's the small dogs that seem to do it. They need to make up for being tiny by trying to have loud voices. Remember, Border Collies only talk when there's something important to say. If you talk all the time, humans stop listening."

"There's one more thing I want to tell you," Mummy said. "Most humans are too silly to be able to understand dogs. But sometimes, you find a clever one who you can talk to and who will understand and talk back to you. If you find one of these humans, they're worth their weight in gold and need to be treasured."

A couple of weeks passed, and two of my brothers were taken away from the barn. Mummy was sad, and I think I even saw her crying when she thought I wasn't looking.

Snuggling up to her, I whispered, "Where have my two brothers gone, Mummy?"

Wiping away her tears, Mummy called all her remaining children, "Come and sit with me a while."

With us all sitting around her, Mummy said, in a shaky voice, "My dear children, two of your brothers have been chosen to live as human dogs. I'm immensely proud because this shows I've brought you up so well that others can benefit from having you around."

The boys all glanced at each other, then at me, and back to Mummy. I wondered if they all felt the same as I did. I wasn't sure I liked the sound of what Mummy was telling us. Did it mean I'd have to leave the warm, cosy barn one day? Surely, I wouldn't need to leave my mummy. Surely Mummy wouldn't let me go away.

But one April morning, I overheard the boys talking.

"They're coming to meet her today. Only a girl will do."

As I joined the chatter, the boys went quiet and huddled around me, playfully hitting, and nuzzling me. Odd, very odd.

I flopped myself down next to Mummy. "What's up with the boys today? They're acting a bit strange."

Mummy explained quietly, "Remember, Beinn Fhada, I've already told you that you're a very special puppy, and before too long, some humans will be coming to meet you to see if you can help them in their lives."

"But I don't want to go away. Please don't let anyone take me away," I cried.

Mummy nuzzled me into her thick, warm coat. "Hush now, there will soon be a different family for you with a new human mummy and daddy. They'll give you a new name but will take care of you and love you just as much as

I do. It's just the way it is. Puppies can't live with their dog mummy forever. I'm getting old, and one day I'll have to take my journey over the dog rainbow bridge. But remember, Beinn Fhada, my love for you will last forever. Call my name whenever you need me, close your eyes, and you'll feel my love surround you. One day, when the time comes, you will need to travel over the rainbow bridge. I'll be waiting for you, and I'll call your name. Until then, enjoy every day of your life, and be the best you can be at everything you do."

I wasn't sure I understood all this, but I knew that if Mummy was prepared to let me go, I must be brave and do whatever she told me to do.

Chapter 2

Becoming Beatrix

13 April 2013

The snow had disappeared, and the green hills around us were beginning to re-appear. A bitter, icy wind still blew around the farmyard when I poked my head through the gate at the front of the barn, but there was something different today. I could sense it, just a feeling.

As I lay with my nose resting on the cold, metal gate, I saw a big black car coming slowly up the farm road, and watched as two humans climbed out, before they disappeared into the farmhouse. I noticed Mummy's ears were pricked up, and she was pacing the floor. I also noticed with some alarm that she wouldn't look at me. But I could smell something different about her today; not a strong odour, but one I hadn't noticed before.

"Boys, what's that smell around Mummy today?" I asked.

"It's fear, you silly girl; Mummy's scared," whispered one of the boys. "It happens every time humans come and take one of her children away."

The farmer's wife brought the two humans down to the barn, and they lent on the gate, looking at us. All the boys were clambering up the metal gate to get to them, to get a cuddle and a stroke. The man stroked all the boys and smiled at them, but thc lady just stood there. She was looking at me, and only me. I didn't know what it was, but I had this feeling. Peering from behind the boys, I watched this lady and cocked my head to the side (as Mummy had taught me). Then I saw it. A tear gently rolled down the lady's face. It was only a little one. I watched as she quickly wiped it away. The lady seemed to watch me as closely as I watched her. She gave a little smile, just enough for me to see, and then she stretched out her arms to me. The boys tried to jump up into her arms, but it wasn't them this lady wanted to hold. It was me. Step aside, boys.

Within a couple of minutes, the lady had hold of me. There was a comforting smell about her which I liked, even though I didn't know her. Then all the humans made their way back into the farmhouse, the lady still holding me, leaving the bemused boys behind.

The farmhouse seemed warm after the cold barn where I'd spent all my life. Logs were crackling on the open fire, and I was amazed at the flames jumping around. There was a lovely smell of food cooking on the stove, and my tummy rumbled. It was so cosy in there, but I was slightly alarmed to see a lamb curled up in a box next to the fire and wondered if they would start training me to be a sheepdog. But the lamb looked at me, giving me a knowing smile.

The humans let me play on the floor, but I wanted to be up on this lady's knee. I nuzzled up to her leg, and she bent down to pick me up again. She seemed so friendly and safe. I wondered if she tasted as lovely as she smelt, so I gently licked her hand. The lady giggled and held me close to her chest. I thought she must have liked that, and she didn't taste too bad, so I licked her face. The lady didn't seem so keen on that but didn't push me away.

Everything seemed to happen quickly after that, and we were now going towards the black car. I didn't feel ready and wanted my mummy. I realised with horror that this must be my day to go to live with the humans.

"Mummy, Mummy," I shouted.

Fear began to rise from the bottom of my tummy, and I saw Mummy standing by the barn.

"It's time, little one," said Mummy gently. "This is your new mummy and daddy. They need you. Take care of them, protect them with all your heart, and in time they'll love you as much as I love you."

I wasn't entirely sure if it was the wind making Mummy's eyes water or whether she was crying.

"Stop, stop. I'm not ready to go," I cried aloud.

But then I thought to myself, oh, hang on. What's this? The car smelt strange. Strange, but nice. And it was warm. The wind didn't come through the windows the same as it howled through the metal gate in the barn.

I heard a click. What was that? There was something around the lady. It was holding her in the car.

Then we were moving. Backwards. Then forwards. Then backwards and forwards again. I wondered if this man knew how to work the car. Was I safe in here? But this lady was holding me tightly. It was so lovely. I could feel her breath on me. I swear I could hear her heart beating through her coat.

Oh my, I never realised what a glorious place I lived in. There were magnificent hills all around, full of colour. I'd never been so far outside the farmyard.

I glanced back as Mummy and my remaining brothers faded away into the distance. Even Daddy, who never spent much time in the barn with us, was now standing alongside Mummy. I could see that Mummy was resting her head on Daddy. With a jolt of shock, I realised I was now a human dog.

Heck! It was hot in the car, and I felt a bit strange, but not in a good way. The car went up and down, and the road was so twisty.

"Stop, stop. Let me out. Something's happening." I cried.

But it was too late, and I couldn't help it. I watched with horror as my breakfast shot out of my mouth and landed all over this lady. Oh, the smell! It was terrible. I felt mortified.

"I'm sorry, lady," I sobbed.

"It's OK, don't worry about it," the lady said, but I did notice her face wasn't saying that.

"I can wash my clothes and wipe the gear stick when we get home," she said.

Home? Where would that be? I wondered.

Hang on one minute, I thought to myself. Mummy said that some humans are clever enough to talk to dogs. This lady must be one of those. Wow. I've found a human made from gold. This lady can understand me, and I can understand her.

I sighed with relief as the lady opened the car windows a little, and I could now breathe with proper air coming back into the car.

I think I'll lie here and cuddle the lady. I didn't feel so bad now, but oh no! That feeling. It was happening again.

This time the lady held me at arms' length as I was sick down her legs and shoes. That same rotten smell filled the car.

I wondered if I'd really eaten that, but I thought I might try and eat it again.

"No, no!" the two humans shouted together.

Rule number one, I made a mental note to myself, human dogs must not eat their own sick. It seemed a bit unreasonable, but it didn't taste all that nice the second time round, so I could live with that rule.

Now the car was going much faster. The road was less bumpy, and there were no twisty ups and downs.

"I've never been so grateful to reach a dual carriageway," the man said with a sigh.

I was so tired. I needed a little sleep. But Mummy said I had to look after these humans. Gosh, I was so tired, and my eyes kept closing. But oh my! That smell was still here. I thought if I could rest my head, I could take a nap. Not for long, mind. I could close my eyes for five minutes.

I was awakened with a start by a sudden silence. The engine had stopped, and the car was now still.

"Come along, Beatrix," said the lady. "Let's show you to your new home."

Beatrix? Who's she talking to? I wondered. What was it that Mummy said?

"You will have a new mummy and daddy, and they will give you a new name."

These humans must be my new mummy and daddy, and Beatrix must be my new name. I tried it out.

"Beatrix, Beatrix, Beatrix, Beatrix," I shouted.

It sounded OK to me, and I felt pleased with the sound of my new name. And this new mummy and daddy didn't seem so bad.

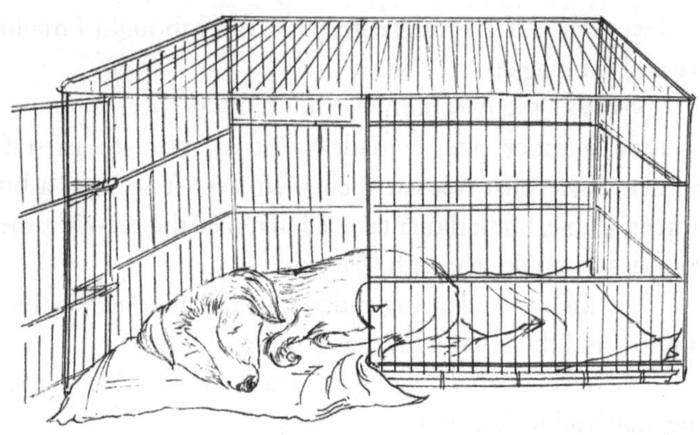

Chapter 3

The Crate

That first day away from the barn was so strange. The humans (whom I will now call Mummy and Daddy) took me inside and told me this was my new home. Mummy put me down carefully on the floor in the spacious room.

Oh yes, I liked it at once. It was so quiet. No other animals were running around, and the ground was so soft. Much softer than the straw in the barn. There were so many new smells, which were all lovely, and I realised I could quickly get used to this new home.

But my tummy was bursting now. What was it my dog mummy taught me?

"Don't go to the toilet near your food or where you sleep."

Right, I'll squeeze my way behind this big seat. It smells like an excellent place to have as my toilet spot. There's no food and certainly no bed back here. So here goes.

"No! Not there!" shouted both my new mummy and daddy together.

Heck, what was all that commotion about? I was picked up and practically thrown out into the garden before I could even start to do my business. Once I'd finished, I was lifted straight back inside the house.

"Oh, but I wanted to smell that grass out there," I cried. It was so different from the farm. There were scents from other animals, but I didn't recognise them.

Back inside, I could run around, lick and sniff everything. There were different smells but no other animal scents in here. There were objects to run around, and Mummy gave me a couple of things to play with. There were so many smells, things to lick and new sounds. It was like a wonderland to me.

They showed me a big bowl with water in it. Wow. A bit different from my usual water. No straw was floating in it, and I had no brothers to fight with to get to the bowl. I tried a little sip. It was OK. It tasted clean and fresh, but I do like flavoured water. The water in the barn always seemed to have something in it to add flavour to it. This water was plain. But I didn't tell Mummy and Daddy what I thought. That would not be polite.

I sat down and looked at Mummy and Daddy. They were smiling at me. I began to think that I was already making them happy.

"Beatrix, come and try out your new bed," said Mummy.

She put me on this fluffy, soft, padded bed.

"Is this really mine?" I gasped.

I looked around. There was nobody else to share it with. Mummy and Daddy were too big, so they wouldn't want it. I stepped on it. Nice. Very nice. I put all my four paws on it and lay down. I felt like I was sinking into it. It was so soft.

Oh, I was so tired again. I thought I'd close my eyes for a minute. Mummy was stroking me.

"That's nice. I think I'll have a nap. Just a little one," I whispered.

I must have slept for quite a while as I'd drooled down my face and onto the bed. I was embarrassed, but nobody seemed to care.

It was such a long day. I explored, sniffed, licked, jumped, played, and had something to eat. I was even becoming used to being picked up and taken outside whenever I wanted to go to the toilet.

I was enjoying my day, but I couldn't help but think of my dog mummy and daddy back at the farm. Were they missing me? Were my brothers missing me? I knew I had to be brave as this was my new life, but I'm so sad now.

I snuggled up to my new mummy, and she stroked me, talking in a lovely soothing voice, just like my dog mummy. I could listen to her voice all day. I felt a little guilty that in a home full of love, I still had that sad feeling deep in my stomach, but I couldn't help it. I realised then that I needed to accept that change has to happen, and force myself to look forward to the future, rather than simply missing my past life. Perhaps this is what growing up is all about.

During the day, Mummy and Daddy kept putting me into a crate, which wasn't too bad. It was soft on the floor, there was a drink in it, and I could get back out of it if I wanted to.

Later that night, once it had gone dark, they put me in the crate and closed the door.

"What's happening? Why are you locking me in here? What have I done wrong? What did I do?" I asked.

Then it was all quiet. Mummy and Daddy had disappeared.

"No! Come back, please. I'm frightened," I cried. "My dog mummy never left me alone at night."

Where have they gone? Will they be coming back? I need the toilet. Well, OK, I did need the toilet. Oh no! I've done it next to the water. I'm so ashamed of myself.

"If you come back, I'll try harder. Please," I cried.

But nobody came. I cried out for my dog family. Suddenly, the light came on, and my new mummy ran down the stairs.

"Phew, thank goodness for that. You came back," I sobbed.

Mummy opened the crate and took me out, sitting on the floor with me, stroking and talking in her lovely, soothing voice.

"It's OK, Beatrix, don't be scared. Mummy and Daddy are just upstairs," she whispered to me.

It wasn't OK. I was scared. But now Mummy's back, I'll be OK.

Oh no! She's locked me back in the crate. Mummy's going upstairs again. At least it wasn't dark this time as she left the light on for me, but I was scared here all by myself. I started crying again.

After what seemed like hours, Mummy came back again. She sat a little longer with me before putting me back in the crate. I was so tired now. I could try a sleep - just a little one.

Where am I? Where's Mummy and Daddy? Help. I'm all wet and smelly. Oh, it's not dark anymore. I can see light peeping through the curtains. It must be morning. That wasn't too bad, I thought to myself. I'd survived my first night in my new home as a human dog.

During the day, things were great. Mummy never said anything about the mess I had made in the crate. She just put a clean sheet in the bottom, and nice fresh water in the bowl for me. Mummy didn't put me in the crate, but the door was left open, so I crept in several times. It smelt so lovely and fresh now, and I must admit to having a little nap in there.

Today I nearly got the hang of doing my business outside. It did mean almost getting thrown out of the door sometimes by Mummy or Daddy when they saw me doing that circling thing. The steps out of that back door are so big, and I can't manage to climb down them all by myself.

Being outside is great. There's grass to play on, and I can sniff everything around the garden. It's so different from the barn I came from, but it's OK, and I'm surprised at how easily I'm adjusting to my new life.

Do you know what the best thing about today was? I realised that I didn't have to share my dinner with anyone. Mummy put my food down, and it was all for me. No brothers to push me out of the way, leaving me with the leftovers. I felt stuffed by the time I'd eaten my lunch, so much so, that I had to nap on the lovely soft rug that Mummy and Daddy had given me.

It quickly became my routine; something to eat, a drink, a play on the rug, a quick run outside to do my business, and then back inside for a sleep.

Night-time fell again, and I suppose it wasn't a total surprise that I was put back in the crate and the door closed. I cried a little, but Mummy and Daddy still went up the stairs. I wonder what's up there.

Once again, it was all quiet and dark. I was a little bit scared and cried out for Mummy again. She came and checked on me.

"It's OK, Beatrix, go to sleep," she said gently. She didn't open the crate but stroked me through the door.

"OK, Mummy. I am tired; I'll try and have a sleep," I said.

Heck. That was quick. It's light again. Mummy's come back. I suppose this crate thing's not so bad. It's cosy, quiet, clean, and dry, and Mummy always comes back for me.

The next few days flew by in a blur. I've learned so many new things. I now sit at the kitchen door when I want to do my business, and I hardly have any accidents inside. Mummy and Daddy said I'm a clever dog for learning things quickly. I've even got my favourite spot outside for doing my you-know-what.

There are plenty of cuddles, giggles, food, drink, and heaps of fun. Life with my new mummy and daddy is simply perfect.

Change is not always such a bad thing.

Chapter 4

Tiny Steps with Mummy

As I adjusted to being a human dog, I became more aware of things around me, especially Mummy and Daddy. Mummy seemed tired most of the time, and often lay down on the couch. I liked lying beside the sofa near her so she could stroke me. She seemed to like that, and I could see that it made her smile when I was next to her. Daddy is fun and always takes me out to play in the garden. He's particularly good at football. Mummy isn't.

I didn't go out of the garden for what seemed like years, but then one day, Mummy announced,

"It's time for your first trip to the vet Beatrix. Then we can start having some exciting trips out."

"Oh, that sounds fun. What happens at the vet place?" I asked.

Mummy was a bit vague, but said, "It's nothing to worry about. It'll be fine."

Her fake smile didn't convince me. You know what I mean. When somebody smiles, but the smile doesn't quite reach their eyes. Something was going to happen at this vet place, and I didn't feel very good about this.

Before I knew it, I was all alone in the back of the black car, but I wanted to sit on Mummy's knee like the last time.

"I'm sorry for being sick over you and the gear stick, Mummy. Please let me sit on your knee again," I screamed and cried, trying to climb over the seats to get to Mummy and Daddy.

"Calm down, Beatrix," said Mummy. "It's OK; we'll be there soon. Lie down."

Lie down! Lie down! How could I lie down with the car wiggling about all over the place? It felt like I was being thrown all over the back of the car, and before I knew it, I'd been sick and had been to the toilet. Oh, the shame. I cried and cried until the car stopped, and Mummy gently lifted me out.

"Don't cry, Beatrix," Mummy said. "It's OK. Let me clean you up."

I was so embarrassed but pleased that Mummy didn't seem cross at all with me for being sick and going to the toilet in the car again.

It was very noisy out of the car. Cars were whizzing around all over the place, and there were so many humans. As I sniffed the air, I couldn't recognise the different scents. I decided I preferred it in my garden and house where there's just me, and Mummy and Daddy. I might even like to be back in the car.

Mummy carried me to the vet place. "Wow," I said. "This place is amazing. And the smell. It's fantastic. I can smell food. Where is it? Can I have some?"

"Not this time Beatrix. Next time you'll be able to," Mummy replied with a little laugh.

I like this vet place. As we waited at the counter, I met some new lady humans who were lovely. They tickled me and said how cute I was (and I wasn't even doing that head-tilting thing). They gave me a couple of little biscuits.

We went through another door, and there was a different human there. Mummy said she was the vet. She seemed nice, but she took me out of my mummy's safe arms and put me on a large, cold table. The lady felt me all over, prodding and poking me, which I thought was rude, given that the lady didn't even know me. Then she stabbed me in my neck.

"Ouch! That hurt," I cried out. "Help! Save me! Oh, don't worry Mummy, she's got more biscuits for me. It's OK."

The lady stroked me as I ate the biscuits, and she didn't stab me again. It was only a little stab. The vet place is really not too bad a place to visit.

Then we had to get back in that horrible car. I cried and cried all the way home. I was sick again, but once we were home, I could play in the garden, and I felt much better.

"Now that you've had your injection, we can take you for a walk to see the world," Mummy told me.

Over the next few weeks, I was taken out for little walks many times during the day. Sometimes Mummy came with us, but often she was just too tired. Mummy or Daddy always tied a long thing around my neck, and they held onto the other end so I couldn't run away (not that I had any intentions of doing that, of course).

I saw many new things on those walks, met new humans and new dogs, and there were so many different things to sniff and lick. I didn't need to do my business in the back garden as I had a whole new world to do this in. It's a bit strange, as Mummy and Daddy watch me all the time, and they pick up anything I do and put it in a bag. Strange humans! But if that's what they like to do, I guess it's OK.

I got so excited when I saw new humans and dogs and wanted to jump up at them. Mummy and Daddy told me off about that and made me sit down. Mind you, when I sat down, I got a biscuit. Sometimes I still forget. It's just so exciting to meet new friends. I see lots of dogs running around without being fastened to their humans. I wonder if I'll ever be able to do that.

I soon realised that when we went for a walk with Mummy, we had to go slowly. Sometimes, Daddy had to ask her a few times before she would agree to come for a walk with us. When I went to Mum and nudged her, she always smiled and said,

"OK Beatrix, let's go for a walk then."

As the weeks went by, I noticed that my little legs were getting longer and more muscular, my paws didn't seem quite so ridiculously large anymore, and I could walk further without feeling so tired. At the same time, Mummy was getting stronger, and didn't lie down on the couch as much. Mummy started to take me for longer and longer walks, and she was getting faster at walking too.

Then one day, Mummy said, "I'm ready to take Beatrix out by myself." And that was it. Mummy and I became walking buddies.

As I became more confident and listened to what Mummy and Daddy said, they would let me off the lead in the park or in the wood.

It was amazing. I never went too far from Mummy and Daddy though, as I didn't want them to get lost. I like walking with Mummy. We have some great chats, and she's always teaching me new things. I know that when she says sit, stay, come, down, and stuff like that, I get a biscuit. Who knew how easy it was to get humans to give you treats?

But then there are trips out to the park with Daddy. My daddy's great. He always has a tennis ball in his pocket, or we take a giant football. He spends hours throwing the ball to me. I'm proud of my Collie-herding skills. I can run right around the park to retrieve the ball. I do that lying on my tummy thing, and everyone says I've got 'the eye'. It's a skill most Collies are born with. We're not skilled at herding sheep by barking, making lots of noise and running around all over the place. No, not at all; we give them 'the eye'. You could say that we intimidate sheep by staring at them and silently commanding them to move where we want them to go. Mind you, I've heard that you sometimes need to give the silly sheep a little nip of their ankles to get them to move in the direction you want them to go.

In my new life, I don't have any sheep to herd, but I can do that with Mummy and Daddy and any other humans that want to get involved. I can stare at them and get them to throw a ball. And if they don't get the ball, I stare at them, then at the ball, then back at them. They can't ignore 'the eye'. Honest, it works. You should try it. I bet I'd have been a great sheepdog.

Now I have the best of both worlds - Mummy's full of energy, thanks to my love, cuddles, and slow walks. Walks are getting longer, and we have such fun. Between the walks I have with Mum, I play with Daddy and my ball in the park.

What more does a dog need?

Chapter 5

Rescuing Mummy from the Rottweiler

"Come on, Beatrix," shouted Mummy from the kitchen. "Shall we go for a walk in the park?"

Do I want to go out? I didn't need to be asked twice and was at the back door before Mummy had time to get her shoes on.

"Don't forget the biscuits for me, and bags for my you-know-what. I'm bursting, so you may need a few bags," I said.

Mummy always fills her pockets with little treats for me and has little black bags to pick up anything I do. It's a bit embarrassing, and I wish she'd look away as I do what I need to do, but as I've already told you, she insists on watching me and then picking it up. Humans can be a bit bizarre. Mind you, not every human does the picking up bit, and it gets a bit messy and smelly on the grass sometimes. I'm already learning to tell which of my dog friends have been out before me by the mess I can smell.

The park we go to is just behind our house, and it's great. There's so much space to run around and no motor cars to stress Mummy. You see, I'm quite partial to chasing cars and motorbikes, but I get into serious trouble when I do.

In the park, there are usually plenty of friends to chat with, chase, and to fight with over a ball or two. Some of the dogs are large and some are small, but mostly they're all good fun, except for that German Shepherd who tried to eat me a couple of weeks ago, so we keep our distance from him now. The humans are not too bad either, as most of them have biscuit pockets, and if I do that cute sitting thing next to them, I get a treat or two.

Today was different, however. Nobody else was in the park, so I had to play with Mummy. But I do like it when it's just the two of us. A bit of quality time with Mummy is always good. She is my best friend (but don't tell Daddy I said that).

"Right Mummy, come on, take that lead off me so I can run around."

But Mummy had stopped walking and was pulling my lead tight. I could hardly breathe.

I looked up at Mummy. She had a strange look on her face.

"What's wrong Mummy?" I gasped. But she didn't speak. She just stood there looking towards the far end of the park. Was she worried about something? I could sense something different about her. There was a bit of a strange aura around her, and I could smell something. Somewhere in my memory, I could remember that smell. What was it? Then I remembered what the boys had told me when I could smell something on my dog mummy, *"It's fear, you silly girl; Mummy's scared."*

Fear. That's it. Mummy is scared. But what's scaring her? I looked around. The only thing I could see was a dog and a human at the bottom of the park. I've never seen that dog before. It seemed OK to me. There was nothing to be scared of there.

"Oh no!" Mummy whispered. I think she was nearly crying and was pulling me on the lead. "Come on, Beatrix, let's go this way."

It's the dog. That's what's scaring Mummy. Is it going to hurt her? I need to protect Mummy. It's my job to keep my mummy safe. I did the one thing I could think of and began barking and growling at the dog. Mummy stood motionless, waiting for the dog and the lady to leave the park. I could sense that Mummy was still scared, so I kept barking and barking to show that nasty dog that I was guarding my mummy, and it couldn't come near her.

At last, the dog and lady did leave the park. My barking saved Mummy. I'm such a brave dog. Mummy seemed a bit better then, and finally let me off my lead for a run-around.

By the time we got home, Daddy was in the house.

"There was a huge Rottweiler in the park off its lead," gasped Mummy. "I was so scared and didn't know what to do. Dogs like that shouldn't be allowed in the park off the lead. What if it had come over to us? The owner would never be able to stop it from hurting us. Rottweilers are so vicious. Beatrix went wild when she saw it, and started barking and pulling on the lead until the owner left the park with her dog," Mummy sputtered. She still sounded like she was nearly crying.

I knew it. It was the dog that had scared Mummy. Well, at least it didn't come near us because I barked. I kept my mummy safe.

For a long time, I did the same thing every time we saw that vicious dog, and I kept Mummy safe. It was a bit strange, because the more we saw them, the closer Mummy would go to them. I kept barking and pulling on the lead, but Mummy kept going closer to them. She even started to talk to the lady. I could sense that the fear was still there, so I kept barking to protect her from the nasty dog. I must be doing an excellent job because the dog never came near us or barked at us.

Then one day, we went for a walk in the wood. I'd left Mummy walking on the path, and I was running around off the lead. It's great in the wood, as there as so many things to smell. There are deer, squirrels, and all different sticks and stones to play with.

Oh no, I thought to myself. As I looked around, I could see that nasty dog walking towards Mummy. But Mummy was talking to the lady and actually standing next to the dog. I was barking and barking as usual, but Mummy was telling me to stop. I didn't know what to do.

The lady was holding out a biscuit for me. I looked at Mummy, and she said, "Sit nicely, Beatrix."

Then you wouldn't believe what happened next. Mummy walked through the wood alongside the lady, and that dog was walking between them. It wasn't even on the lead. And the dog didn't eat Mummy.

It turns out that the dog is called Sally, and she's really nice. She smiles at me when I bark at her, which makes me feel silly. But I must bark because that keeps Mummy safe from Sally the Rottweiler.

I learned a big lesson from Sally. We should never prejudge someone by how they appear. If you look deeper, the person may be quite different from what you expect. My mummy assumed that the Rottweiler she saw at the other end of the park was a vicious dog, when in reality, Sally the Rottweiler is the calmest, friendliest, and most obedient dog you could ever hope to meet.

Sally tolerated me barking and jumping at her repeatedly. She never reacted, other than to smile and kept on walking. I feel a bit foolish about the whole thing now.

Once I'd got to know Sally the Rottweiler, I realised she was getting old and not as well as she could be. She often complained of sore hips and knees, but still never barked. Sadly, not long after I became good friends with her, Sally had to go over the rainbow bridge, where all dogs go eventually. I hope that if she were still here, she would laugh at my story about her, and how silly I was before I knew how adorable she was.

Chapter 6

The Train

It took me a little while to adjust to travelling in the car, and I don't mind admitting that I hated it at first. OK, I was terrified. I was sick and did a poo a couple of times. But now, I absolutely love the car. Long journeys, short trips, I don't mind. Car journeys usually mean we're going somewhere exciting.

It was not long after I'd realised the absolute joy of being driven around on our different adventures that Mummy announced,

"I think it's time we introduced Beatrix to the train."

"Do you think she's ready?" asked Daddy.

My ears pricked up. The train, what's that? I wondered. It must be something special if I need to be ready for it, I thought. Is it a thing? A human? Another animal, or a place?

"Now that she loves the car, we could drive to Croy and get the train to Edinburgh," said Mummy, rubbing my ears.

"We could make a picnic to have in Princes Street Gardens. That way, Beatrix can run around, do what she needs to do, and then we can enjoy lunch in the gardens."

Even though I still didn't know what the train was, I was up for it if it involved a picnic and a run-around.

The next day Mummy beckoned me to the car. "Come on, Beatrix, we're off on a train ride."

"What actually is a train?" I asked, jumping into the car.

"It's great. You'll see. You'll find it a bit noisy at first, but you'll get used to it," replied Mummy.

I was a bit nervous as I'm not a massive fan of noisy things, but if Mummy said it was OK, then I guessed it would be.

Daddy drove us to the station car park.

"This is Croy Station, Beatrix," Mummy said, as she opened the car's back door, and fastened my lead onto me. "Have a good sniff around, as there's plenty of time before the train arrives. You need to remember this is the station where you get off the train to come home."

"Debra! Beatrix is never going to travel on the train by herself," laughed Daddy. "Just leave her in peace and stop stressing her."

"You never know what might happen. You scoffed at me when I taught Beatrix to cross the road at the pelican crossing, and to wait for the green man," snapped Mummy. "It's the same thing. Just as waiting for the green man might save her life if she tries to cross the road herself, knowing Croy Station is her place to get off the train, might help her to get home one day."

Mummy and Daddy always have these discussions, which usually end with Daddy's eyebrows raising, and Mummy rolling her eyes. But they're the best of friends really, I'm sure.

We left the car in the car park. I wasn't happy. Did this mean we were not going on an adventure?

We walked up the hill and over a little bridge, before stopping at a patch of lovely grass. I don't know about you, but I like to do my business on grass. I hate having to go on the road or pavement.

I remember one day being out with my human brother Benjamin and his dog, Alfie, or Al as we all called him, in a lovely little village in Yorkshire called Horton in Ribblesdale. Al did a great big poo right in the middle of the pavement. I was disgusted with him.

"What are you doing?" I cried.

"Don't be such a prude," Al laughed. "The humans always pick up our poo. It's like a special treat for them."

I'm still not convinced and prefer to go somewhere private if I can. By the way, I never saw Al again after that!

"Come on, Beatrix, do what you need to do," said Mummy. "You'll have a long time on the train, and there's nowhere to go to the toilet once we are on it."

I took my time sniffing each blade of grass and finding my perfect spot; then I did a big wee and another. And I did a little poo just to be sure I wasn't taken short on the train thing, whatever it was.

As we walked down a winding path, Daddy asked, "Have you got hold of her lead tightly?"

"Of course. Do you think I'm stupid? I know she's going to be frightened when she sees her first train," said Mummy crossly.

"Oh, Mummy. I'm scared now. You're both making me nervous. I don't think I want to see the train anymore," I cried. Tears started to roll down my face.

"It's OK, stay calm. Do you see that yellow line?" asked Mummy.

"Yes," I whimpered.

"Well, you must make sure you wait behind the yellow line at all times, until it's time to get on the train," said Mummy.

"But what about all those stones down there by those metal lines? Can't I get one to play with?" I asked eagerly. I can't resist stones. There were stones everywhere. This train thing was turning out to be a bit of an adventure.

"No!" Mummy shouted. "You must never, ever go onto the train lines. When the train comes down the track, it will be fast and noisy, but sit next to me and don't move. The first train that comes won't stop here, and it will speed past us, making a loud noise, and if you're not behind the yellow line, you could get caught in the wind that the train makes and find yourself dragged onto the track and under the train."

"Oh my," I gasped. "That doesn't sound very good. I'll stay right next to you and not move, I promise."

"Then there'll be another train going to a place called Alloa," said Mummy, holding my lead so tightly I could hardly breathe. "This train always arrives a couple of minutes before the Edinburgh Train. This train will stop, the doors will open, and people may get on or off the train. Ignore this train and the people."

"You're giving her too much information," said Daddy. "Look how nervous she is now."

Then suddenly, I could hear this rumbling sound in the distance. It got louder and louder, growling, but unlike any animal I'd ever heard.

"This is the fast train," said Mummy, bending down next to me, pulling my lead even tighter.

Mummy was right. The train came zooming towards us, with two big eyes looking at us. I was terrified and tried to hide behind Mummy.

The train roared as it passed us, and I could feel the gust of wind that Mummy mentioned.

"Wow," I exclaimed. "Just think how strong that gust of wind would be if you didn't stand behind the yellow line."

"Exactly," said Mummy. "So, you've seen your first train. It's not so bad, is it? Remember, the next one is not our train. Listen for the announcement telling you where the train is going."

Then a voice in the air said that the next train was for Alloa. Mummy must be psychic, knowing what the voice would say. I did exactly as Mummy told me to and waited behind the yellow line for the train to stop. There was a beeping sound before the doors opened, and humans seemed to come out from nowhere, but I ignored them. The train's doors closed again like magic, and the train set off.

I wasn't sure I wanted to get on a train now, but a voice in the air said, "The next train is for Edinburgh Waverley."

"This is ours, Beatrix. Wait for the door to open, then jump over the gap onto the train."

"OK," I whispered. But when that next train arrived and the doors opened, I saw the huge gap and the big drop down to the stones and metal lines; I froze.

"Jump Beatrix," Mummy urged as she tried to get on the train. But I couldn't do it. I was scared.

Bending down, Mummy picked me up in her strong arms, and we both got on the train, with Daddy following us.

As Mummy put me down, she just about dropped me. I looked around the train. It wasn't so bad. There were so many different smells, dogs, humans, and other strange odours, and to my delight, food. I heard the beeping noise, and the doors closed behind us. It felt all wobbly for a minute as the train started to move.

Mummy tried to sit on one of the little seats in our bit of the train, but I wanted to get closer to the food. I could see lots of humans further along in the train, and humans always have food.

"Come on, Mummy. Let's say hello to everyone," I said, pulling her behind me.

It felt strange on the train, like it was swaying from side to side. Every so often, the voice in the air (who must have got on the train with us) said things like, "The next stop is Falkirk High." I wondered if the voice thought everyone would forget which train it was, because the voice kept repeating that this was the Scotrail train to Edinburgh.

But the best thing about the train was that all the humans wanted to stroke me.

"Oh, would you look at that lovely dog. It's so cute. Is it a sheepdog? Is it a boy or a girl? Can I clap her?" asked one of them.

"Why does she want to give me a round of applause?" I whispered.

Mummy laughed. "She wants to stroke you. That's what she means by clapping you."

Humans and their silly sayings. But I did that cute puppy dog eye trick throughout the train journey, and I was stroked and tickled many times.

The train stopped a few times. There was a beeping noise, and the doors opened with a whooshing sound, letting some humans get on and off. I kept an eye on Mummy to see if I needed to help her to get off the train, but she never moved from her seat until the voice told us we were approaching Edinburgh Waverley.

"Come on Beatrix. This is our stop. Wait nicely for the doors to open, then carefully jump across the gap onto the platform," Mummy told me. "Do you think you'll be able to jump this time, or do you need me to lift you again," she asked.

"No," I said, puffing out my chest. "I think I've watched enough humans jumping onto the platform on their two long legs to know that if they can do it, I'm sure a clever Border Collie like me can do it too," I replied indignantly.

The train shuddered and groaned, then stopped. Mummy waited for the light to flash on the button, then she pressed it, and the doors whooshed open.

I panicked but remembered what Mummy had said about not looking down. I jumped and pulled Mummy out of the train, and we were in a different station, much bigger than Croy. I swear there must have been a million humans and so many trains. It was both fantastic and terrifying at the same time. Of course, I had to sniff everywhere. There were so many new benches, posts, steps, and floors to smell.

Before I knew it, we were out of the station and into the open air. There were loads of cars and buses, and the air was too smelly for my liking.

We stopped at one of those pelican crossing things and waited for the green light to flash. It was like a trick. The light flashed, the cars and buses stopped, and lots of humans swarmed across the road. Some humans nearly bumped into me because they were looking at their phones instead of where they were going.

"Let's go straight into Princes Street Gardens to the grass so that Beatrix can go to the toilet," said Mummy.

"Good idea," I whispered. "Now you've mentioned the toilet; I'm bursting."

Mummy and Daddy found an excellent patch of grass. It was huge, almost like a field. I sniffed around to find my perfect spot.

"Come on Beatrix. Do you have to sniff every blade of grass before you decide where to go?" groaned Mummy.

"Well, actually, yes, I do. How do I know what I'm standing on and who else has been to the toilet there before me if I don't sniff everywhere?" I asked, looking up at Mummy.

With my business done, it was playtime. Mummy took my lead off me and allowed me to run around, chasing the ball. Daddy always has a ball in his pocket. He is just the best daddy ever.

"Right, time for lunch," announced Mummy.

Daddy and I didn't wait for Mummy to ask us twice. The ball is good, but food is better.

And there, in the quiet, relaxing gardens, only a few minutes away from the busy, noisy, smelly station, we had a lovely picnic: roast ham, cheese, crisps, and some water. Mummy and Daddy had tea from their flask. I was so tired that I even had a little snooze. It's exhausting learning about trains and being around so many new humans.

"Back to the station now," said Mummy, packing up all the picnic bits; not that there was much food left to pack away. Mummy and Daddy always pick up all the papers and rubbish and don't leave it on the ground. Mummy says we should leave nothing but footsteps when we're out. It's a pity other mummies don't teach their little humans that!

Then it was back across the pelican crossing, watching out for the clumsy humans. We were soon back at the train station. It was so busy and noisy, and oh, the smells; it was like sensory overload. And none of it was pleasant.

"This is our train coming. It's the Glasgow Queen Street train, but you must make sure it stops at Croy, where we'll get off," Mummy told me, holding tightly onto my lead once more.

"Look Mummy. Those humans are standing past the yellow line. Are they stupid? Do they want to fall under the train?" I asked in amazement.

"Exactly! You concentrate on keeping yourself safe and ignore what other people are doing, said Mummy."

I could hardly think straight. The noise was hurting my delicate ears. Daddy wears a hearing aid, and he sometimes has to turn it off in noisy places. I wish I could turn my hearing off right now.

"The train's coming," Mummy said.

And our train came groaning and whirring to a stop in front of us. There was that bleeping noise, and the doors opened.

"Oh no. It's too crowded. I can't see the step Mummy," I cried.

"Step aside and let all these people get off the train. You don't need to rush, and you don't need to pull to be the first onto the train. Have some manners Beatrix."

"But I do. It's so that I can make sure it's safe for you and Daddy," I muttered.

The panic was over, and we were soon on the train again. There were not so many humans this time, and we went further into the carriage.

"Come and sit under the table Beatrix," said Mummy. "The trolley needs to come past."

It was a bit of a squeeze getting under the table with Mummy and Daddy's legs and the post from the table, but I managed it just in time before this metal thing on wheels came past. Wow, I thought. That would take the tail off any dog. But it wasn't such a bad metal thing because Mummy and Daddy could get drinks from it and a little biscuit, which I shared with Daddy. Mind you; I kept my paws and tail out of its way when it trundled back up the carriage.

During the journey, the voice in the air was back and kept telling us that this was the Glasgow Queen Street train. The voice also said the train would stop at Haymarket, Linlithgow, Falkirk High, Croy and Glasgow Queen Street.

"Croy. That's our stop," I said excitedly, recognising the sound.

Smiling at me, Mummy turned to Daddy, "Look, she already knows where we're going."

That voice in the air never shuts up. All the way back, it kept saying the same things over and over again. I was still worried I wouldn't know precisely where to get off. I knew the sound of Croy, but I still had to learn the different sounds and smells.

Every time the train slowed down at a station, the sounds changed, and I could feel how the train was moving: fast, slow, bumpy, and even jerky. At each station, the light on the button flashed and had a bleeping noise, and the doors opened with that whooshing sound, letting new smells and sounds into the train.

Finally, I heard the voice in the air announce that the next stop would be Croy. I looked up at Mummy and Daddy, watching as they put on their coats and picked up their backpacks. It was time to go.

"Come on Mummy. We need to get to the door."

I pulled Mummy forward and stood with my nose almost touching the door. I could feel the train slowing down and drawing to a halt. As I watched for the flashing light, and listened for the bleeping sound, I waited for Mummy to press the button. She told me to keep calm and to remember my manners. I want to be a well-mannered dog, but I can't see the point of Mummy telling me to wait my turn at the door. I have to be the first to get off the train to make sure it's safe for everyone.

At last, the doors opened. I took a deep breath to take in the smell of Croy Station. I was pretty sure that if I were ever on the train by myself, I'd be able to recognise the sounds and smells to tell me I was at Croy Station.

It was a relief to jump across the gap from the train to the platform and breathe fresh air. Trains and cars are OK, but you can't beat being in the open air.

Once I'd had my first experience with train travel and had overcome my fear of the noise, and the gap between the platform and the train, and learned to resist the stones down by the metal lines, I could relax and enjoy our train journeys. I now believe that trains are even better than cars. There's lots of room and food under nearly every seat, and all the humans want to stroke your coat.

We go on trains quite often now. I think I'm the luckiest dog ever because when I tell my dog friends in the park about my train adventures, some of them don't even know what a train is.

I've been on train trips that have been great fun, but I've also been on some that have been quite awful. One of these journeys was coming back from a place called London. My human brother, Benjamin, was living there, and we were going to join him to celebrate Christmas.

"Beatrix, you're going to the capital city of London," Mummy announced one day. "We have to catch our usual train from Croy into Glasgow Queen Street, but then we have to walk through the city centre to Glasgow Central Station."

"Oh no. I hate walking through Glasgow. It's so busy with humans who walk into me all the time. They all seem in such a rush. There are too many sounds and smells for me. It's horrible," I moaned.

"I know what you mean," said Mummy. "But it should be quiet today as we're going early. We'll take you for a little walk on some grass when we get to Glasgow. Make sure you do everything you need to do, as it's a long journey from Glasgow to London."

I was so looking forward to it as I saw the purple box on wheels was coming with us, but I didn't see Daddy making up a picnic.

"Why are we not taking a picnic on the train if it's a long journey?" I asked.

Mummy laughed. "Well, today we're travelling by something called First Class. As it's your first long journey, I decided you needed to be comfortable. The good thing about First Class is that we all get drinks and food during the journey, so we don't need a picnic. We will, of course, have some treats for you, but we don't want you to have too much to eat or drink as there's nowhere for you to go to the toilet on the train," explained Mummy.

And we were off. As I'd expected, we took the car to Croy, got the train to Glasgow Queen Street, and began the short walk to Glasgow Central Station. Mummy was right; there were very few humans in Glasgow. As promised, I was allowed to play on the grass next to a big river. I wanted to go in the water, but Mummy said no. Something about nobody should swim in the Clyde.

We then headed to a new station for me, Glasgow Central. This is a massive station with a high roof. I'm not sure if it's the same for humans, but it was awful for me and my acute hearing. All the noises (and so many of them) seemed to merge and echo around the station. And, of course, there were a whole host of new smells.

"That's our train, London Euston," said Mummy.

We made our way down the platform along this colossal train. There was something different about this one. It appeared important, and it was so long. I could jump up easily onto the train once Mummy had found our carriage.

"Wow Mummy. It does feel posh in here. Look how much space there is between the tables. I don't think I need to worry about getting my tail trodden on by clumsy humans or that trolley thing," I said as I sniffed around the train.

"That's right," said Mummy smiling. "Sometimes we just need to feel special, and your first long train journey is one of those times."

Well, I got myself comfortable under the table and before long, the train was off, and I was sleepy. Just as I was nodding off, a smart-looking man stopped at our table.

"Would you like something to eat?" he asked Mummy and Daddy.

"Two sausage sandwiches, and two cups of tea please," replied Daddy.

This train was getting better all the time. I popped my head out from under the table and did that puppy dog eye thing at the man.

"Well, would you look at you? How cute are you and so well-behaved. Would you like a sausage?" the man asked, stroking my head.

I tell you; you don't get that sort of treatment on the train to Croy.

Once I'd eaten my sausage, I had a long, relaxing sleep, waking only when the voice in the air said,

"The next stop is London Euston."

I want to tell you some incredible tales of how wonderful London was, but it wasn't very pleasant. I thought Glasgow and Edinburgh were busy places, but they seem like villages compared to London. There were humans, cars, buses, vans, and bikes everywhere. The noise. The smells. Oh, how I hated it. The only good thing was that we could see Benjamin for a few days.

When the holiday was over, it was time to go back on the train. Only we didn't have posh seats on the way back. This train was jam-packed with humans and their big boxes on wheels. It wasn't just that we didn't have posh seats; Mummy and Daddy didn't have any seats at all, because something had gone wrong with the booking system. We were standing in the door area, and humans were pushing us. I thought I would get squashed under a box on wheels until Daddy lost his cool a bit.

"Will you all show a bit of common sense and stop shoving? We have a dog here who's frightened by your stupid behaviour. There's no point in trying to get us out of the way as we have nowhere to go. Do not push any more suitcases against my dog."

Go Daddy! At least the pushing stopped a bit. And that's where we stayed for the whole journey. Mummy and Daddy ended up sitting on their box on wheels. However, Mummy became a bit of a star when she handed out chocolates to the humans around her. I didn't know Mummy knew how to share chocolate.

I can't tell you how pleased I was to get to Glasgow Central Station again. It made me appreciate what a calm, peaceful place I live. I can't pronounce Kirkintilloch, but I'm glad we live there and not in London.

Chapter 7

Walking with Grief

I've already told you this, but life with my humans is better than I had ever hoped. There are lots of laughs, plenty of treats, loads of food, amazing adventures on the hills and, well, just lots of happiness.

But sometimes humans have to deal with terrible sadness. I saw this first-paw with my mummy.

Things were rather good. I'd been walking with Daddy while Mummy was baking in the kitchen, which is always good because I usually get a few bits to taste – so long as there's no chocolate.

But then the phone rang. Mummy answered it and suddenly started to scream. It was awful. I've never heard such a noise in all my life, and I hope I never hear it again. Daddy cuddled her, but I was so scared that I lay on the kitchen floor watching Mummy. I didn't know what was happening and I didn't know what to do.

All the happiness suddenly vanished from the house. Mummy was crying, Daddy was sad, and nobody was talking. Then Mummy came downstairs with that big purple box on wheels. I'd usually be excited when I see that because it means we're going somewhere on holiday. But I knew this time it was not the same.

What's going to happen, I wondered.

Then Mummy got in the car and left. I jumped up at the window.

"Mummy, Mummy, come back. Don't go. Please, I'll try to help you if I can, but I don't know what to do."

Daddy was standing at the window, waving as Mummy drove away. He was so sad. Oh my, he needs a cuddle. I'll sit next to him, and that will make him feel better. But it didn't work.

Over the next few days, it was terrible at home. Daddy was so sad, and the house seemed empty without Mummy. I heard Daddy talking on the phone many times, and he said something about death. I knew something terrible had happened, but I didn't understand. I just knew it felt like sadness in the air at home.

Daddy took me out to play in the park, but he wasn't any fun. In the evening, he just sat on his chair, stroking me. It was like his heart wasn't in throwing the ball for me. I don't know how to explain it, but I felt that I was doing a good thing being there and letting him stroke me.

"Oh, listen Daddy. Is that our car coming down the street? I'm sure it sounds like it," I shouted, jumping onto my window seat.

"Yes, yes, it is. Mummy's back. Mummy, Mummy, Mummy. You're back," I cried.

Mummy came into the house and gave a little smile. No, that's not right, I thought. That's not Mummy's proper smile. She's still sad.

"Come on, let's go for a walk Beatrix," said Mummy.

Daddy asked if she wanted him to come with us, but she shook her head. Oh gosh. I didn't know what to do. I'd never seen anyone like this before.

We walked through the park and down to the wood, where Mummy took the lead off me. Usually, I'd run through the wood, play with the sticks and stones, and smell everything. But today, I knew I shouldn't do that. Mummy needed me. So, I didn't do any of my usual playing tricks. I didn't bark or run around. I just walked next to Mummy, letting my coat brush against her. It was silent in the wood, except for Mummy crying. We walked together in silence.

When we got home, Mummy sat on the floor in the front room and cuddled me.

"Thank you, Beatrix," she whispered.

I learned another big lesson today. Helping somebody doesn't always involve you doing something. Sometimes it's enough just to be there. It's not your role to put things right; it's your role to offer support. That can be silent support.

Chapter 8

Are you dead, Mummy?

During the winter of 2018, Scotland had some crazy weather, all thanks to something called the Beast from the East. Winds, extremely low temperatures, and deep, deep snow everywhere that lasted for ages.

Mummy, being Mummy, still took us out on some adventures but turned back when the weather became too bad. Mummy says it's a braver person who turns back on the mountains without reaching the top than somebody who makes it to the top and has an accident or even worse. That's the thing about my mummy, even though she's a bit clumsy, she likes to have adventures and a bit of excitement, but doesn't really like being scared and never puts us in danger on purpose.

Three weeks ago, we tried to get to the top of Ben Lawers but were beaten back by this so-called Beast from the East. I'm not entirely sure what the Beast is, but that day, I must admit that the weather was frightening even for me. You could hardly see your own paws in the snow that suddenly began to fall. Mummy had her compass out, which told me she was worried about getting lost, and I had to show her the way again. We had a bit of a chat and decided that the best thing to do was to go back down the hill and try again another day.

"When will I ever get to the top of Ben Lawers with you?" sighed Mummy. I felt sorry for her because I knew it was her favourite mountain. It must be spectacular up there because I've been to many mountains with Mummy, and they are all my favourites.

But today, we were going to try and climb Ben Lawers again. Daddy said that Mummy had lost her marbles. I've never seen Mummy with marbles, so I don't know what he means.

"Don't worry about us," Mummy said to Daddy. "I know there'll still be lots of snow up the hills, so I'll pack plenty of layers of clothes and crampons, ample food supplies, Kendal Mint Cake, and a flask of hot tea. We'll be fine."

But, marbles or no marbles, we headed up the hills through Glen Lyon to tackle Ben Lawers again. What a difference today. We had lovely clear blue skies and a bit of warmth in the sunshine.

Ben Lawers is one of those high Munro mountains. To get to the top of this hill, you first climb up Beinn Ghlas, another Munro, so Mummy says we were aiming to get two for the price of one, or something.

We had a wonderful time climbing up Beinn Ghlas, playing in the stream, chasing the stones, and rolling down the icy slopes (me, not Mummy, of course). The views, unlike last week, were amazing. I like to take in the sights and gaze at all the mountains in the distance, just as

Mummy does. I often wonder how we will ever find the time to climb all the hills I've seen. We'll have to live to be about four hundred years old!

Mummy had told me that the final climb up that troublesome Ben Lawers is a steep section you get to by crossing a narrow ridge. Today this was a broad ridge, suggesting lots of overhanging snow. Mummy had fastened herself to me to get over this ridge, but I stopped and looked around. I wasn't happy. What if this snow gave way, and Mummy dragged us both over the side of the ridge? I did my sitting down thing, looking at Mummy.

"Well Beatrix," said Mummy. "I think you're right. This is a bit too risky. We've climbed one Munro today, so that Ben Lawers can wait for another day."

"Thank goodness. I'm glad you agree. Can we have our lunch now?" I asked. Daddy does pack us an excellent picnic.

We were both a little disappointed not to be getting to the top of Ben Lawers, but we'd already had a great climb. It had been a bit icy and snowy at times, and cold in the wind, but well worth it for the views from our lunch break at the top of Beinn Ghlas.

As we headed back down, I looked back up the mountain and saw two humans coming down the hill towards us in the distance.

"Well, I never," gasped Mummy. "Skiers on Ben Lawers."

I don't think I'd ever seen skiers before. Now, as you know, I'm a Border Collie. I'm also a Border Collie who likes to chase sheep, squirrels, and cats. I looked at Mummy, and she looked at me with a don't-you-dare glare.

But I couldn't help it. I was off.

Sadly, what I had not realised was that my silly mummy, who was balancing on the steep icy slope using the metal claws she had fastened to her boots, and was using her sticks with metal bits on the ends to keep herself from falling, had clipped the extending lead onto my collar. Even worse, she had not locked the lead, so as I set off to run, the lead just extended out.

Now I'm not one for bragging, but I swear I am the fastest Border Collie from a standing start, and I can go from 0-60 miles per hour in seconds. I set off like a bat out of hell.

Unfortunately, because Mummy had not locked the lead and didn't let go of her end, I dragged her prostrate down the slope. But she stopped once she hit some rocks.

Of course, when she stopped so suddenly, it nearly pulled me off my feet too. But I quickly found my composure and looked back at Mummy. I watched in horror as she lay face down, not moving for what seemed like hours.

"Oh no!" I cried out. "I've killed my mummy."

I ran up to her and began licking her face. "I'm sorry. I'm sorry. Please don't be dead," I sobbed.

Fortunately, the skiers had seen what had happened and came to our aid. By some miracle, Mummy had landed with her arm underneath her, taking her full weight rather than landing face first. With a bit of help from one of the skiers, she was able to sit herself up.

I could see she was badly shaken and had a sickly look about her, but she was moving all her limbs, and there was no blood. Something was running down her face, and to my horror, I realised my tough Yorkshire mummy was crying in front of strangers.

It was a long, slow walk back down the mountain to the car, and Mummy kept her arm tucked away in her jacket.

I could see she was having a bit of a cry to herself. "Don't worry Mummy, you'll be OK," I said gently. "I'm really sorry. I couldn't help it. I didn't mean to hurt you."

"It's OK Beatrix," she said through gritted teeth. "I'll be fine. I'm a bit battered and bruised, but I'm OK. You realise I'll have to tell Daddy because he'll be able to tell that something is wrong."

"Oh no! What if he grounds us, and we can't go on any more adventures," I wailed.

But when we got home, Daddy listened silently to Mummy's story, made her a cup of tea, then sent her to bed for an early night.

"When will the pair of you ever learn?" Daddy said, shaking his head as we shared our supper of hot buttered toast.

Chapter 9

Real Christmas Trees, Baby Jesus, and The Beauty Parlour

Life as a human dog continues to get better and better. I've done exactly what my dog mummy told me to. I love my human mummy and daddy with all my heart and tell them so every day. It's amazing because I honestly believe they do love me as much as my dog mummy loved me.

Oh, I feel a bit sad now. I wonder what my dog mummy is doing. What if all her children have been taken away, and she's all alone? She has my dog daddy, and I know that they love each other. They didn't think I could hear them, but they always said soppy things to each other, like I love you to the moon and back.

Still, it would be nice to be able to see my dog family again, to get one of Mummy's special cuddles and for me to be able to tell them that I still love them. I never told them enough. Everyone should remember to tell their loved ones how special they are and how much they are loved.

I know how lucky I am with my humans. Every day is precious. But Christmas time at our house is an extra special time, and there's always a fantastic real Christmas tree. Mummy says that whenever she can afford a real Christmas tree, we'll have one because when she was growing up, she only ever had a little plastic pretend tree. What's the point of a pretend tree, I wondered?

If you've never smelled a real Christmas tree, then you don't know what you're missing. They have such a unique smell, sweet but rustic, and trust me, the water the tree stands in is the best-flavoured water you'll ever taste. I bet there are not that many dogs whose human parents buy them a proper indoor tree. I've only cuddled up to it and drank the water. I'm not like one of those nasty male dogs who feel the urge to go to the toilet against every tree they come across. That would be horrible inside our lovely house.

Mummy gets really excited as December approaches, and putting up the Christmas tree is a big deal for her. The tree gets picked up a couple of days before the end of November.

"Don't touch the Christmas tree Beatrix," said Mummy. "I'm going to stand it in the corner so it can find its own shape before we decorate it."

She says that every year, but I can never understand that because the tree looks perfect to me when Mummy and Daddy bring it into the house. What sort of shape do humans want their tree to be?

Then on the last day of November, the decorations come out. It's so exciting. There are sparkly things, round things, and shiny things - hundreds of them. Mummy takes them out of the box one at a time and shows them to me. She does this every year, and it's the same things she shows me each time. But I don't mind. It's exciting trying to guess what will come out of the boxes next. Sometimes I remember, but often I forget, and it's like seeing things for the first time. It is indeed a special time. I sit next to Mummy as she decorates the Christmas tree. I'm not allowed to touch the decorations, but I can smell each one. Sniffing is usually much better than feeling anyway.

Once the decorations are on the tree, Mummy turns out the big room lights and switches on the twinkly lights around the tree. We sit back and admire our work. Turning on the Christmas tree lights must be one of the best things I've ever seen. It turns our already peaceful front room into a Christmas wonderland. Mummy always sits on the floor with me, and we have a few minutes just looking at the tree and taking in the moment. I don't think Daddy's quite so excited about the decorations, but I'm like Mummy, I love them.

After the tree, it's time for the musical toys. Now I'm not quite so impressed with these. You know what I mean, those toys where you press a button, and they sing and dance to a ridiculous tune. We have a dancing tree, dancing birds, dancing dogs, and let's not forget the enormous ugly singing reindeer.

"Please Mummy. Enough! You've got so many now. There's hardly room for me on the floor next to the tree anymore," I said, as she introduced some singing penguins to the toy gang.

"Don't worry Beatrix, there will always be room for you, but you know that we need a new musical decoration each year," laughed Mummy.

Sometimes Mummy turns them all on at the same time, and what a din that is. She forgets that I have such acute hearing, and these high-pitched singing monstrosities hurt my delicate ears. But it makes Mummy smile, so I can cope with it. It's only a couple of minutes each day throughout December I suppose.

Mummy and Daddy are always telling me how proud they are of me because I don't touch things that are not my toys, and I really don't. I don't even touch food until I've been told I can have it, though I do slaver over any food if it's close enough. But we have this thing called a Nativity Scene. Apparently, Mummy made this herself many years ago when her human children, Benjamin, and Chlöe, were little. I can't imagine Benjamin being a little boy as he is so tall, but I guess he was a baby once.

Anyway, I don't know why, but I can't help but pick up that little Baby Jesus thing from the Nativity Scene. It smells so amazing, and when I put Baby Jesus in my mouth, it kind of crinkles.

Now stop all that screaming!

I don't bite Baby Jesus. Don't be ridiculous. I don't chew anything I'm not going to eat, and I'm certainly not going to eat Baby Jesus. But Baby Jesus has some sort of strange attraction for me. I think I've become infatuated with it.

The first time Mummy saw me put Baby Jesus in my mouth, she shouted at me to put it down.

"Don't you dare eat Baby Jesus," she cried.

"Get real Mum. I was never going to eat it," I muttered.

But it has something special about it. Mummy and Daddy say that maybe it's because there's straw in the cradle, and I must like the smell of the straw. Well, between you and me, Baby Jesus had some straw in its cradle when I first saw it, but it's like this. It's never crossed my mind to eat Baby Jesus, but that straw in the crib was delicious. The smell, the texture, the look; it was too tempting. So, although Baby Jesus is still with us in the lovely Nativity Scene, the crib is now devoid of straw.

Sometimes when Mummy and Daddy are out, I play with Baby Jesus and throw it around the room. Usually, I hear when they're coming back in the car, and put Baby Jesus back where it was, but sometimes I don't quite manage it. Once, I only heard them at the last minute, so I pushed Baby Jesus into the gap under the big cupboard in the front room. Well, there was an outcry. Mummy noticed straight away that Baby Jesus was not in the crib.

"Where is Baby Jesus?" Mummy cried out.

I wasn't going to tell her at first, but then she got all worked up, with Daddy joining in the panic.

"Oh no! What if she's eaten Baby Jesus?" moaned Daddy.

I tell you, they got themselves into such a state that I had to do something. Obviously, I couldn't tell Mummy and Daddy that I'd put Baby Jesus under the cupboard, because that would be admitting to playing with it. So, I did that eye thing. I looked at Mummy, and then at the cupboard. I looked back at Mummy to ensure she was paying attention, then I looked back at the cupboard, and lay down on my tummy, facing where Baby Jesus was.

Well, you'd have thought that Baby Jesus was worth a million pounds the way Mummy rejoiced once she found it under the cupboard and had realised that I'd not eaten it.

Now I try to play with Baby Jesus when the humans are not about, to stop them getting so worked up.

Mind you; it was different when that noisy little Minnie Violet, the human granddaughter, came to our house for Christmas one year. She got away with everything, acting like butter wouldn't melt in her mouth. Minnie was allowed to pick up all the toys, and nobody shouted when she put Baby Jesus in her mouth. And, by the way, nobody complained when she put my toy chop in her mouth either. By the time she left to go home, most of my toys had baby slaver all over them. Disgusting!

I must admit that most of my memories around Christmas are good, except for one. Now, Mummy and Daddy like to have a theme for their Christmas. There have been many different themes - Beatrix Potter, Ugly, Victorian, and Roald Dahl. They do silly things. Nothing that costs them a lot of money, just fun things, like finding an old book, an ugly teapot, telling a joke, or making some Victorian punch.

The memory that still brings me out in a cold sweat was the year the theme was a Posh Christmas. Mummy said that it would be great if I could be involved. I wasn't too worried at that point.

"We should take Beatrix to the dog groomers so she can be a posh dog for Christmas," announced Mummy.

I wasn't sure what she meant, but the look on Daddy's face told me I wasn't going like it.

So off we went. At first, I thought it wasn't going to be so bad. We went to my favourite shop, the vet place - lots of lovely smells and treats on the counter for me. OK, sometimes a lady there gives me a little stab, but generally, it's an OK place to visit.

But this time, they took me through a door I'd never been in before. Then Mummy and Daddy left me. Well, listen here. I have never been as affronted as I was that day. The woman there soaked me. She rubbed smelly soap suds into areas I didn't even know I had. She brushed and cut my hair (even in my private bits). Then she used this great big dryer thing. It was so noisy. I'm not ashamed to admit I was pretty scared at one point. I may even have had a little cry.

At last, Mummy and Daddy came back, and I heard them asking the lady how I'd gone on.

"Your dog displays trust issues around her back end," the lady told them.

Trust issues around her back end! If somebody you'd never met before started touching you in your delicate bits, you'd display trust issues too. Please!

Let me tell you, I gave Mummy and Daddy such a look that they knew exactly what I thought of the dog groomer.

It didn't take me long to get myself sorted when we went out in the wood later that afternoon. I quickly managed to get my coat back to its usual condition and get rid of all that horrible smelly stuff they put on me. It was vile so I rolled myself in some lovely fox poo.

I'm pleased to report that Mummy has never again suggested they take me to the dog beauty parlour.

Chapter 10

Eating Too Many Snacks

The years are flying by, and I'm no longer a tiny puppy. One day I was in the park with Daddy when my dog friends started laughing at me because I called my humans Mummy and Daddy. They said only puppies say Mummy and Daddy. I was a bit confused and couldn't wait to run home to talk to Mummy about it.

"Mummy, my friends are laughing at me for calling my parents Mummy and Daddy," I sobbed.

"Oh Beatrix, that's nothing to be worried about. Sometimes as children grow up, they call their parents Mum and Dad. It's OK if you want to do that. But it's OK if you still want to call us Mummy and Daddy. You decide, and don't let your friends force you to change your mind." Mummy stroked my ears. She always knows the right things to say and do. I love having my ears rubbed.

Over the next few days, I thought about what my friends and Mummy had said and tried it out in my mind.

Mummy, Daddy, Mum, Dad. I decided that as I was no longer a puppy, I should start to talk a bit more like a grown-up, and I'd call my humans Mum and Dad. It seemed a bit strange at first, but now it sounds natural, and I can't imagine going back to calling them Mummy and Daddy. But in my heart, they will always be Mummy and Daddy.

A few years before I became a human dog, my human mum and dad (heck, it still seems a bit strange not writing Mummy and Daddy) were married on the Isle of Skye. I'm not sure what this marriage thing is, but it seems to be something Mum and Dad like to celebrate every year because they've chosen to live together for the rest of their lives. I get to go everywhere with them, so celebrating is always a good thing in my book, but I'm a bit confused as to why they don't celebrate being together every day, not just once a year.

"Mum?" I asked. "Why do you and Dad only celebrate being together one day each year? I want to celebrate every single day now that I'm a human dog and get to spend my life with you and Dad."

"Beatrix, you're such a clever dog. But just because we don't say it aloud doesn't mean we don't celebrate each day we're together. People are not as straightforward in their emotions as dogs, and sometimes we don't let others know how special they are."

And with that, she went over to Dad and gave him a big kiss and a cuddle.

I've already told you that Mum is my best friend. We chat all the time, planning different adventures and hoping that Dad won't ground us if, or when they go wrong. This particular year, Mum discussed with me the different ways she and Dad could celebrate their wedding anniversary. Mum is like me and will go out on the hills at the drop of a hat, no matter what the weather is doing. Dad is different. I love him to bits, but oh my, he does moan about the weather. It's too cold, too windy, or too wet. Mum and I just get on with it and love nothing better than walking in the wind and rain or, even better, the snow. We're not sun worshippers at all.

Now, around this time, Dad's knees were still recovering from a recent trip up one of the big mountains he had climbed with Mum and me. He'd told Mum he thought he'd have a break from going on mountain hikes with us for a while.

One night, Mum asked me, "What am I going to do? I'd like to go up to the Highlands and walk in the hills for our wedding anniversary, but I don't know how to get Dad to believe that it was actually his idea."

But then fate seemed to take over. My human brother Benjamin was coming to stay for a few days. Mum told me he would be starting a new chapter in his life on the Isle of Skye. I wondered if that's a big book or something.

Mum explained that Benjamin needed to get on the West Coast train to Skye the following Monday, which happened to be Mum and Dad's wedding anniversary. Dilemma indeed.

"Dad likes a train journey. And you know how he likes to travel on that West Coast train. Make sure he has lots of butties, and he'll love it," I giggled to Mum.

Soon our plan began to appear. Mum got the maps out, and we looked at them together. Mum sat back, smiling at me.

"Mm, I wonder," said Mum. "What if I tell Dad that we're going to celebrate our wedding anniversary in a cosy hotel, with a trip on the lovely West Coast railway? Benjamin could join us for part of the way, but he could stay on the train right up to Mallaig," said Mum excitedly.

"I bet you could build in a walk too, Mum. Just remember to give Dad lots of sandwiches and a KitKat, and he'll soon agree," I replied, already looking forward to the adventure. I love train journeys; they're so relaxing and always involve lots of food.

And so, the plan developed. Mum explained it to me. We were all going to get the train from Croy, and then Benjamin would stay on the train up to Mallaig. Mum, Dad, and I would get off at Tyndrum station. We'd then have a little walk of six miles on the West Highland Way up to the hotel at Bridge of Orchy, enjoy a lovely night in the hotel, having a hearty breakfast the following day before coming back home on the train.

I tell you, when Mum sets her mind to it, she certainly does come up with some exciting plans. Would she get Dad to agree to it though?

That night, as Mum and Dad did that cuddling thing on the couch, I heard Mum begin to work her magic on Dad.

"I thought we could have a night in a posh hotel to celebrate our wedding anniversary, my sweet," she said into Dad's ear.

"Enough detail for now Mum," I whispered to her. "You can release the rest of the information to Dad at appropriate intervals."

Excitedly, now having Dad on board with our plan, Mum phoned the hotel to make sure we could get a dog-friendly room booked so I could go with them. Why all rooms are not dog friendly, I can't imagine. Not only did she book a room at short notice, but she also got a deal on a separate cottage next to the hotel. Perfect, I thought to myself. I wouldn't have to protect Mum and Dad from anybody walking past the hotel room, and I wouldn't need to do the barking thing that even Mum doesn't like.

"Have you seen the weather forecast for Monday and Tuesday?" Dad asked. "It's going to be pouring it down both days."

Now Mum and I know that Dad's idea of bad weather and our idea of bad weather are poles apart.

"It'll be OK," replied Mum. "We're only walking on the West Highland Way, and the guidebooks tell us we don't even need a map or a compass, and we have a lovely cottage next to the hotel to stay in."

"Go Mum. You sell it to him," I laughed.

Dad did that eyebrow-raising thing he always does at Mum's plans.

"Oh, we're doing a walk, are we?" he sighed.

Mum did that smiling sweetly thing that Dad always falls for, and discussed the plans for the two-day trip, telling Dad he needed to travel light as he'd be walking for six miles carrying everything, including his picnic, for the overnight stay.

"Risky giving him all that information," I said.

Before too long, Mum had everything planned. Benjamin had arrived at our house, and we were all enjoying a relaxing evening until Mum read out a message from her human friend, Salena.

Have you seen the weather warnings for the West Coast? You must be mad, the message read.

Now it's one thing ignoring Dad's warnings of severe weather, but hearing this Salena mention the weather made my ears prick up. Mum doesn't call her DCI Riley for nothing.

Mum quickly changed the plans. Mum explained that there was a yellow warning for torrential rain covering Crianlarich, Tyndrum and Bridge of Orchy. Rather than risk walking in the flood plains from Tyndrum in dangerous weather, we'd get the train straight to Bridge of Orchy, then go for a walk once we had arrived there.

Sounds good to me I thought. Even Dad seemed to think this was better because he wouldn't have the six-mile walk. He is so easy to please. Surely Dad realises that Mum will have something else up her sleeve. But bless him; he always goes along with Mum's plans.

Then Mum said she needed to make a second adjustment of the plan. Due to the bad weather forecast, all the ferries across to the Isle of Skye were cancelled for Monday, so Benjamin couldn't get to Armadale.

"That's OK Mum," I said, snuggling up to Benjamin. "I don't see my brother often, so it would be lovely to have him stay at the hotel with us. Please Mum," I begged.

"It's our wedding anniversary Beatrix," Mum whispered to me. I didn't quite understand why that was an issue. Humans are strange sometimes.

"Problem solved," announced Mum. "I've sorted Benjamin out with some accommodation by the ferry terminal at Mallaig, ready for when the ferries start to run again."

Dad's eyebrows, by this point, were not just raised; they were nearly falling over the back of his head.

The following morning, at some ridiculously early hour, I could hear the alarm going off upstairs just as I stretched out from a long sleep. I don't mind early starts at all. There's also the added benefit that some humans can't seem to eat breakfast when they have to get up early. Mum and Dad nibbled at their breakfast toast before dropping most of it down on the floor for me to eat. Benjamin, of course, ate all his breakfast; he's always eating. Mum says Benjamin has hollow legs. That must be where he puts all his food, and why he always wears boots with laces to hold it all in. But he does share it with me sometimes, especially when I do that excessive drooling.

After a short taxi trip to the local train station at Croy, then a ten-minute train journey, we were in Glasgow Queen Street station. We had an hour to wait before the next train, so I kept all the humans in the station amused, going from one person to the next, getting cuddles and strokes. Well, you know how it is; there's always the possibility of a biscuit or two if I do the puppy dog eyes.

Time passed quickly for me, and we soon got settled on the next train. I don't know about humans; but it always seems an exciting time getting on that train up the West Coast. Listening as the voice in the air calls out the names of the stations fills me with joy. Crianlarich, Tyndrum, Fort William, Arisaig, Morar and Mallaig. I've been lucky enough to go to all those places. Yes, I do understand the train announcements. How do you think I know when to get off the train?

This journey for us was going to last about three hours, although Benjamin had about six hours to go. Just think how many treats I could get if I could go to Mallaig with him.

I had a little sleep to prepare for the picnic, and ten minutes later, I was awake and hungry.

"I think we should wait for our picnic until we get off the train," announced Mum.

"What!" I cried.

Benjamin and Dad had a look of horror on their faces too.

But the picnic gods must have been looking down on us. Just outside a place called Helensburgh, the train came to a standstill.

The voice in the air announced, "Ladies and gentlemen, there will be a short delay. The track on this line is single track in several places, and we need to wait for a delayed train coming in the opposite direction."

I looked at Mum. She was busy doing that crocheting thing, so she wasn't going to be in a rush to get the picnics out. I looked at Dad. He was drumming his fingers on the table. Possible. He might give in. I looked at Benjamin. His fingers were fidgeting with his rucksack on the seat next to him. I knew I could rely on hungry Horace Benjamin.

"Go on Benjamin. Get the picnic out. You know you want to," I whispered.

It worked. It wasn't long before the picnics started to creep out of everyone's rucksacks. Of course, Benjamin is always the best person to sit next to because he can't resist my puppy dog eyes and my drooling, so he always gives me treats.

I was just getting into the swing of the picnic when Mum told Dad and Benjamin that they had to stop eating their picnic as we all had a long day ahead of us – some longer than others.

"And Benjamin. Don't give Beatrix another thing," she said sternly.

With that, we put the picnics away. Mum can be a spoilsport at times. Dad and Benjamin looked as sad as I felt.

Eventually, the delayed Caledonian Sleeper train came down the track, and we were on our way again. Once beyond Arrochar and Tarbet, the views should have been amazing, but the rain moved in, so you needed to use your imagination. Mum tried to tell us that she could see The Cobbler in the distance, but I think she was dreaming. I know that mountain very well, and I couldn't see it.

Being in charge of the humans, I like to prepare myself for when it's time to get off the train, so I'm always watching Mum to see when she starts to put her crochet away. That's always a clear sign that we'll be getting off soon.

"We will soon be approaching Upper Tyndrum," the voice in the air announced.

I looked at Mum. The crochet was going away, and she was getting her coat on - time to get ready.

"We will soon be approaching Bridge of Orchy," the voice in the air said.

I pulled Mum towards the train door. I need to get to the doors and stand with my nose almost touching them. That way, I can feel the vibrations and hear different noises from the wheels on the tracks. If you listen, you can tell when the train is slowing down, and the carriage floor feels different, so you know you're approaching the station. When we're on our usual train, I know that we always get off at Croy, but on different trains, I have to look for clues to know which station we're getting off at. I also know when we are getting to Halifax as I know that station well because Mum likes to go there as often as she can.

The train slowed gradually to a stop. We hugged and kissed Benjamin and said our goodbyes. Once the train doors opened, we left the train for what Mum had told us would be a short five-minute walk to the hotel.

I know we were in the Highlands, but the rain pouring down was ridiculous. Mum has this expression when she says it's raining cats and dogs. Well, I couldn't see any cats to chase or dogs falling from the sky, but I can tell you, by the time the three of us got to the hotel, we were all wet through. I have my lovely Collie double coat, and Mum and Dad have their good waterproof stuff, so we were OK. As Mum always says, there's no bad weather, just bad clothing. I'm not sure that Dad entirely agrees.

We checked into the hotel, only to find that the lovely cottage Mum had promised Dad as part of the deal had flooded due to the inclement weather, so we were moved to a different room. But all was well again when Dad discovered that the lovely hotel manager had removed the added charge for me and had even given Mum a further discount for the inconvenience.

"OK, now it's time for a walk," I said, pulling on my lead. "We have new hills to explore."

Dad was obviously on his best behaviour, saying he was happy to do what Mum wanted as it was her anniversary treat.

Clever man, I thought.

"Let's walk along the West Highland Way towards Inveroran," announced Mum.

The hotel man gave Mum a map and told us about a round trip we could undertake in about three hours to the top of Mam Carraigh, drop down to the Inveroran Hotel and back to our hotel. With my excellent hearing, I did think I heard the manager mutter under his breath, "You're mad."

And we were off. I was in the lead straight away and ready to explore - so many new smells. Within the first five minutes of the walk, we'd reached the mud, and there was so much flood water. Mum and I were bubbling with excitement, but Dad started moaning straight away, saying that it was too wet to go any further. I heard a bit of a discussion between the two of them as Mum pointed out other humans were walking through the mud who'd not come to any harm, so we'd be fine.

Mum is just the best and bravest person I know. It was difficult to see at this point whether it was the rain on Dad's face or if there were actually some tears as he reluctantly agreed to follow us.

Before too long, we were through the deep mud, and the path started to climb steadily to become a stream to walk in rather than a mud bath. Reaching a forest, Mum declared she'd found the perfect lunch spot, sheltered from the rain and with a few logs to act as a table. Lunch, exciting, I thought. Mum and I love outdoor picnics.

The warm tea and food seemed to cheer Dad up a little. I'm not sure he was quite so sheltered from the rain, and he did slide off the fallen tree that Mum had said was a perfect table to sit at, as it was just too wet and slippery. But we had a lovely lunch, with Mum and Dad sharing their treats with me. I'm a bit embarrassed to say that Mum and Dad even managed to share a cheeky anniversary kiss. I looked away, of course.

Once we had set off again, I ran up in front of Mum and Dad to make sure everything was safe for them. I noticed that the rain was getting heavier, and the wind was getting stronger, but it was fabulous. There's something special about walking in a place you've never been to before. It's so exciting. The views were non-existent, but Mum announced she could see the Inveroran Hotel at the bottom of the hill through the clouds. I must have run up and down that hill four times, waiting for Mum and Dad to get down to the bottom of the hill - they were slipping and sliding so much. I even noticed that Mum wasn't so smiley now either.

Then we were on a narrow road. I don't like roads as they can be hard on my feet. I love to be on the grass, in the mud, or in the water. A river ran alongside the road, but Mum told me I couldn't swim in it, as if I would! There was no way I would even try to get in that river. It was way too fast. We dogs know when it's not safe.

Before long, we arrived back at the hotel. I was very wet, and Mum and Dad were equally dripping.

I realised then how much I liked the hotel man. Mum cried with alarm that she had forgotten to pack a towel for me and asked if the man had an old towel she could borrow. But an old towel was not good enough for him, and he kindly gave us a lovely fluffy bath towel. I can tell you; I was impressed. The towels at home are nowhere near as big and soft as the towel he gave to Mum. I felt very special indeed.

We finally got to our lovely room, but the wooden floors were slippery with all the dripping water from Mum and Dad. Whilst they had hot showers and put on dry clothes, I spent the next half hour sniffing all around the room, then settled down to have a little snooze, laying on my fluffy towel next to the glass door overlooking the fast-flowing river. If you're ever searching for a cosy, friendly hotel in the middle of nowhere, then the Bridge of Orchy Hotel is simply perfect.

The best thing was when we went down to the restaurant. Oh, the smells. I was beside myself. There was a lovely fire too and lots of humans. What more did I need? A room with heat, humans, and food meant I was in for a good evening.

Mum and Dad chatted away with lots of humans as they had their food, but I was the star attraction again and had lots of treats dropped down on the floor for me. Mum was a bit of a spoilsport for the second time that day when she said we had to go back to the room, as people would keep giving me treats, and I'd eaten enough already.

You can never have enough treats!

All was going well until the early hours of the morning. I woke up and had that funny feeling in my tummy. It must have been the accumulation of treats stretching from Glasgow Queen Street, the train journey to Bridge of Orchy, lunch in the rain and the restaurant goodies. I was ashamed when yes, on the hotel room floor before Mum or Dad had the chance to get dressed and get me outside,

I was sick. But it was OK because the floor had no carpet. When Dad took me outside for some fresh air, Mum cleaned the hotel room floor, and all was well again.

Mum and Dad had a little discussion about how well their wedding anniversary was going, but ten minutes later, I felt back to my usual self and snuggled up on my lovely bath towel, acting as though nothing had happened.

Happy Wedding Anniversary Mum and Dad.

Chapter 11

Me, a Hero

30 April 2018

It's going to be an exciting day today. Mum's come down the stairs with her purple walking bag, the one she puts clothes and treats in. That can only mean one thing.

"Do you know what you're going to do today, Beatrix?" asked Mum.

"Going for a long walk with you?" I replied, smiling.

"Not just a long walk Beatrix," she said. "Today, I'm hoping you finally get to the top of my favourite mountain. We're going to tackle Ben Lawers again. I know you've already been up lots of hills and mountains, but it would be wonderful to get to the top of my favourite mountain with you."

For some reason, Mum absolutely loves this hill. We've already had a few attempts to get to the elusive summit of this mountain. Yes, it's the same mountain where we saw the skiers. Mum says she's forgiven me, though. Of course, the chapter Left on the Mountain, is later in the book, but I like to forget about that one.

We were up bright and early as Mum always worries that she'll not get a space in the small car park at the start of these walks. Between you and me, she's not the best at getting her car into small spaces, and I've learned one or two new words when she's had to do this.

We had a funny incident on the drive from Callander to Killin. If you don't know this stretch of road, it's a bit like a mini roller coaster. I used to be terribly travel-sick in the car even though Mum always takes her time driving, especially along bumpy roads. It helps that I'm a bit taller now though, so I can see out of the windows.

At the time, we still had our big black car where the seats folded right down, and it gave me the whole back area to myself, and I could stretch out and have a snooze if I wanted to. But really, when I'm in the car with Mum, I like to look out of the windows watching the magnificent scenery and trying to work out where we're going and which mountain we'll be tackling.

On this day however, as we went alongside Loch Lubnaig, I didn't feel comfortable seeing a van driving very close to the back of our car. Maybe the driver was trying to get closer to me, but I wanted him to keep his distance. Mum's always telling Dad to keep his distance from cars, and that only a fool breaks the two-second rule. I'm not sure what this rule is, but I bet this silly human driving the van was breaking it today. I could sense that Mum was not too happy about him either. She kept looking in the rear-view mirror, and I could see her angry eyes. Trust me, if my mum's not happy, she can have very angry eyes.

At last, after a few more twists and weaves on the road, the van flew past us. I sighed with relief.

"How stupid was that man? Did you see how quickly he passed us at such a ridiculous place? There's no way he could have seen if anything was coming the other way," Mum shouted.

She sounded really cross, and I'm glad she wasn't angry with me.

We laughed together as we approached Killin, and the same van was at the side of the road with the passenger leaning over the side of the wall doing that being sick thing. Oops!

Mum soon had our car safely parked at the Ben Lawers car park, and we were heading up to the two Munros - Beinn Ghlas and Ben Lawers. I was hoping we'd get to the top today, but there was a nip in the air, and clouds cuddled the mountain tops.

Mum has told me on quite a few walks that it's no shame to have to turn around before you get to the top. Sometimes this has happened to us because of the weather or Mum was too tired. I'm always disappointed not to get to the top because it's a great feeling sitting at the big pile of stones on the summit. If the weather's good, Mum always lets us rest and eat some of our picnic goodies at the top. But you should always head home if you don't feel safe or you feel unwell. The mountains will always be there for another day.

Mum was wearing plenty of clothes and had that bag on her back with some tasty titbits (which I have to share with her). She always has lots of spare clothes, but I don't know why. It just seems like something extra to carry, but I'm sure Mum knows what she's doing.

Thankfully, today Mum did none of that falling down thing she does so often, and I didn't chase any skiers.

Now I know you humans think you're the only creatures to enjoy the views on the hills, but you're wrong.

I love to be on the hills and see the mountains around me. Often Mum and I sit together and watch the views. We don't talk. We just sit and enjoy the peace. Today, the views were not brilliant, but every now and again, the clouds cleared and gave way to allow us to do some mountain spotting.

As we approached the top of Beinn Ghlas, it was getting windy and very cold, so we had a little stop for a snack, and for Mum to put on another layer of clothing and her gloves (on herself, not me). Of course, being a proper Border Collie, I have my double coat – an outer layer of fur and an undercoat of shorter, softer hair. This undercoat also helps to keep me cool in hot temperatures. I know some of my friends at home whose human parents insist on shaving almost all their fur off in summer, and they can't keep themselves cool at all. Thankfully, my mum doesn't do that to me.

Making our way along the ridge between Beinn Ghlas and Ben Lawers, it was blowing an absolute hoolie. I was a bit worried at this point as Mum is probably the clumsiest human I know, and I was mightily relieved when she fastened herself to me with the lead. At least when Mum's attached to me, she follows me, and I can make sure she takes the correct route.

It was the furthest I'd been up this mountain, so I was taking my time, looking, sniffing everything, and listening. I needed to remember every single sight, smell, and sound, so that the next time we come up here, I'll know exactly which route to take, just in case Mum forgets.

Finally, we reached the top of the mountain and even managed to get our photo taken by another human.

"Congratulations Beatrix. You've now climbed my favourite mountain. Wait till we tell Dad. He'll be so proud of you," gushed Mum, giving me a big cuddle.

I'm not sure what all the fuss is about this mountaintop. It was so cold, there were no views, and even though there was a big pile of rocks at the top, Mum said we had to descend a bit and get our lunch later once we were back down and out of the wind.

After a while, Mum took the lead off me. I looked around, sniffed, decided that she was safe enough to walk alone, and started to skip my merry way down the path.

As I was running around, I thought I could hear a strange noise. It was like a cry, but it wasn't the sound of a sheep. What was it? I wondered.

Mum was still coming down the hill, so I thought I'd have a bit of an investigation. I could smell something different, so I went a little further off the path and could see something in a hollow.

What was it? Was it a sheep? No. I was a bit nervous now. What was I going to find?

Then I saw her, a little human hiding behind a rock, curled up, shaking, and doing that crying thing. She didn't have any of the big boots on that Mum wears, just some silly little shoes. Her clothes looked too thin and were blowing in the wind. It was a bit strange because she was holding a jacket rather than wearing it. Why didn't she have any of the nice warm clothes like Mum always wears, I wondered?

What was I going to do? Mum would never come down here off the path. Something was definitely wrong here, and I needed Mum to see this little girl. So, I did the one thing I knew would make Mum come to me. I sat there bolt upright. I didn't bark or jump about. That way, Mum would realise I'd seen something.

I could see Mum looking for me and calling my name. It was so hard not to run down to Mum. But then I saw it was working. Mum had stopped walking and was looking over at me. I willed her to come over to me. And she did. Phew! Mum will know what to do now.

Mum did the thing I love about her. She gave that little girl one of her smiles and put her arm around her shoulder.

"Are you OK?" Mum asked her.

"I was with some friends, but they wanted to go to the top of the mountain, and I was tired, so they left me here to wait for them to come back down," the little girl sobbed.

I thought to myself that her friends didn't sound like very nice friends at all.

Then Mum's voice changed. She used that stern tone and said, "Come on, get up, put that jacket on and let's get you walking down the path and out of the wind."

"It's not my jacket; I'm holding it for my friend until he gets back down from the top," said the little girl.

"Well, your friend's not here, and you're cold. Put the jacket on," said Mum firmly.

"Oh! What about our lunch? Are we not having anything to eat yet?" I barked at Mum.

"Soon Beatrix, we need to get this girl out of the wind, or she'll end up with hypothermia," said Mum sharply. "Just be patient."

Once we were down the ridge, away from the chilly wind, Mum saw the two men we'd been chatting to earlier in the day, who were now sitting in a sheltered spot eating their lunch. Heck. Everyone's eating but us. But I didn't say anything. Mum was already worked up, and I didn't want her to be cross with me.

Mum and the men talked about getting this little one sorted and down the hill. Mum pulled her mat out of her backpack and made the little girl sit on it, then made her put on the spare jacket that Mum always carries. So that's why Mum takes it with her - for when she meets silly humans who don't have the right clothes with them.

One of the men had a spare pair of gloves and put them on the little girl. Then Mum took out her flask of tea (don't forget we'd not had our lunch yet), and I watched as she helped the shaking girl to drink some of it. Mum was stern with her and made her eat some of the horrible minty stuff that Mum raves about – Kendal Mint Cake. Mum told the men that the girl had no food to eat but that she could spare her a piece of her lemon drizzle cake, and asked if they had any chocolate they could give to the girl. Phew! At least our sandwiches were safe, so I'd still get something to eat.

Before long, now wearing the spare clothes, and with the hot tea and food inside her, the little girl had stopped shaking. We turned our heads as her friends caught up with us. They're going to be in serious trouble, I thought. Mum is really cross.

Do you know how I said that I learned a few new words when Mum was trying to park her car? Well, I learned more new words today as Mum spoke to these friends. Let's just say they quickly knew what Mum thought of them leaving their friend alone on the mountain.

Mum and the two men were then able to get the little girl walking again and help her down the mountain. Disaster averted.

Mum and the men (not the friends) kept cuddling me and calling me a real hero.

"You know Beatrix, if you hadn't seen this young girl, I'd never have found her, and the cold may have killed her," said Mum, rubbing my ears.

One of the men patted my back and said, "We hadn't seen her either, so well-done young Collie. You're a real hero."

Me, Beatrix, the Hero.

Chapter 12

And Dad Came Along Too

I'm used to Mum planning adventures for us, and usually, it's just the two of us, with Dad staying at home to make our tea for us on our return. He blames his bad knees, but I think he secretly tries to avoid any adventures planned by Mum.

During one particular spell of hot weather, Mum decided we'd have a hike up Ben Lomond.

"I think I'll come with you," announced Dad. "It might be the last time I get to go up a Munro before my knees give up for good."

I was pleased that Dad wanted to come along but was equally concerned about this act of heroism as he's not done any hill walking for some time, and Ben Lomond is a big mountain.

"Do you think he'll be OK Mum?" I whispered.

"Yes, he'll be fine, don't worry. We can always turn back if it's too much for him," replied Mum.

"Go Dad," I said, feeling a sudden surge of pride for him wanting to have a last go at the mountains. And at least it wouldn't be too cold for him today because, oh boy, he can moan about the cold.

Mum and Dad took each Monday and Tuesday off from their tearoom. Mum says she likes to walk on Mondays, so she has time to recover before returning to work. A good move I'd say, given some of the adventures we've had.

So come Monday morning, lunches were packed, flasks of tea made, rucksacks filled with spare clothes, and walking boots sorted. I get so excited when I see the walking bags being brought downstairs, as I know this means a play day on the hills. Mum always tells me to calm down and not worry because I'm going with her. As if she'd dare go without me!

To get to the start of the walk, the last few miles from a place called Drymen to Rowardennan is a bit of an adventure. The single-track road dips, weaves and meanders its way to the banks of Loch Lomond. But soon enough, we were there.

I was glad to be out of the car; even with Mum's careful driving, my tummy had been starting to feel a bit funny. Once Mum and Dad were out of the car and had their rucksacks on their backs, I could look for a stone to carry up the hill. It's a Collie thing.

I couldn't help but laugh at Mum and Dad with their bags of clothes. It was a lovely summer's day, but as I've mentioned before, Mum always has spare clothes just in case. Mind you, I remember when I found the girl on Ben Lawers. She had no jacket on, and she was suffering from hypothermia, so perhaps Mum's right.

Mum was in a strange mood. She was doing that singing thing and pretending to play the drums. She said something about giving people an earworm with a song about taking the high road to Scotland along the banks of Loch Lomond. I guess it was quite a good song as we were going up Ben Lomond, even with Mum singing it, but don't tell her I said that. I never did see any worms.

Today the mountain was full of humans. Most people like to walk in the summer. I prefer walking with Mum in the winter when often we don't see another person all day.

The hike up Ben Lomond is glorious, but a bit steep at times, even for me. I heard Mum telling Dad that the National Trust for Scotland has done an excellent job sorting the eroded paths to prevent Ben Lomond from disappearing.

"It also helps us folk who think we're real mountaineers by giving us access to these wonderful hills," said Dad, already puffing, panting, and having a rest.

The views today were terrific. At one point, we watched in amazement at the clouds rising from the valley in front of us. The hills and mountains around us were in and out of the clouds all day.

Mum always has to tell Dad which mountain is which. Even I can recognise the mountains now. The Cobbler (Ben Arthur) across Loch Lomond was as clear as I have ever seen it. That's one of my favourite hills, you know.

At one point, you could see in all directions, and I could imagine that I was looking at every mountain in Scotland. I was glad that Dad seemed to like looking at the views as much as Mum and I did. I'm always surprised that some humans don't seem to take the time to enjoy their surroundings, and often seem too busy rushing up and down the hills to appreciate the fantastic scenery around them.

Running ahead of Mum and Dad to ensure the summit was safe for them, I could feel the midges start to nip at the skin on my face.

"You'll need to get your smidge out when you get up here?" I shouted down to Mum. I know she likes to use some of that smelly stuff to keep the beasties from biting her. Sometimes she even tries to put some on my nose.

"Which way are we going back down?" I asked. "Look, there's a path leading off the top that way."

"No, that's the Ptarmigan Ridge and it has too many steep drops for my liking," replied Mum. "We'll go back down the same way we came up." As you know by now, Mum's a bit clumsy, so I was pleased to hear that. What with Dad and his bad knees, the last thing we needed was Mum falling down any steep drops and me having to rescue her.

Mum took lots of photos, and it seemed to take forever for her to stop and let us have our picnic. But eventually, we enjoyed a lovely lunch, and the three of us lay together enjoying the heat of the sun. It didn't take long for Dad to fall asleep, and he was soon snoring away just like a pig. I was so embarrassed. I quickly grabbed my stone and dropped it on his tummy. That woke him up and stopped him from making that awful noise.

Mum was shaking her head.

As you leave the summit, the path is steep and rocky. Mum's always saying that she takes each step as though it might be her last, so she's never in a rush going down the hills.

By this time, I'd started to realise that walking in summer was great fun as there were hundreds of humans to fall for my Border Collie charms. My mouth ached from smiling, and I was getting a crick in my neck from the cute head tilting. But so many humans were talking to me, hugging me, stroking me and, much to my delight, throwing my stone for me.

I chuckled, listening to Mum talking to Dad,

"I feel like I'm out with my teenage daughter. She came along in the car with us but has spent the rest of the day chatting and playing with everyone else. Maybe she hoped all their rucksacks would also be filled with goodies for her."

There always seems to be something, or someone, to spoil the fun. I was having a wonderful time playing with a group of humans, and they were, even though I say it myself, totally taken in by my charms. I wasn't bothered that these people spoke in a foreign language as they could still stroke me, cuddle me, and throw my stone.

Now I'd noticed a couple of sheep on the hill, but I was far more interested in how many humans I could get to throw my stone rather than chasing the boring sheep. In the distance back up the hill, breaking the peace, I could hear a man shouting. His voice started to get louder and louder, turning into a roar. As I looked up at the mountain, it was like something from a cartoon. Sheep were running in all directions, chased by an enormous brown dog. The dog was being chased by its owner, who was howling at it to stop, and he was using some very short, fast words. The crowds of humans walking, sitting and lying down on the hill, became aware of the chase as the sheep and humans scattered in all directions. It looked like a game of human skittles. Glancing over at Mum, I could see that she was also aware of the chase. I could read her thoughts, and I knew she could read mine. She knew I was going to give chase and sort this mess out (well, I am a Collie). Mum joined in the fracas and shouted to the humans playing with me to grab hold of my collar.

It became a game of charades as these humans obviously didn't understand the simple command, 'grab her collar'. Sadly, for me, but fortunately for the sheep, they realised just in time what Mum was trying to tell them and grabbed me off my starting block before I could join in the chase. If looks could kill! I was not happy Mum had spoiled my chase.

With the disaster averted, we went back down the hill safely to the car and home again. Mum said she has aching legs, Dad had sore knees, and I could feel myself twitching on the rug as I did a re-run of the day in my mind.

I'm pleased to tell you that no dogs, sheep, or humans were hurt in this story.

Chapter 13

Left Behind on the Mountain

13 August 2019

Mum wrote about this event in her book, The Magical Tearoom on the Hill, and between you and me, I'm dead chuffed how I was once again declared a hero. I wish my dog mum could see me now. I always pray she'd be proud of the dog I've become.

But Mum told the story in her book in her words. I wanted to tell you how this scary adventure felt for me.

Since starting my life with humans, I've realised that dogs and humans are much the same. I need to eat, sleep, and go outside for some exercise to keep my body fit and healthy. I've got my favourite foods, walks, and of course favourite game, where I play with a ball in the park. Mum's a bit the same; she loves cakes and biscuits, which she always takes with us on our walks up the hills. She has her favourite walks too, with Ben Lawers at the top of her list.

This mountain has already been featured in previous chapters, including when I found a girl freezing with the cold, and when I pulled Mum down the hill when I chased the skiers in the snow!

This particular adventure will be stuck in my mind for a long time. Dad says he'll never forget this day either, but Mum says she's trying to forget about it and get on with things as much as possible. She acts like nothing bothers her and tells everyone she's a tough Yorkshire girl, but I know better. Underneath her tough appearance, she's just a big softy who cries like a baby at the drop of a hat.

As adventures go, this was a pretty frightening one, and I honestly believed I might never see Mum again. Let me tell you all about it.

As usual, Mum and I were heading out onto the hills without Dad. Poor Dad. His wonky knees hurt him so much now that he can't come out to play on the mountains with us anymore.

"Right Beatrix let's get ready. It's a good day for another hike up Ben Lawers. I bet there'll be plenty of bilberries ready for picking up there," announced Mum.

"Oh, I remember the bilberries. They smell lovely, and the heather around them is like a soft blanket. I love that mountain."

Mum packed her backpack with plenty of warm clothes. Dad made a picnic for us, a flask of tea, and a bottle of juice to drink. Of course, Mum put in some Kendal Mint Cake too. She loves that minty sugary treat, but I think it's disgusting, and I'm glad she never wants to share it with me. Actually, I don't think I've seen Mum sharing her Kendal Mint Cake with anyone except that girl who was freezing with the cold, who I rescued a while ago. That girl had no coat on, silly girl!

The drive up to Glen Lyon can be a bit of an adventure, and even though I don't drive myself, I can understand why humans sometimes find the single-track road a bit scary. It's narrow and twisty, and there are big drops at either side of the car in places.

Today arriving at the car park, the views were already great. A few black clouds were racing across the sky, and a gentle wind blew around us. I love walking in the wind. It makes my black and white coat look pretty, and humans always tell me what a beautiful dog I am.

I think Mum was finding it a bit chilly as she'd already put on her long trousers and jacket before we left the car. My coat's perfect, whatever the weather. I often think it must be much easier being a dog than being a human.

This mountain is one of Mum's favourite climbs. She always talks about it, showing me maps of the area and pointing out the routes, as if I need a bit of paper to know which way to go. Mum says it's not just because it's a high mountain that makes it her favourite climb but because of how remote it feels up there. Mum and I are so alike as we both like walks where we don't meet many humans, allowing us to enjoy the peace. We've been up the mountains before and never met another person. Dad says we're as mad as each other.

We were having a fabulous day. Mum chatted with a few different people, including a lovely lady and her son, who threw lots of stones for me.

As we began climbing up the hill, Mum was beside herself when she saw all the massive bilberries growing.

"Look at the size of these bilberries," she squealed. "I'll pick some of these on the way back down, and Dad can make some wild berry jam with them."

Mum does get excited about the strangest of things. I'm not so keen on eating these tiny berries, but I do love running in the heather around them. It seemed like a good plan as I'm always a bit tired at the end of this long walk, and I'd be able to have a little rest in the heather as Mum picks away at the berries to her heart's content.

Before long, the heat of the sun and the shelter of the mountains brought out millions of midges. Mum stopped, smothered some of that midge spray over her face and hands, and even rubbed it into her hair, which was not a pretty look, I can tell you! These midges must do nasty things to humans, but they don't bother me. It all seemed a bit of a waste of time, because before too long, it started to rain, forcing Mum to put on her waterproof jacket and trousers.

As we worked our way up the twisting path of the first mountain, Beinn Ghlas, I found my perfect stone for the day and encouraged everyone we met to throw it for me. We Collies have a way of letting everyone know exactly what we want you to do. Trust me!

It was turning into a glorious day. The views were stunning, the sun was now shining, and Mum had a great big smile on her face. As you near the top of Beinn Ghlas, there's a little respite where you seem to be walking along a grassy field. You've conquered the steep twisting climb, and there's a good long section of level walking before the final haul to complete the first Munro of the day.

The wind started picking up as we climbed higher and higher onto the open mountain. I love the wind. I waited for Mum at the top of one of the large rocks, enjoying the feeling of my coat blowing in the wind. Mum now had on her woolly hat. She always likes to wear something on her head when we're on the hills, and I worry that one day she'll try to make me wear a hat too.

Once over the final ascent to Beinn Ghlas, we got our first view of the summit of Ben Lawers, and the route began to descend over a ridge. As soon as I see the steep drops along either side of this ridge, I wait for Mum to clip her lead onto me. I've said before that Mum's a clumsy human, and I mean clumsy. I always feel relieved once she's fastened onto me because she usually needs my help over this section.

As we began the short descent, we chatted, and I got a couple of my biscuits; Mum had some Kendal Mint Cake and took lots of photos. She must love me as she's always smiling when taking pictures of me.

Approaching the last section of Ben Lawers, Mum stopped to talk to a couple of walkers who also had a Border Collie. The other dog and I had a run about together as Mum chatted away to the walkers for what seemed like forever. Parting company, the other walkers headed down the mountain, and Mum and I set off to finish Ben Lawers, with me leading the way, of course.

That's when things started to get a bit strange.

At this point, Mum's usually keen to get to the top of the mountain, but the next thing I knew, she was sitting on a rock.

"Come on Mum," I called to her. "You've just had a rest. Let's get to the top so we can have our lunch."

I ran back down to her, sitting beside her. I watched as Mum got out an apple from her rucksack. Maybe we were having an early lunch. But she only took one bite of the apple, then threw it on the ground. I must admit Mum looked a bit odd. She was pale and no longer smiling.

"Come on Beatrix," she said. "I don't think we'll bother with the summit today. We'll go down the old deer stalker's path. We can have our lunch break further down there."

"What!" I cried. "Not go to the summit. Why not? It's not snowy or icy? What's wrong Mum? We were having a wonderful time until now. What's the point of coming if we're not going to the top? Please Mum. Please let us go to the top."

"Don't whine Beatrix. Not today," Mum replied.

As I watched Mum stand up from the rock, I was slightly alarmed at how wobbly she seemed. But we started to walk down the track. Going along the path on a slight descent is usually a walk in the park. Mum was behaving oddly. She was going so slowly and barely putting one foot in front of the other. I looked closely at her. She was a horrible colour and was rubbing her chest.

We'd only gone a little way down the track when Mum plonked herself down on a big flat rock. I couldn't believe what she did then. She got out her phone and started to take pictures of herself.

"Don't bother with photos," I told her. "You look a bit too rough for that."

I was pleased she listened to me and started getting our lunch from her rucksack. Dad always packs a lovely lunch for Mum and me to share. There are usually sandwiches, cakes, biscuits, and a flask of tea for Mum. I'm not bothered about the tea as I drink the fresh water from the becks and streams. Each hill has different flavoured water you know. You should try it.

But today was different. I watched expectantly for Mum to eat her sandwich and then give me the end bit, but she only had a little nibble, then dropped the whole sandwich down to me, before sighing,

"There you go Beatrix; you can have that. I don't feel like eating today."

Usually, I'd gobble up the sandwich, but it didn't feel right today. I looked at Mum. She didn't seem well at all. I was beginning to feel worried about her. I suddenly lost my appetite and sat beside her with my nose on her knee. That usually makes her smile. It didn't work today.

She got out her phone again and started pressing the buttons. It clearly didn't do what she wanted it to because she used some of those naughty words that I'd heard her use before when things were not going well.

Right, I decided. I had to take charge of this situation. Mum was not well, and she needed some help. I looked around. It was all quiet, and there was nobody near us. Further back up the hill, I caught sight of the lady and her son, who'd been throwing stones to me earlier. I didn't want to leave Mum, but I knew I needed them to come back and help her.

I started to bark. I have a really loud bark when I want to. You know what I mean, the bark that the postman can hear through the double glazing and the bark that Mum says goes right through her. I barked louder and louder. We were in a bealach, and as I barked, I could hear the sound echoing across the valley.

"Wow! That's loud," I gasped.

But it was working. The lady and her son were running down the hill towards us. When they finally got to us, Mum told the lady she didn't feel very well.

"I think she can see that Mum," I whispered.

They talked about phones and that there was no signal. The lady said she'd go back up the hill as she knew there was a signal up there. I didn't know what that signal thing was, but I hoped it would come and make Mum better.

Then the lady left.

"Oh no!" I cried. "Don't go. Please don't leave us alone again. What am I supposed to do?"

Now Mum wasn't sitting on the rock anymore; she was lying on the ground. She wasn't moving at all. And she certainly wasn't smiling.

I kept barking to try and get more humans to come and help. It had worked to get the lady down to us, so it might get more humans to come. I kept licking Mum's face.

"It's OK Mum. Everything's going to be fine."

I collected lots of little stones for her and put them on her jacket. I don't know about you, but I always feel better with a few stones next to me.

My barking obviously worked as soon more humans ran down the hill to Mum. They pulled out all Mum's spare clothes from her backpack and wrapped her in them. There was even a new blanket I'd never seen before. It was a shiny, silver one which didn't look cosy to me, but it seemed to be helping Mum. Then other humans were putting their own coats on Mum too. One lady was lying on the ground beside Mum, holding her hand. Usually, I wouldn't like it if humans got too close to Mum, and I've never seen her hold anyone's hand except for Dad's. I didn't understand what was happening, but somehow, I knew it was OK for this lady to be so close to Mum. I was glad she was.

I kept barking because that was the only thing I could think to do. Other humans were now throwing stones to me. I was a bit torn. I wanted to sit next to Mum and make sure she was OK, but I can't help chasing stones. I ran for the stones, and then came back to check on Mum. The lady was taking care of her quite well, so I went to play with the stones again.

Then somebody put my lead back on me and stopped me running around. What was going on?

"Please look after Beatrix when it comes. She'll be frightened," I heard Mum say.

"When it comes?" I whispered to her. "When what comes? I'm already frightened."

Then I could hear a strange noise. The humans around Mum were all looking up at the sky, and one of them was standing up, waving a large orange plastic bag in the air.

I looked into the distance where the noise was coming from and saw a red and white thing in the sky. It was getting closer and closer, larger, and larger. It was so noisy, even louder than my bark. I started to bark at it. I needed to protect my mum from the noisy monster.

It flew above us in a circle for a couple of minutes before finally landing on the hill near us. Humans came running out of the monster, and one knelt by Mum and started talking to her. I saw him put something in her mouth, but I didn't know what it was.

Then they put Mum in a carrying thing and began taking her to the monster.

"Oh no! Please don't take her away. I love her. Bring her back," I kept shouting to them.

But they took her away. I couldn't reach Mum to rescue her from the noisy monster because I was on my lead, and the person was holding me so tight that I couldn't move.

I kept barking and crying.

"I'm trying to save you Mum. I love you. Come back."

But the monster went back up into the air with Mum inside it. I wondered if I'd ever see her again.

Then I realised I was all alone. How was I going to get back to Dad and our house? I knew how to get down the mountain to the car, but I couldn't drive the car myself. What was I going to do?

But the humans who'd been helping Mum spoke nicely to me, and we all began to walk along the track back down the mountain to where the car was. It was a bit of a strange walk. I didn't know these humans, but they seemed nice enough. It wasn't like walking with Mum; she only put the lead on me when I needed to help her over dangerous ridges and rocks - this time I had to walk back all the way down the mountain with the lead on. I never even got to play in the heather by those bilberries Mum had raved about.

As we got closer to the car park, I could see a car that I recognised. It was Buster's car. Buster's one of my friends who lives across the road from me with his human Mum and Dad. My dad was standing next to Buster's dad, waiting for me. How he knew I needed him, I don't know. I wondered if he also knew that somebody had stolen Mum from us.

"Dad, Dad, you're here. Mum's been taken away. I tried to save her, but the noisy monster took her. I'm sorry," I barked.

Dad took the lead from the lady and thanked her for bringing me down the mountain. I thought he'd be happy to see me, but he looked sad, although he did give me a little cuddle.

Then we were in our car travelling home. Dad never spoke all the way home. I wondered if he was cross with me because I didn't keep Mum safe. I lay down on the back seat and closed my eyes, feeling as sad as Dad looked. I'd let Mum down. I hadn't kept her safe.

When we got home, Uncle Danny was there waiting for us. Dad packed a bag for me with some food, little black bags for you-know-what, and my stretchy lead. I thought Dad must be upset with me, and that was why he was sending me away. I was beside myself.

Off I went in Uncle Danny's car. But Uncle Danny was lovely. When we got to his house, he let me sit on the floor next to him, stroked me and chatted with me. Uncle Danny didn't seem to be cross with me at all, and I thought living with him might not be too bad after all.

The next few days passed quickly. I'd been to Uncle Danny's house many times before, so it wasn't strange being there. I had lots of cuddles, food, a lovely warm home, friendly humans, and plenty of walks. What more did I need? Well, apart from Mum and Dad, of course. I was scared I'd never see them again; it was all my fault.

Then one day, Uncle Danny packed my bags and put me in the back of his car. I was excited and thought we were going on an adventure. But I recognised the route we were taking and realised he was taking me home. What had I done wrong at Uncle Danny's for him not to want me anymore? I thought I'd been very well-behaved. OK, so I dug up his garden a bit and pulled concrete from around the drainpipe, but he had some lovely stones that needed re-arranging.

Uncle Danny's car pulled up outside my house. He let me out of the car, opened the front door of my house and let me go inside. I ran in, hoping Mum and Dad would be there, but the house was empty.

"Oh no! I've got nobody. Everyone's left me. They must hate me because I didn't rescue Mum," I sobbed.

I sat on my window box, looking out onto the deserted street. But then, before I knew it, Dad was pulling up into our driveway in our little red car, and who was sitting next to him? Mum. My mum. She was safe and back with us. I was jumping up and down. I got a ball out of my basket for Mum to play with.

"Mum, Mum, you came back. I've got a ball for you to play with," I cried.

Dad told me I had to sit down and be careful. Mum still seemed a bit out of sorts, so I didn't fuss over her too much. I was just glad she was home, even if she didn't want to play with the ball.

It wasn't long before she was lying on the couch, and I was snuggling up on the floor beside her.

"Do you know how proud I am of you Beatrix? You really are my hero. I've missed you so much, and I was so worried about you having to come down the mountain without me," Mum said, stroking my ears.

She never said anything about being cross because I didn't save her. I don't know how Dad rescued her, but I love him even more now.

I knew then, as I had done all those years ago when I first became a human dog, I had to take care of Mum and get her strong again. I never left her side and kept checking on her all the time.

A few weeks passed with Mum taking her time, finding her feet again and taking short walks through the park and into the wood near us. But it wasn't long before Mum was getting back to her usual self, and we were heading up the hills. Dad told me he was worried about Mum going out in the mountains again but that he knew I'd look after her as much as possible. I promised him I would, so long as there were no noisy red and white monsters.

More adventures, here we come.

Chapter 14

Has the World Gone Mad?

March 2020

"It's late; what's going on? Where are you, Mum? I'm bursting for the toilet. When are you coming down to take me out?" I cried, at the bottom of the stairs.

Usually, every morning it's the same. I hear the alarm going off upstairs (I still don't know what happens up there), and Mum comes down to take me for a walk. Then it's back home for some breakfast. I don't care much for the porridge stuff that Mum loves, but Dad always makes two slices of lovely hot buttered toast, one for him and one for me. Then it's all a bit of a blur whilst they get themselves sorted and put on their uniforms. As soon as I see the white shirts with purple writing and the matching purple jackets, my heart sinks as I know I will get left at home again.

But today was different. Eventually, Mum came down, and we went out for a walk. There was no rushing and, if

I'm honest, Mum seemed a bit sad. I told myself that she'd feel better when we got on the farm track that we usually walked along. She'll soon feel the fresh air around her, and perhaps we'll see the deer.

Mum didn't seem to cheer up. There were no deer in the fields, but we saw a few other humans who seemed sad too.

Something was odd.

Mum's usually very chatty with humans and laughs with them, but she didn't seem to want to be near them today.

Dad had breakfast ready when we got home, but there was still no rush. We ate our toast, and I went to lie on my window box to get ready to do my sad-looking face to them when they set off in the car and left me. I've got this sad eye look mastered to a tee now.

Hang on a minute, I thought. Mum and Dad are not getting ready in their usual work clothes. They're just sitting around. Don't they know they're going to be late for opening their tearoom?

"Wow," I sighed. "This is amazing. You're not leaving me. Are you and Dad staying at home with me? What a fantastic day this is going to be."

I realised I didn't need to make that sad-looking face or wait for Trisha from Campsie K9 to take me out. Oh, mind you, I do like going out with Trisha and playing with my friends. She's great and takes me on long walks and spends hours talking to me. Trisha is another one of those golden humans who can speak to dogs and understand them. But that's OK, I told myself. I'm happy to stay at home with Mum and Dad. I love being with them. I hate it when I'm left alone.

And that was it. Mum and Dad stopped going to work. They began to stay at home with me all the time. Had they realised how sad I was without them? Did they know I missed them so much that they had to stay home with me?

I tell you, life as a human dog is just getting better for me.

Strange things started to happen though. When Mum or Dad went out, they started covering their mouth and nose with masks. I began to see more humans wearing masks. What's all this about, I wondered? I noticed that humans stopped getting close to each other too. They seemed to be keeping each other at arm's length. When we were on the canal, Mum kept stopping and moving away from the path if other humans were coming the other way. It was like she didn't want to be near them, and nobody wanted to be near Mum except for Dad and me. Mum and Dad kept saying how stupid people were because they didn't know how far two metres was. Mum said she would start going out holding her walking pole in front of her. It's all very odd. I love being near Mum. What's wrong with everyone?

Let me tell you about the masks. Humans are now wearing all different ones. Some are plain, some coloured, some have pictures on them, and sometimes humans cover their faces with their scarves. I've never seen anything like it in my life. There are even some dirty masks lying about on the ground. Has the world gone mad?

Luckily, I can still understand what humans are saying because, as everyone knows, your eyes say far more than your mouth. I can tell what humans think just by how they look at me, raise their eyebrows and whether their eyes sparkle. I can tell whether to trust somebody by looking into their eyes. You can't lie with your eyes. Do you remember earlier in the book, I was telling you about me having 'the eye'? Well, this is a bit like that. You can get humans to understand what you want with your eyes. Try it. Look at somebody, then look at a stone you want them to throw for you. Keep looking at the person, then the stone, and before long, you'll make them understand what you want them to do. Go on. Try it. See what you can make a human do by using 'the eye'.

I'm not entirely sure what's happening. There was lots of activity in the garden. Mum and Dad painted the fence and the hut in a strange new colour, a bit like the colour of sky. I've had to keep my distance as they are messy when they paint.

The big signs I remembered being at Mum and Dad's tearoom, where I sometimes went for a special treat, were now in the back garden and fastened to the newly painted fence.

It's wonderful though. The weather is perfect; sunny, dry, and warm. Now that the paint on the fence and hut has dried, I can move around the garden and find the perfect spot to sunbathe for a while, and then I can move into the shade when I get too hot. Mum and Dad have tables and chairs in the garden, and they seem to live outside during the day. Mum says they're eating al fresco, whatever that is. I don't think I've ever eaten any al fresco! But Mum and Dad are eating their meals outside in the garden, which is simply perfect; I sit near them, and if I do that excessive drooling thing, I get lots more treats than I would when I'm inside.

Life is more relaxed now. There is no rushing around, and I don't get left alone. I miss Trisha and my dog friends, but I like this new lifestyle.

Mum says we can't go on long walks because somebody called Boris has ordered the country to be in lockdown. Well, I don't know who this Boris is, but thank you for giving me more time with my Mum and Dad.

Chapter 15

Just Throw the Flipping Stone

28 February 2021

One of the benefits of having parents who work for themselves is that my mum can pick the days we will have as playing-out days. Mum says we're fortunate to live in East Dunbartonshire because this puts us within easy reach of the Campsie Fells. With the current travel restrictions, I'm probably one of the few dogs who can still access wonderful scenery without breaking any of the COVID-19 Lockdown rules. Or so Mum tells me.

The Campsie Fells, to the unsuspecting eye, could be just a little hill that you see from our home in Kirkintilloch and nothing much to shout about. The summit of Lecket Hill is nowhere near as high as a real mountain or one of those big Munros, but it's no mean feat, I can tell you, especially in wet weather when humans can find themselves waist-high in peat bogs. OK, waist-high is an exaggeration, but with my mum, anything is possible. Of course, I know exactly where to step and only ever get my ankles dirty.

The walk around the Campsie Fells from Clachan of Campsie, up Cort-ma-law and across to Lecket Hill in wet weather is similar to one of my favourite Yorkshire Dales hikes, Pen-y-Ghent. I've been up this with Mum and Dad, my human brother Benjamin and even my human sister Chlöe. This, too, is not a giant of a mountain. However, it is a serious undertaking in wet and wild weather, but given the right conditions, the view from the top is unbeatable. I don't think Chlöe will be doing any more walks with us because when Benjamin persuaded her to climb Pen-y-Ghent, it rained all the way round, and she said something about never again. I don't think she liked sharing her lunch with me either and certainly didn't like me doing the drooling thing over her.

You know I've told you about my brave Mum, well I'm trying to get her fit again after she had that little heart attack thingy, but things keep getting in the way. I managed to help her climb Ben Ledi last year and was delighted with her, but we haven't climbed anything significant since. I'm a little anxious now because Mum says we'll go back up Ben Lawers this year. You know the one, the mountain where noisy monsters come and steal humans. Thankfully, I've heard her talking to Dad. She's arranging for Benjamin to go with us once he's allowed to travel again between England and Scotland. Mum said that having Benjamin with us would stop Dad from worrying all day. I don't know about Dad, but I'd be pretty worried too if it were just Mum and me. I'll be glad to have Benjamin there to help me keep Mum safe.

With the lockdown thing in full swing, we're only allowed to travel five miles from our county border, so the Campsie Fells are the most extreme hill climbing we can undertake just now. We had a couple of epic walks over these fells last month in the snow when it was a little bit like Narnia up there. Then we had weather warnings for rain and high winds. But this week, Dad, our chief weatherman, said Saturday would be the best day to go walking as the weather was going to be good.

Now, Mum is my best friend, and we've had many adventures together. Most of the time, I act like a very obedient dog, and will come to heel at a slight nod or whistle and do almost anything Mum asks when I see a biscuit being offered. I'll sit to command and even run to Mum when she says, "Let's put your lead on." But let's not forget that I'm a human dog, and I have to confess to having one bad habit, which is a bit of a Collie trait. I'm obsessed with stones. I've been known to choose a stone at the bottom of the mountain and carry it all the way to the top and back down again. Mum doesn't like me playing with stones and is not particularly good at throwing them for me. I've tried playing with the tennis balls that Mum sometimes brings, but the stones are so unique. They feel lovely against my teeth, all taste different, and it's fantastic to see them fly through the air when humans throw them for me to chase. Mum says it's my own fault that I've broken a couple of my teeth doing this. She ignores my requests to throw the stone when I drop it at her feet. I do understand this now, and, in my mind, I know she'll not throw the stone, but I still try in the vain hope that she might do so.

However, when other humans are on the hills, I can't resist taking my favourite stone to them and dropping it at their feet as I do the Collie lying-down thing. Despite the chosen humans declaring how cute I am and how lovely I look; they don't always know what they should be doing with the stone. I can't bear this stupidity, so I get up and tell them, in no uncertain terms, that they should be throwing the stone for me.

Last time we were up the Campsie Fells, Mum was a bit cross with me when I talked to the humans.

"Beatrix. Stop that. You're scaring people. Not everyone understands what you're saying. It's just a bark to them."

"But you know I'm a soft dog. Why would humans be scared of me?"

"Yes, you are the softest dog anyone could hope to come across, and I know you have no aggression in your bones at all," replied Mum. "Unfortunately, you have the deepest bark I've ever heard from a dog, which can be intimidating. Also, that Collie smile that you do when you want somebody to do something, involves you showing lots of huge, sharp teeth."

"But you always laugh at my smile and tell me how wonderful it is," I cried.

"Yes, but all that the strangers can see is a big dog barking loudly, baring teeth, and running towards them. It's not a good look. This causes them to panic, and people try to run away from you because they think you're a savage dog. And you, Beatrix, make things worse when you continue to run around them, barking and showing sharp teeth. It's so humiliating and frustrating for me."

After that walk, I didn't speak to Mum for hours. I was affronted. I was distraught that she said I looked like a savage dog. Savage indeed!

I was a bit worried a few days later, overhearing a conversation she was having with Dad.

"I can't bear to go back up the Campsie Fells with her again," said Mum. "With the lockdown, it seems like the whole of Scotland is walking those hills, and she's making my walks so frustrating. I'm going out this week by myself and leaving her at home."

Dad laughed until he realised that she was serious.

"Surely not. Beatrix will cry for you. You can't be so cruel to her. And you know she looks after you on the hills," argued Dad.

"Go Dad. You tell her," I whispered to him.

"No," Mum declared. "You can't make me feel guilty. I just want a walk, in peace, with no barking dog upsetting everyone."

When she went upstairs, I went into the front room to get a cuddle from Dad.

"Dad, will she really go for a walk without me," I sobbed.

"Don't worry Beatrix; she wouldn't be able to do that to you. You know she loves taking you up the hills with her," he said gently.

Saturday morning arrived, but there was none of the sunshine that Dad had promised us. Mum took me out for a walk before breakfast.

"Mum, I'm sorry I was naughty and barked at the humans. Please let me come out with you today. I'll not bark at anyone, I promise," I said to Mum in my saddest voice (I'd been practising).

"OK, if you promise. I'll give you one last chance," said Mum.

I was so happy, and soon, we were getting ready to set off up the Campsie Fells again. Dad made us our packed lunch and a flask of tea for Mum.

"Dad obviously got the weather wrong," moaned Mum. "We'll not need suntan lotion today, but at least the wind will keep the midges away."

Before long, we were on the hills, with Mum clad top to toe in her waterproofs. I felt a bit sorry for her because I could imagine every other place in Scotland was basking in the sunshine.

"Not to worry about the weather Beatrix," Mum said. "The bad weather will keep the folk away."

Well, I can tell you that there were hundreds of humans climbing the Campsies. But there was a thick mist today, and I could see very little. This always puts me on high alert because my sight might not be the best, but I have excellent hearing and a great sense of smell. I already knew that lots of humans had set off from their cars as we made our way up the hills.

It quickly became a scene of absolute bedlam. As the mist started to clear, humans appeared like magic. I ran around, dropping stones and smiling at them. But the humans ignored me. The more they ignored me, the more I smiled at them. When they still ignored me, I started shouting at them, which made some of them scream and cry.

It wasn't long before Mum fastened herself to me with that lead thing. We walked in silence. I could tell Mum was cross, so I followed her without saying anything.

Away from the madding crowds, Mum found a small stile to sit at for our lunch.

"I thought you promised me this morning that you wouldn't bark at people," Mum said sadly. "Honestly Beatrix, it was like a scene out of a horror film when you started barking, showing your big sharp teeth, and people were screaming. I'm very disappointed in you. You've ruined the peace again."

"But Mum," I cried. "Why don't the silly humans just throw the ******* stone then?" (Rude word censored in case little people are reading this).

Mum told me off for my foul language, but she did laugh – I did learn the word from her, after all.

So, I apologise to all the walkers I disturbed and worried that day (and for those humans I meet on the walks to come when I'll probably do the same).

Perhaps Mum could make me a sign to hang around my neck that reads, 'Please Throw My Stone for Me'. That would make things much simpler.

Chapter 16

I Bet You're Glad I'm With You Today

3 March 2021

It seemed like Mum had forgotten her frustration of the last few walks up the Campsie Fells with me barking at everyone, and it came as no surprise to either of us that we were looking forward to going back up the same hills for another adventure. Of course, looking forward to yet another hike up the Campsies is stretching it a bit. That Covid thing is still here, and the lockdown is stopping us from travelling any further than our local hills, and to be honest, even I'm a little weary of hiking the same route repeatedly.

Dad, our personal weatherman, informed us that Wednesday this week would be a good day; cold but clear.

"Why don't you take yourself up the hills when you can?" he suggested.

Mum didn't need asking twice.

"Beatrix," she called. "Come and look at the map with me."

Mum loves a map, and because I love my mum, I pretend to love maps too.

"I think we'll do a different route. We can start further up the Crow Road at the layby where you would usually come down the hill if you were doing the circular route."

"Wow, are we going the whole way round the Fells?" I gasped.

"Not this time. We'll start further up the road where there'll be fewer people for you to bark at," she said, raising an eyebrow at me. "As it's been so wet recently, it'll be too boggy in some places, so we'll go as far as our usual lunch stile, then come back down the same way. I know it's nice to do a circular walk because you don't spend all day thinking about the route you have to go back down. But sometimes doing a walk in the opposite direction can make it seem different," explained Mum.

Armed with our picnic, flask of hot tea and warm clothes, Mum was soon parking our car in thick fog on the desolate Crow Road.

"I thought Dad said it was going to be fine today," I moaned. "I don't mind the bad weather, but even I think it's about time we had some dry walks."

Mum gave a little laugh.

But soon, we were off on our merry way and crossing the new wooden bridge taking us over the bubbling beck that we used to have to wade across. Now for you humans, this new wooden bridge is a godsend, but for us dogs, it creates a bit of a challenge as the slats are a little bit too far apart, and dog paws can get stuck between them.

Mum laughed at me as she watched me trying to cross the bridge. It was far easier without the bridge.

Fumbling through the gate in the new deer fence, I was amazed at how the ice formed in front of our eyes. As the gate closed behind us, a cracking noise caught our attention. We watched as the ice broke away from the gate and fence, crashing to the ground like shards of glass.

"Wow," we both cried.

"That's an unusual sight, especially so low down the hills," gasped Mum.

The start of the walk is a bit of a pull, but nothing too steep, and it's now a well-trodden path. Mind you, the well-trodden path was the only thing I could see as the fog descended thickly and quickly around us, but there was no wind. It was also incredibly cold. We'd only been walking a few minutes when Mum stopped and took her backpack off.

"Yes, snack time. Good idea Mum," I said.

"Give me a break Beatrix," said Mum. "We've only been walking twenty minutes. I've only stopped to put my gloves on."

But Mum couldn't resist my puppy dog eyes, and laughing, she gave me a couple of my biscuits.

I glanced around and breathed in the calm, peaceful, silent air. There was not another human in sight, so there was no point finding a stone. Mum never throws stones for me.

As we headed up the hill, I ran around in large circles, playing in the frozen grass. If there were to be no stone games, I could still have fun.

Before too long, I was vaguely aware that the visibility had dropped, and the fog wrapped silently around us. Our coats glistened with the developing frost, but we were having fun. On days like this, we don't do a lot of talking. We enjoy the peace and walk together in silence.

Mum stopped and looked back down the hill towards the car. I could see about as far as the end of Mum's walking pole.

"Well Beatrix, this walk will be trickier than I imagined. I'll have to keep my wits about me across the tops where the path's not so well-defined."

Sometimes Mum treks along without a care in the world, especially on days like today, with no noise, no humans, and no cars. But today seemed different.

Looking around, Mum announced, "I'm not absolutely convinced I know exactly where we are."

"I bet you're grateful you didn't leave me at home now," I muttered under my breath.

Dad calls Mum the pathfinder because she's so good at route planning, map reading and using a compass, but sometimes I know I need to be the leader. My pathfinding skills are something else. There's no marching along and hoping for the best with me.

I skipped and ran a little way, then stopped and stood for a minute, while sniffing the air to use my incredible sense of smell to tell me which way to go. It's well known that Border Collies have a highly developed sense of smell and an excellent memory. Mum also knows that once she's taken me on a walk, I remember the route, right down to where we stopped for snacks, where the cairns are, and where we had lunch. There have been times when I've been walking with Mum, and she's decided to take a different path, and I've had to sit myself down on the track I know we should be taking. Mum's grown to trust me and my instincts for following the correct path, not that she'd admit to relying on it, of course.

When we have boggy terrain to cross, Mum always watches me to see which way I go as I always seem to skip across the muddy bits, and not even get my paws wet. Of course, my weight's much more well-distributed, being on four legs rather than you mere humans who try to walk awkwardly on two legs across the soft ground.

"OK Beatrix, please don't tell Dad I've asked you this, but which way do we go now?" asked Mum.

I was at once on high alert. I was in charge now.

To be fair to Mum, the fog was thicker and colder than before, and navigation by humans would be almost impossible. I took a breather. I thought about where we'd walked from and where we wanted to be. Although the path was a bit vague in places up to the top, there was at least a track. Remembering from earlier trips up here, I knew that if we found ourselves walking on big tufts of grass, I'd know we were off the path. I've walked the Campsie Fells many times with Mum, and she says she thinks she could walk them with her eyes closed. Today she may as well have had her eyes closed.

"If you could just get us to the summit, the clouds will have cleared a bit, and then we can take our usual long walk back to the car park. We can then walk the mile or so up the road to where we have parked the car," Mum said quietly.

I could smell that fear thing about Mum now, so I wasn't going to mock her for getting lost, but I did wonder what would happen if the clouds hadn't cleared once we reached the top. Mum must have heard my thoughts.

"These hills are not incredibly high and don't have any real cliff edges, so the worst thing that could happen would be to find ourselves in Lennoxtown, with the car back up in the layby on the Crow Road."

"You'd have to tell Dad you were lost then," I said, trying not to laugh. "Just follow me, and you'll be fine."

We continued to skip along. OK, I skipped while Mum plodded. We even managed to negotiate, without too much hardship, the stile and fence with no dog flap. These bits are always a bit of a laugh for me. I wait for Mum as she works out the best way for us to get across. Then I'll show her which is really the best way.

"I'm fairly sure this is the track that would take us across the hill to the stile we usually sit at for lunch. Then we can follow our usual path back down to the Crow Road car park," Mum said, with a bit of a cheer in her voice.

I'm pretty sure it's not, I thought, but I didn't say anything.

This bit of the walk was a bit boggy, to say the least, but Mum had her walking poles with her to check the depth of the bogs before setting her feet down on them. I was trying to imagine what Dad, Mr Health and Safety, would say if he knew what the conditions were like.

"There's the fence Beatrix. That's where the stile is. We're not lost anymore," cried Mum.

"Watch out for that deep bit of bog just there," I shouted.

Too late! With her next step, one of Mum's legs disappeared into the depths of the soft, deep bog. I watched as she quickly got her walking poles dug into the firmer ground around her. I observed with amazement as she shifted her weight until she was horizontal, spreading her weight, (which, of course, is slightly more than mine). I panicked, thinking she would sink and never be seen again, but then I thought how ridiculously melodramatic I was being. I did worry that if she pulled her leg out too quickly, she'd lose her boot and then have to walk another five miles with just one boot on. Fortunately, she was wearing gaiters which fastened over the bottom of her boots and then her waterproof trousers over the gaiters, so her boot was firmly attached to her leg. Slowly, with a sucking noise and a lovely peaty smell, she was able to pull her leg free and roll herself over on to the firmer ground.

This time, I couldn't stop myself from laughing out loud.

Mum glared at me.

The next obstacle was yet another stile with no dog flap. Again, with no arguing or pointing out to Mum that we were at the wrong stile, I let Mum lift me ungainly over the stile, which is no mean feat with a large dog. But there was no way I was going to try jumping over it. She brought us this way, so she could jolly well lift me over.

Once over the stile, Mum used it as a table and chair and got out our picnic. Peanut butter sandwiches, hot tea, and a jam slice today. I, of course, had my own biscuits but shared Mum's buttie too. Just what the doctor ordered.

"This fence post is a bit higher than I remember," Mum said, reaching up to rest her flask of tea on the post.

"That's because it's the wrong fence post," I pointed out.

"Don't be silly Beatrix. I can see the two paths leading from the stile, and there's that little hill we usually walk up to get to the main path. No problem. What does it matter if the fence post seems a bit taller today?"

"Whatever," I sighed.

Refreshed by our lunch, Mum packed everything back up (leaving nothing but footprints, of course) and set off up the short hill to get to the main path. Lo and behold, out of the mist appeared a large cairn, just to confirm to Mum that the stile we had made our way to for our lunch stop was not our usual stile.

"Don't you even say it," hissed Mum.

By now, any panicking from Mum over finding the route in the thick fog was over, as we were now on the side of the hill that we both knew like the back of our hands and paws. Gone were the deep bogs, so there would be no further risk of Mum being swallowed up, never to be seen again. Even though I didn't admit to it to Mum, I was relieved to be out of the mist and fog.

We made our way along the tops of the hills, and finally the route began to descend steeply down to the Crow Road car park. Of course, now we were at the popular side of the hill, there were a few humans for me to get to throw my stone, but nowhere near as many as on previous walks.

Once we reached the main road, I was a little disturbed that we were now walking up the road and not stopping at the car park as usual. Remembering that our car was a mile further up the road, I suddenly felt tired.

It's not that far back up to the layby we parked at, but it felt like another five miles today. I was, of course, rallied by the fact that I get a biscuit every time a car comes past. That all started when I was a puppy and, in proper Border Collie form, I'd try to herd up the vehicles. To get me out of what Mum said was a dangerous hobby, she offered me a biscuit whenever I allowed a car to go past me without chasing it. I quickly discovered that biscuits were better than cars. To be honest, now, if we ever have to walk on roads, I pray for traffic.

Once back at the car, Mum dried me with a clean towel and let me get into the car.

"Now remember Beatrix, it's only the good bits we tell Dad about, or we'll be grounded," whispered Mum.

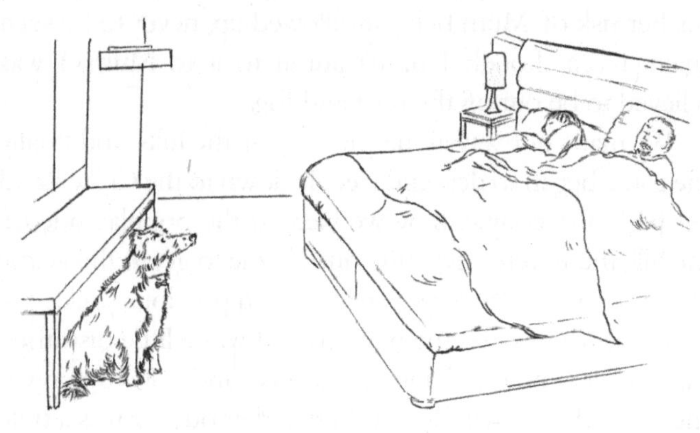

Chapter 17

The Christmas Best Forgotten

December 2021

As I've told you in one of my other stories, Christmas with my family is always special. This year was gearing up to be spectacular after the cancelled celebrations in 2020 due to that Covid thing.

I knew things were getting exciting when Mum brought down the big purple suitcase. This means only one thing - Mum and Dad are going away. And when Mum and Dad go away together, they always take me with them.

Early in the morning of the 23rd of December, Mum was back and forwards, packing the car. I was so excited, even though I knew it meant me having a journey in the back of our small car with only half a seat. But I wasn't caring. We were going on holiday.

Then we were off. Dad was driving to start with as he's OK on the motorway. Mum doesn't let him drive on the country roads as he forgets where he's going and gets into a bit of a panic.

It was an uneventful trip, with a quick stop for us all to do you-know-what at Gretna services and to have a picnic in the car. Mum and Dad said they didn't want to go into the services to eat, because it was too dangerous, and they would just nip into the toilet. I couldn't see anything scary, so I didn't understand what they were panicking about, but I wasn't bothered as I got my own patch of grass to use. If they were that scared of going into the services, I don't know why they didn't use my patch of grass to go to the toilet next to me.

A couple of hours later, we stopped outside a house. I wasn't exactly sure where we were, as I'd not been to this place before, but Mum ran in, so I followed her. My lovely human sister, Chlöe, gave me a big smile and a cuddle. But then I spotted that Minnie person and, not only that but there was also another little human.

Minnie was all over me. She grabbed me, put her fingers close to my eyes, in my mouth, and grabbed my tail. I looked at Mum. She pointed to me and told me to be nice. She also pointed to Minnie and told her to be gentle with me.

Do you know what Minnie did? She pointed at her grandma and giggled. If I'd done that to Mum, she would not have been happy. Mind you, thinking about it, when I give Mum a paw, she does smile at me. I wondered if giving the paw was the same thing as pointing.

The tiny human, Harley, was different. He's a little cutie, and just tickled me and giggled.

Taking in my new surroundings, I saw a huge basket of toys, way bigger than the basket at home. And what was on top of all the toys? A giant Peppa Pig was sitting there like a big soft lump of bacon. I thought I'd have a little play with it. I grabbed it out of the basket and started shaking it like I do with my toys at home.

Well, Minnie was hysterical. She was laughing so much that she fell over. It was a good job she had a nappy on, or there would have been an accident on the floor.

Mum was not happy with me and told me off, saying I must not play with the children's toys. It was different when Minnie was at my house, and she was putting my toy chop in her mouth, getting baby slaver over everything. Nobody told her off then. And can I remind you that was when Minnie put Baby Jesus in her mouth.

As for Chlöe, her face was even scarier than Mum's. She was certainly not a happy human.

Dad saved the day by getting my tennis ball from his pocket. It's amazing the stuff he keeps in his pockets. Mum's always telling him he's like a boy scout.

Minnie (or Mad Max as Mum now calls her) wasn't so bad then. She played with me quite nicely, like a proper little girl, and I've realised that my lovely smelly tennis ball is much better than a soft, fluffy Peppa Pig.

The peace didn't last long though, and Minnie went back to prodding and poking me, so I growled at her and pushed her away. Mum decided we'd all had enough of each other.

We set off in the car back up the road to the hotel where we were staying. Once I'd sniffed around the place and checked it was safe for us, we went back down the moving floor thing into the exciting food place.

Benjamin, my human brother, came to meet us. I was so excited as it'd been ages since I'd seen him. He's always so pleased to see me. He strokes me, talks nicely to me, and always drops some nibbles from the table when he thinks nobody is watching. I like Benjamin.

I found it strange in the food place as there were a lot of flashing lights and people sitting at tables around the room. One person was up there singing at the top of his voice (which was hurting my ears), and everyone kept clapping. I thought they were clapping for me to get up and dance, but no, they were just humans being humans.

Then it was back up to the room for a good night's sleep before returning to Chlöe's house.

Minnie was much better behaved, for a while. I toyed with the idea of getting Peppa Pig out of the toy basket, but then I remembered Chlöe's scary face and thought better of it.

Mum was quiet in the morning, but I was distracted by activities in the kitchen. Chicken and beef were being cooked for dinner. Oh, the smell. I was starting to drool already.

Suddenly, Mum said she was taking me for a walk, but she wasn't much fun at all, just plodding around the park, kicking the tennis ball for me, and not throwing it at all. She didn't even talk to me.

When we got back to the house, the smells were incredible. Who needs Peppa Pig when you have chicken and beef to look forward to?

"I feel a bit sick," said Mum. "I think I'll go for a lie-down."

Even more chicken for me, I thought, but then I felt a bit guilty and selfish.

Mum came back down as dinner was being served. It was so exciting; all this food and little humans who love dropping food under the table to me.

Then Mum disappeared upstairs again only to re-appear just as the food dropping was beginning to get interesting.

"Can we go back to the hotel?" she asked Dad.

No! I thought. I've not had any chicken yet.

But off we went, with Dad driving, so things had to be bad.

Once at the hotel, Mum went straight into the little room, making lots of strange noises. I tell you, when she came back out, she was as grey as the winter sky. And she just slithered her way onto the big bed.

I wasn't going near her! Dad could take care of her. She was in and out of the little room so many times she was making me dizzy. I found myself a cosy, comfortable space under the table, where I was well out of the way but could keep my eye on the two of them.

Well, would you believe it? Dad started going in and out of the little room too. It wasn't long before he was looking as grey as Mum.

The next twenty-four hours passed very slowly for me. I was worried about the two of them but didn't know what I could do. There were times I was bursting for the toilet, but I had to hold it in. Usually, Mum and Dad are good with me and take me for lots of walks, but they were lying on the bed, not moving, not talking, and crawling in and out of the little room.

I heard them talking about viruses with names like Covid and Nora.

Worse was to come. Usually, when we go away, Mum always packs my food into bags, and Dad then puts some cheese or ham on top of the dry food. Not this time. The only thing that was being offered to me was a dry oatcake. Some Christmas this was!

The following day, Mum and Dad slowly packed all the bags, and we were back in the car for a little stop at Mad Max's house to say goodbye to everyone. I've never seen such a sad, poorly lot of humans in my life. The only ones laughing and smiling were Minnie and Harley.

Back into the car and Mum said she had to drive through the Dales until we got to the motorway as her stomach wouldn't cope with being a passenger on wiggly roads.

In the back of the car, I could sit up and look out of the window. I know the route well now and recognise lots of places.

Leaving Halifax, the weather looked as sad as Mum and Dad, and you could hardly see anything through the fog. As we travelled out of Calderdale, up to the heights of Denholme Gate and the Flappits, the fog lifted, and it turned into a pleasant trip.

Just before darkness fell, we pulled into our drive at home. At last!

And it's been a quiet time since then. There has been no festive spirit and noticeably short walks. One good thing about this whole sad affair is that Mum hasn't had all those musical toys playing every day like any other Christmas holiday. I feel sorry for her though, as she loves Christmas, and this has been a miserable time for her this year.

She says this makes her even more determined to have her own Christmas Tearoom, where it will be Christmas every day.

Chapter 18

Revisiting the Helicopter Hill

30 May 2021

I was having a snooze on my window box. Feeling the sun's heat on my back through the window, I knew summer was just around the corner. I thought I might have to move from my box, as I was getting so hot lying there. But I was so comfortable.

As I debated whether to get down or burn, I overheard Mum chatting to Dad in the kitchen.

"It's time I went up there again."

My ears pricked up on hearing this. Where did Mum need to go? I was down from my box and in the kitchen before you could say the word 'biscuit'. This was a conversation I needed to be part of.

"Where do you need to go again, Mum? Am I coming with you? When are we going? Does Dad need to make us a picnic?" I asked, nudging into Mum's legs.

"If you think you're ready, then yes, it's time," said Dad, biting into a rich tea biscuit.

Oh, Dad's got biscuits. Real biscuits. I ran around the table and sat by his feet. Dad always shares his biscuits with me.

"It's time to go back up Ben Lawers, you know, the one where I had to be taken away in that helicopter," said Mum.

"No! No! Not that one," I shrieked. I was slightly embarrassed that such a high-pitched noise had come out of my mouth, but I was so shocked.

"Why do you need to go up that hill again? There are so many other lovely walks. Not that one. Please Dad! Tell her she can't go up there again."

"Beatrix, calm down," said Dad. "Mum needs to do this. It's her way of proving to herself that she's better. We must let her do it."

Dad dropped me a biscuit.

"It's OK Beatrix. You'll be there, and Benjamin has agreed to come along too, so there's really no need to panic," Mum said, smiling at me.

I noticed that Dad wasn't smiling quite so much.

Suddenly I'd lost my appetite for biscuits and walked slowly into the front room, jumping back onto my box. In my mind, I was back up that stupid hill. Mum was lying on the ground, and that giant, noisy monster was coming to take her away. I remember being so frightened that I might never see my mum again. Why did she need to go back up that mountain?

A few days later, Benjamin arrived at our house, and all the talk was about Ben Lawers. I was still a bit worked up about going, but at least Benjamin was going to be there, so he could help me to keep Mum safe. It's a big responsibility to be in charge all the time, and it will be nice to share the burden. After all, what's the point of having a big brother if he doesn't help you every now and again?

Then it was time. Dad was getting the picnics ready. Mum and Benjamin were packing their bags with spare clothes and getting their big boots ready.

Dad took me out to the car and fastened me in.

"Look after her for me Beatrix," whispered Dad in my ear. Was that a tear I saw in his eye? I wondered.

I realised then that it wasn't a burden having to go up that hill again with Mum; it was a privilege. If Mum was brave enough to get back up that mountain, then, of course, I'm going to be with her, and I will keep her safe.

I was still glad Benjamin was coming.

As always, the drive to get to the walk was fun. I've told you in earlier stories that the journey to the start of Ben Lawers is a bit exciting, and today was no exception. Along the lovely roller-coaster of a road passing alongside Loch Lubnaig, Benjamin kept saying how beautiful the scenery was. When he saw the loch, I thought he might even jump out of the car as he was chatting so much about wanting to swim in the glass-like water.

Glancing in her rear-view mirror, Mum smiled at me. We're used to the views, but we never grow tired of them.

As Mum turned onto the single-track road leading up to Ben Lawers, Benjamin didn't look quite so smiley or excited.

"Oh! Take your time Mum. It's a bit narrow this road, and there are some big drops. There's no rush," he said in a quiet, little voice. I thought Dad was a bit of a scaredy-cat up this road, but Benjamin was even worse.

"Don't worry Benjamin. She's an expert on this road now," I called to him, but I kept a close eye on the steep drops by my window.

I've never seen any human get out of a car as quickly as Benjamin did when we finally arrived at the car park.

Then it was the usual wait for the humans to get themselves sorted. They take so long putting on their different boots and choosing which jumpers or jackets to put on. Benjamin decided he needed suntan lotion, and Mum insisted she had to rub on some of that smelly smidge stuff. I'm always ready.

Then we were off.

"Is that the top we can see Mum?" asked Benjamin.

"No. You don't see the summit of Ben Lawers until we get up to the top of Beinn Ghlas," replied Mum, holding my lead as I helped her across the road to the start of the walk.

"Can we see where the helicopter landed from here?" asked Benjamin.

"No, not yet. Not until we get up to the top of Beinn Ghlas," replied Mum.

"Do you feel OK?" Benjamin asked, putting his hand on Mum's arm.

"I'm fine, honestly," replied Mum as she took off my lead.

"Is he going to keep asking questions like that all day Mum?" I whispered to her.

Mum smiled.

It was a strange day. I was glad to be back on Mum's favourite mountain, but I could still remember the last time we were here and well; you know what happened then! I felt like I had butterflies fluttering around in my tummy, but if Mum was OK, then everything was fine.

It was fun having Benjamin come along with us, as he throws more stones than Mum does. Mum hardly ever throws stones; that's why I have to ask other humans to throw them for me (then I get into trouble for talking too much to them as I forget that not all humans can understand dog talk).

As we began to climb the first mountain, Mum and Benjamin chatted with lots of different humans, and we had plenty of little rest stops. I did wonder if this was because Mum couldn't walk as quickly as before, or whether it was just to enjoy the views and have more biscuits. It seemed to be working though because Mum looked to be having a wonderful time.

I knew we were getting near the top of Beinn Ghlas. The wind was building up, and the walk got a bit steeper. Watching Mum and Benjamin was like watching twins. Mum would stop to put on her hat, and the next thing I knew, Benjamin was putting on his. They copied each other without thinking, if you know what I mean. They are so similar. I wonder if I'm like my dog mum.

We had a lovely little break at the top of Beinn Ghlas, and Mum still seemed to be having fun.

Leaving the summit to walk along the ridge, with Mum safely fastened onto the lead of course, I started to get a little bit uneasy. Not quite scared but a bit panicky. In the distance, I could see the big stone where Mum had started to feel unwell on that last walk up here. I needed to keep Mum away from that stone. I couldn't let her sit down on it. I didn't want her to become ill again. Trying to walk faster, I pulled Mum on the lead.

"Don't pull so much Beatrix. Slow down," Mum complained.

As we walked past the giant boulder, Mum put her hand on it.

"Don't touch it Mum. Don't touch it!" I cried.

Mum tickled my ears and unfastened me from the lead.

"This is as far as I got last time," Mum said to Benjamin.

"We don't need to go to the top of the next mountain. We can go back now if you're a bit nervous," said Benjamin, looking worried.

I looked at Mum. Was she nervous? Was she scared? Now I was a bit anxious. Was she going to be ill again? Would a noisy monster take her away once more?

Fastening her coat up a little more against the wind, Mum smiled and said, "No. I'm going to get to the top today. Nothing is going to stop me."

She is so brave. I love my mum.

As we made our way up the final mountain, I ran between Mum and Benjamin, laughing and giggling. There was a massive patch of snow just before the top, and Benjamin called on me to play in the snow with him. He kicked the snow about, and I rolled a stone across it. Mum took pictures. This is the life! - climbing hills with your favourite humans and having snow to play in.

The top of Ben Lawers is a bit rocky, and the actual summit is small, with a square lump of rock that everyone likes to stand at and have their photos taken. Mum and Benjamin were no different.

The best moment of the day had to be when Mum stood by that lump of rock and threw her arms in the air. Benjamin stood alongside her. She had the biggest smile on her face that I'd seen for ages. I could feel the happiness oozing out of her.

"Well done Mum, you did it," said Benjamin, putting his arm around her.

For a moment, I couldn't move. I had a lump in my throat and thought I might cry. I was so proud of Mum. She had taken on this mountain again and beaten it. What a brave human she is.

"Are we having lunch now," I asked excitedly.

"No, I think we will go down the hill until we've passed the helicopter spot, then we can all enjoy our food," replied Mum.

I skipped down Ben Lawers to the big stone on the ridge. I was making sure Mum didn't sit down on it again, but she was skipping too, and we were soon back on the track heading down the back of Beinn Ghlas.

I had an uneasy feeling about me as I walked down the track, as this was the point where Mum became really ill the last time. Actually, this is where I thought she was going to die.

"Over there is the spot where the helicopter landed," said Mum pointing. She didn't need to tell me. I have thought about that day many times and know every single step of that fated walk.

"And that's where I was lying," sighed Mum.

Benjamin didn't say anything.

"Ten more minutes down this track, and we can have our lunch," said Mum in her cheery voice, breaking the sombre mood.

Soon we were sitting down on Mum's blanket and enjoying the splendid picnic Dad had packed for us. Mum and Benjamin were laughing and smiling together, I no longer felt anxious, and Ben Lawers had been well and truly conquered.

I couldn't wait to get home to tell Dad all about it!

Chapter 19

Is He Dead, Mum?

After *The Christmas Best Forgotten* had been forgotten, and my humans started behaving somewhat normally again, Mum began planning my first family holiday. According to Mum, we would have two fantastic weeks in a caravan (or house on wheels, as I like to think of them). There would be Mum, Dad, and lots of people from my human family - Chlöe, Neill, the demon Minnie, cute little Harley, gentle Leo, and myself. My big human brother Benjamin and his new dog Zeb would be coming to join us too.

One day I was listening to Mum and Dad chatting. Mum went on about how much she was looking forward to the holiday and staying in a caravan.

"It's been years since I went on a holiday to Primrose Valley as a child. We're going to make so many new memories as a family there," said Mum, her eyes glistening. Dad glanced over his glasses at me.

Sitting on my box, looking out of the front room window, I could feel my stress and anxiety building. Of course, I get stressed and anxious - I'm a Border Collie.

Evie, our own little house on wheels, was parked in our driveway. Now I like going away in Evie, but it's a bit of a tight squeeze. Mum and Dad have such long legs and big feet, and they always seem to put them just where I want to lie down. Not that there are that many options for me to choose from. I can lie under the table with Mum's legs right up against me, by the door with Dad and his legs over the top of me, or I can lie in the aisle next to the fridge. That's my favourite place, as I like to see what's being cooked on the little stove and check that the corned beef and cheese for my treats are still safe in the fridge.

Mum and Dad sleep at night in a bed, which they have to climb up a couple of steps to get into. Dad always has a bit of a huff and a puff about that. But then, he does a lot of huffing and puffing about everything nowadays.

I've heard Mum talking to other humans, telling them she loves spending time in Evie and how Dad tolerates it. As for me, I'm not bothered about where I stay. So long as I have plenty of food, treats, water, a nice dry place to lie down and my mum and dad, I'm quite content. A tent, a house, a caravan. I'm not that fussy. I suppose I should have put Mum and Dad at the top of my list of priorities, but then, it's that Maslow's hierarchy of needs thing that Mum told me about once.

Jumping down from my window box, I nuzzled up to Mum's legs as she was sitting on the couch doing that crocheting thing she loves so much.

"How are we going to fit everyone into Evie?" I asked in my most concerned voice.

Mum looked down at me and started laughing and tickling my ears.

"You silly thing. We're not taking Evie. There'll be a huge caravan for you, Dad, Benjamin, Zeb, and me. Chlöe, Neill, and the children will be in another caravan."

Phew, I thought to myself. I like the idea of a family holiday, but I'm not entirely sure I could cope with being prodded and poked by the demon Minnie all day long, every day, for two whole weeks.

The cold, snowy winter months had passed. Mum and I are always sad when winter's over, as we both love the snow and cold. Dad hates it. He moans all winter long about the cold, the rain, the snow, the short days, and the long nights. My humans really are like chalk and cheese.

Gradually, spring turned into summer. The dark nights had been forgotten, and we were enjoying long, long days when it never seemed to get dark. I could sit in the back garden all day and late into the evening. We had our meals outside. What I mean by that is Mum and Dad had their meals at the table in the garden, so it was even easier for me to do the puppy dog eye trick to get them to share their meals with me. Of course, my own food bowl and water stayed inside where it was cooler. Don't worry; I had an old baby bath in the garden filled with fresh water for me each day. If I'm honest, I like it when it's been there a day or so as it has a better taste, but my humans seem to think I need it to be fresh each day.

This year the days just got hotter and hotter. It's hard to keep cool when you're a Collie, but Mum and Dad are great with me and take me down to the canal. I don't like to go in too far. I'm a good swimmer, but I don't really enjoy swimming. I prefer to stand in the water and chase sticks and stones.

It became so hot outside that Mum told me I couldn't play out during the day as I might burn my paws on the hot pavements. I got used to going for a walk early in the morning before the sun warmed up, then lying around in the garden after lunch before going for an evening stroll, once the sun had cooled down again.

It's interesting watching how humans' clothes change during the year. In winter, they wear so many thick clothes, hats and gloves and wrap scarves around their necks. They put on woolly socks in their great big shoes, sometimes with things underneath them to grip the icy ground. Then as it gets warmer, they wear different things, their trousers get shorter, and their big shoes are replaced with shoes that show all their feet and toes. Sometimes they don't even wear socks. I tell you; some humans don't have nice-shaped feet at all. There are funny-shaped toes, wiggly toes, and painted nails, but at least most humans have the most wonderfully smelly feet. Don't forget; my nose is usually very close to these feet.

I'm so glad I'm a human dog and not a human being. I'm happy with my black and white coat and claws on my paws, thank you very much.

Finally, the big day arrived for us to set off on holiday. I was alarmed at the number of bags and boxes on wheels that Mum was putting in the car and wondered if there would be room for all of us. Dad was doing his bit by making the picnic and flasks of tea. I sat in the garden to keep an eye on Mum as she packed the car, making sure she didn't go on holiday without Dad and me. As if she'd ever consider that.

"Where exactly are we going? How long will it take us to get there?" I asked excitedly.

Pausing to catch her breath, Mum replied, "Primrose Valley, near Filey, in East Yorkshire. It's a long way and will take us about five hours or so to get there."

I flopped to the ground and rested my chin on my paws, sighing. I like journeys in the car, especially if we're going on holiday, but five hours! That's a long time.

"Don't look like that," said Mum. "There'll be plenty of stops, and we'll have a picnic or two."

I have to say, the thought of picnics did perk me up.

Soon we were on our way. Mum let Dad drive as we were on the straight motorway so he couldn't get lost.

I'm not sure how fair it is that Mum and Dad get a whole seat each to themselves in the front of the car, and I always seem to be squashed up in the back with everything packed around me. I'm not one to complain, so I just get myself as comfortable as possible and try to relax into the journey. Mum always makes sure it's nice and soft for me by covering everything in a blanket, so there's nothing sharp for me to lean on. However, she doesn't realise how tempting it is for me to be so close to all the food she packs for the journey. She thinks I don't know it's there just because she hides it under the blankets. But I do. I never try to get to it, but the smell is sometimes almost too much for me, and I pray for us to stop for a break.

Before too long, we were pulling into the services at Gretna. I recognise these stopping places now, and I get so excited as I know there'll be a chance to stretch my legs, go to the toilet and have a snack.

Rested, relieved, fed and watered, it was back into the car for a nap. Mum was driving now, so I knew I didn't need to worry too much about us getting lost. And that's how the rest of the day passed.

After what seemed like days, OK, hours, we finally arrived at a place with lots of houses on wheels. Mum found ours, and once I'd had the chance to sniff around, we had a bit of a walk to see Chlöe and the rest of my human family. I was secretly relieved that our house on wheels was not right next to Chlöe and that Minnie. Close but not too close.

If I'm honest, Minnie wasn't so bad this time, and it's a little bit cute how she called me Beetic. Mind you; I don't want people to think I'm related to those tick things. I've had those beasts on me before now. Ticks might be tiny, but they simply latch onto your skin when you're not looking and try to suck all the blood out of you. Dad had to use one of those special tools to pull them off me.

Minnie's still a bit in my face, if you know what I mean, but I've realised that she means no harm. And she does like to play ball with me and take me for a walk. I have to remember to walk slowly when she's holding the lead, as she only has little legs. But I must admit to having a little chuckle to myself when I pull her over. She's as light as a feather! For some reason, Chlöe is not quite so happy at me pulling Minnie around, giving me that stern look of hers. She is so much like Mum. Maybe that's what happens when you become a mum - you learn how to give fierce looks. My dog mum used to do that too.

Over the next few days, we all played games, explored the houses on wheels and had plenty to eat and drink. The sun never stopped shining, and when the sun shines, humans are much more relaxed and smile more.

I think I love family holidays.

Then, do you know what? We found the little track that takes you to the beach and the sea. What an amazing place Filey is. It has one of the best beaches I've ever been to -

miles of lovely smooth sand and so much sea to play in. Where the beach meets the cliffs, there are so many stones and seashells to play with. They smell amazing and still have a pleasant taste about them. It was like getting a taste of fish but not eating any. I heard Mum telling Leo that this is where you can find lots of fossils, and there are some big caves around the bay. Maybe on one of the days of the holiday, we can visit the caves.

Filey is my new favourite place. We spent days simply playing on the sand, running into the sea, chasing a ball, and having picnics in a little tent that had no door. The tent got a bit crowded and messy at times, with Minnie, Leo, Mum, Dad, and I all trying to stay out of the hot sunshine and to eat our snacks without getting sand everywhere. Mum kept rubbing thick, white suntan lotion on the little humans. What a terrible smell. I'd sprint back down to the water when I saw the suntan lotion bottle coming out. Sometimes I couldn't help myself and had to have a good shake to get the seawater out of my coat, but everyone would shout at me to stop and push me out of the tent.

I had a fabulous time.

Halfway into the holiday, my human brother Benjamin came to join us, bringing along his new dog, Zeb, to meet me. Zeb must be the smallest dog I've ever seen, but he's a cute little thing. He doesn't bother me, and I don't bother him. Zeb leaves my stones alone, so I'm OK with him being around me. He's a bit of a live wire though, and Benjamin keeps telling him to calm down and have a sleep in the tent when we're on the beach. I think that Mum fusses over me too much, but Benjamin is even worse with Zeb. I even saw him rubbing suntan lotion into Zeb's fur.

It's always an adventure when Benjamin comes along. It's as though he brings out the Action Girl in Mum. This time he was getting Mum to go swimming in the sea. Seeing her happy and having a good time in the water was nice. Dad said he was happy just putting his feet in the water. I'm inclined to agree with Dad. The seawater was freezing. It was OK for paddling, but there was no way I was going swimming. Not only is the sea very cold, but it tastes of salt, and if I drink too much of it, I need to go to the toilet, and it is very messy, if you know what I mean.

Trying to play ball with Dad and keep an eye on Mum, Benjamin, and Leo swimming was hard work. How I was supposed to keep everyone safe, I just didn't know. Zeb had the right idea; he stayed in the tent and had a little snooze.

One day it all got too much for me. The three of them, Mum, Benjamin, and Leo, had become used to the cold water and were going further and further into the sea. More humans were going into the water too. The waves were coming in over them so high that I couldn't see whether they were OK or not. I couldn't bear it and charged into the water, barking as I swam out to save them.

"Come on, you lot. Get out of the water now. That's enough," I shouted.

But it was as if everyone had gone deaf and could no longer hear or understand me. There were screams and shrieks from little humans and even grown-ups, including Dad. Why couldn't they recognise I was just watching out for the silly humans in the sea.

Eventually, they did come out of the water, and I could go back to enjoying playing ball with Dad. Of course, I kept running back up to the tent because you can guarantee that there's food to be had wherever my brother Benjamin is sitting.

I even enjoyed playing with little Minnie on the beach. She only went into the water to paddle, but she loved throwing the ball for me and had such a cute little laugh. Perhaps she's not so bad after all.

Everything was going so well. Minnie wasn't bothering me quite so much, even on the nights when she slept in our house on wheels, and she even started to stroke my head nicely.

Then one day, all my humans decided to do their own thing. Mum and Dad said they wanted to walk into Filey along the beach as it was our last day before we went home.

The three of us set off. Mum and Dad walked in the water, along the edge of the sandy beach, thankfully just getting their feet wet and none of that swimming in the deep water. They kept throwing the ball for me to chase, and I was having a great time. But then, Mum put my lead back on me and started to walk up the little hill away from the sand.

"I want to stay here," I sobbed, pulling on my lead, trying to drag Mum back down to the beach.

"Come on now Beatrix. You've had plenty of time to play. Mum and Dad would like a nice cup of tea somewhere in the town. There'll be a biscuit or two for you as well, then we'll walk back to the caravan along the beach, so you'll get to play on the way back," said Mum in that stern voice of hers.

"OK," I said, trying to catch my sobs.

Climbing up some steep steps, Dad held my lead - my extending lead. We were going slowly as Dad's knees are so bad now. Trying not to let Dad know I was a bit fed up going so slowly, I let my mind wander, thinking about the fun we'd be having walking back along the sand later. There were just a few more steps to the top, but suddenly, I saw something. I think it was a cat or a squirrel. Well, it was something that moved. I couldn't help myself, and before I knew it, I was running down the steps.

In my defence, how was I to know that Dad wouldn't let go of that silly extending lead?

I heard Mum shout, "Beatrix," and I turned around just in time to see Dad following me down the steps. OK, so I might have been pulling him. I stopped. Whatever I was chasing vanished with the scream that Mum let out. But to my horror, I could see Dad wasn't stopping. He just kept running, well hopping down the steps, faster and faster. Then he fell over and started rolling like a sausage roll down more steps. Oh no! It was like the mountain and the skiers all over again.

Mum dropped her bag on the floor and ran down the steps to Dad. I watched, in shock and horror, as she knelt next to him, stroking his head.

"Is he dead?" I whispered to Mum. She glared at me.

Finally, Dad sat up. He looked a bit pale, but I'd definitely not killed him. Phew!

"What happened?" asked Dad in a shaky voice.

"It's that blasted extending lead. It's going in the bin now. That's twice Beatrix has nearly killed one of us pulling on that lead," hissed Mum.

She said lots more words, but I won't repeat what they were in case little humans are reading this.

"I'm sorry Dad. I'm sorry. I didn't mean to hurt you. I couldn't stop myself."

"It's OK Beatrix. I know you didn't do it on purpose. Let's forget about it," said Dad.

What a hero my dad is.

Dad hobbled up the rest of the stairs with Mum helping him. I walked nicely beside them. They didn't even need to hold the lead now. I was going nowhere. At the top of the steps was a bench, and Mum made Dad sit on it. Dad took his sandals off, and there was a lot of blood. It was horrible.

I wondered if dog blood smells as nasty as human blood. I thought I should have a go at licking the blood off Dad but was relieved I didn't need to when Mum pulled out some tissues from her bag. You can rely on Mum to have everything you need in her bag. She even had some sticky things she wrapped around Dad's toes.

I couldn't help but think if this had happened in the winter, Dad would have been wearing his long trousers, hat, gloves, a thick coat, and some proper shoes. I bet he'd have been able to stop himself from falling, and his toes wouldn't have been cut to shreds. I kept that thought to myself though.

With his toes bandaged up, Dad simply said, "I need a cup of tea. Don't worry Beatrix. I'm OK."

I was mortified. I love my mum and dad so much, but now I'd nearly killed both of them. I was so pleased to hear Mum would be throwing that extending lead away. I never liked it anyway. It was always getting me into trouble.

Before too long, we were sitting outside a café, and Dad didn't look so pale anymore. A lovely lady brought us all some drinks and put some food on the table. I was still too ashamed to even ask for some of the food, but Dad gave me a little bit of his biscuit.

He still loves me.

Part 2

Life and Magic Entwined

Chapter 20

Revealing More Mysteries

Mum and Dad often told me that I had grown into a beautiful, caring, unassuming dog. I was never aggressive to people or other dogs and animals, although I would give a low growl to unpleasant people and bare my teeth if another dog tried to become too friendly with my private bits or tried to steal my ball or stick.

In truth, I'd become a bit of a loner. They do say dogs become like their owners. I enjoyed my own company and the peaceful life I lived with Mum and Dad. In my house, there was no television, no loud music, (except when Mum played her Bruce Springsteen CDs) and no screaming or shouting. Life was good.

When it suited me, I could be sociable, and I especially liked it when visitors came to see Mum and Dad. I always found lots of stones to put on their knees, but I was disturbed that people in their posh, clean clothing didn't always fully appreciate my friendship gestures.

I enjoyed walking the hills with Mum, especially when it was just the two of us. The solitude and freedom in the mountains suited the pair of us.

We'd often sit awhile on a rock or mound and take in the peace, breathe in the clean, fresh air, and admire the views, which at times were so breath-taking that they would bring a tear to Mum's eyes (and mine). Mum would rub my nose, and I would nuzzle up to Mum's legs.

We were true soulmates.

It was on one of these tranquil hikes that I told Mum of my secret missions.

"We've had so many adventures, sad, happy, and sometimes frightening," I whispered to Mum.

"Yes, and you've helped me and others on so many occasions," said Mum, smiling.

"There have been many more adventures you don't know about," I said.

"What do you mean?" asked Mum.

"The times I disappear into the light when I chase my tail," I said, lying with my front paws crossed.

Mum looked lovingly at me. "I often see you vanish into the light, but time almost stands still until you come back with another little gift. I've not asked you about this before because I thought you'd tell me when you were ready," she said.

"I'm ready now. Would you like to hear some of my stories?" I asked.

Chapter 21

Yorkshire Accents, Dark Caves, and Insulin

One of my earliest secret adventures happened during my first-ever trip to the Northwest Coast of Scotland. From my home in Kirkintilloch, it seemed such a long, long journey, and I did at one point wonder if we'd ever get to wherever we were heading.

Not only was it my first visit to the beautiful Highlands of Scotland, but it was also my first time staying in one of those Bed and Breakfast places. According to Mum and Dad, there are not that many B&B things that allow dogs to stay, which is ridiculous. Where are humans supposed to go on holiday if they can't take along their most important family member? Anyway, this one was a dog-friendly place near Camusdarach. If you've never been, I urge you to go. I was amazed by the miles and miles of empty white sandy beaches with loads of sand dunes to play on. The sea there seemed very gentle and was wonderful to play in. My coat was so clean and soft after being in the water there. But the effect the area seemed to have on Mum and Dad was the nicest thing to see. I could almost feel the happiness oozing from them. Mum told me it's no surprise that filmmakers used this location in the film Local Hero, starring Burt Lancaster. It has the equally fabulous soundtrack, Going Home, by Mark Knopfler. We laugh with Dad because he says he loves that tune so much he wants it played at his funeral!

But let's get back to the journey. We had an exceptionally long but lovely drive to get there, and I was certainly glad that we stopped a few times to do what I needed to do and have a picnic or two. That's the thing about going places with Mum and Dad. It's not all about getting somewhere quickly - the journey is the adventure, not simply the arrival. There are always plenty of stops and picnics to share.

When we finally arrived at the bed and breakfast place, I was slightly startled by the two giant dogs running around. They had to be the biggest dogs I'd ever seen. Those Tibetan Mastiffs were huge, but also some of the friendliest dogs I'd ever come across. The man from the B&B put them in their field while I was there, telling Mum and Dad he didn't want any misbehaving. I wasn't entirely sure what they expected us to get up to.

That B&B had so many firsts for me. It was the first time I'd had a big bone to chew on. Oh my! How grown up I felt. It tasted delicious, and I loved sitting outside on the veranda, chewing away on it whilst Mum and Dad drank some of that tea stuff they seem to like so much.

I also had my first experience with a mirror. Heading into the bedroom where we were going to sleep, I was walking (OK, jumping and running along – it was so exciting) next to my mum, when I suddenly caught sight of things moving in the glass thing on the wall. I was convinced there was another mum right in front of me. I couldn't work it out and was so confused, if not a little scared. I do love my mum, but this second mum was too frightening. I'm sure Dad wouldn't be able to deal with two mums, either.

I'm not allowed to jump up at humans, but I lunged at this second mum, only to find my paws hitting the glass. How strange. The second mum was moving around exactly the same as my mum who was standing next to me.

Mum and Dad said they were worried I would break the glass, and they put a blanket over it so I couldn't see the second mum. With hindsight, I can laugh about it, because I now understand the concept of glass and reflections, though they sometimes still take me by surprise.

Another memorable thing about that long weekend was the weather. The whole of this weekend was lovely and warm. I heard Mum and Dad say that it was absolutely roasting. So many of my adventures with Mum, good, bad, and sometimes even frightening, seem to take place during winter when we are surrounded by snow and ice. Not that I'm complaining. Like Mum, I love the snow and the cold.

I know everyone always jokes about it raining or snowing in Scotland, but that weekend the sun seemed to smile down on us constantly. The sky was that fabulous blue colour, with not a cloud in sight. We spent lots of time on the beach and splashing in the clear blue sea. It was bliss. The views across to the Cuillin mountains on the Isle of Skye were the best. One day I'm sure I'll be having adventures up those mountains with Mum.

We'd travelled to the B&B in the car, but we also managed a train ride, crossing over the Glenfinnan Viaduct. This railway line is supposed to be the one that is seen in a Harry Potter film. I don't know much about that film, but we travelled through the most fantastic scenery, with mountains all around us. Mum told me this was one of the world's most beautiful train journeys, and I would certainly agree. Mum was spellbound by the mountains and pointing out all the different summits. Research by scientists (I think scientists are clever people who wear white coats and conduct experiments), shows that dogs and their owners become like one another in looks and personalities. Mum and I are so alike. I'm surprised she's not grown a black and white fur coat to match mine.

Dad, as usual, was too busy eating his sandwiches and KitKat to see the views.

Travelling on this Jacobite train from Mallaig, we alighted at the Glenfinnan station. We had a stroll along a peaceful track towards more mountains, but when it became too hot, Mum decided that the best thing for us all was to be around the water. There was a lovely river down the hill from the track, and we headed to it. There I played in the water, finding lots of stones for Mum and Dad to throw for me, and I was having one of the best days of my life.

I could sense something in the air though. I looked around but couldn't see anything out of the ordinary, but I had a strange feeling in my tummy. Do you know what I mean? When you know something is happening but don't know what it is. You can feel it's important and need to do something about it. That's how I felt.

I looked over to Mum and Dad, and I saw that they were chilling on their picnic blanket, watching over me as they ate their sandwiches. I told you there's always time for a picnic with Mum and Dad.

Something in my mind was taking me back to my dog mum, and her saying I'd know when the time was right for me to chase and catch my tail. That day, I knew the time had arrived.

Slowly, I began to walk around in circles, getting faster and faster. As my spinning increased, I was aware of a strange mist building around me and I could hear the most gentle, soothing, humming sound. A bright light shone in the distance, and I knew the light was searching for me.

I could see my tail, but the faster I ran, the quicker my tail moved away from me. I was determined though. If my lovely dog mum thought it important for me to know when to catch my tail, I would make sure I did. I wanted my dog mum to be proud of me.

With a last grasp, I caught the end of my tail with my sharp teeth.

"Ouch! That hurt," I cried, letting go of my tail. The spinning stopped, the mist cleared, and the humming faded away. A white light shone brightly in front of me, and I was being pulled towards it.

I didn't know where I was going, or for what, just that I had to go towards the light quickly. Was I scared? You bet I was. But I was excited, sensing that something big in my life was about to happen. I had a feeling that this was just the beginning. I knew that somebody needed me.

Running into the light was like going into another world. The air was different, with strange smells and new sounds. And oh, the heat! The sun was beating down even stronger than back in Scotland, but there was a breeze blowing, helping to make the temperature bearable. Where was I?

I stopped and looked around me. A golden sandy beach seemed to stretch for miles. I noticed how prominent the white cliffs were all down the coastline as far as I could see. On the cliff tops were rows and rows of tiny white houses on wheels. The sand was soft on my paws, but as I ran down to the water, the sand became harder and easier to run on. It reminded me a bit of my last family holiday in Filey.

This was not like the quiet, secret beaches of the West Coast of Scotland. There were so many humans sitting on brightly coloured chairs and shading themselves under equally colourful umbrella things or small tents. Some humans were pulling carts that were full of blankets, tired children, and even some dogs. I hope that I'm never so tired, or old, that Mum has to put me in a cart to carry me around. That would be so embarrassing.

All I could hear was screams, shouts, and lots of other different noises I didn't recognise. The sea was rolling up and down in the distance, and I could hear it thundering down onto the sand. It was difficult for a dog like me to know who was screaming with happiness and who was screaming because they were scared. When dogs bark, we have only half a dozen different noises, so you humans have no excuse for not understanding us. There's a bark for being scared, hungry, worried, tired, happy, and, of course, a bark telling you to throw the stone. How difficult can it be? But many humans don't get it and think that we only bark because we're fierce.

I don't like crowds of humans, but I was pleasantly surprised to see that most of them seemed to be eating sandwiches. This was going to be a great adventure. Humans always seem happy to share their food with me for some reason. I think it's that cute head tilt thing I do. I must remember not to do that drooling thing, as that makes humans shoo me away.

I noticed that most of the voices sounded very much like my mum. Mum and Dad talk differently; Dad has a strong Scottish accent, but Mum has this cute Yorkshire accent. Whenever humans ask her where she's from, she says she is from God's Own Country. Oh my! I must have died and gone to heaven, and I was now surrounded by all God's humans. But I couldn't be dead. I could feel the hot sand on my paws and the wind blowing through my coat.

I was confused. Why was I here? What should I be doing, and would I ever return to Mum and Dad?

Slowly I started to mingle with the humans on the beach. Some of them waved me away. That was OK. I understand that many humans don't like dogs, and to be honest, there are many humans I don't like.

It was so hot. I was really thirsty. I knew from up in Scotland that the sea is not so good to drink as it's too salty, so I needed to find a river or something.

Walking past a family, the children seemed pleased to see me and were stroking and cuddling me.

"What a lovely, well-behaved dog you are. You must be thirsty," said the mum. She put some water in a little dish for me. It tasted like nectar. I drank it all up and allowed the children to cuddle me a bit longer as a thank you for the drink.

Sitting under the umbrella's shade was nice, feeling the breeze blowing over me and drinking clear, chilly water. I could have simply settled down and had a bit of a snooze.

But I still had that feeling in my tummy. Nobody needed me here. I forced myself to leave the comfort of the nice family. I knew I had to leave the crowds and go towards the cliffs and rocks in the distance.

Then the beach began to change. Rocks, pebbles, and shells, which were a bit sharp on my paws, replaced the smooth sand, but I knew I had to keep going. As I continued, the ground became rock, with deep pools of water. The surface of the rocks was slippery because of the seaweed. I had to take my time to ensure I didn't end up falling into one of the many pools, although they did look exciting, with lots of colours and loads of stones for me to play with.

The more I moved away from the crowds, the stronger the feeling in my tummy got.

"Go into the caves beside the cliffs Beatrix," a voice in my head shouted.

I looked around. There were no humans near me. Oddly enough, the sea was not so far away now, and the waves were splashing over the rocks every minute or so. I was sure the water was getting nearer and nearer all the time, even though I was running away from the sea. Was it chasing me?

As I scanned the cliffs in front of me, I could see lots of caves. Some were large, some small and some too full of seawater to even get into them.

I wish my mum were here now. She'd know what to do and where to go.

Continuing to make my way along the bottom of the cliffs, I was surprised to see the opening of a gigantic cave that looked like you could fit the entire world in it. OK, a bit of an exaggeration, but it was massive.

I needed to go into that cave; I could sense it.

I looked around again. There were still no humans, and the sea was getting closer. I wasn't just getting my paws wet now; the sea was covering them.

At the entrance to the cave, I peered in. My eyesight's never been brilliant, and I certainly couldn't see much in the darkness of the cave. I stopped for a moment and sniffed the air. Salty and damp.

Slowly and cautiously, I began walking into the mouth of this colossal cave, noticing that the ground was turning from rock to sand, and I was no longer stepping into water.

As I continued further up into the depths of the cave, I could feel the temperature dropping. The sound of the wind and sea was getting quieter. I was nervous. My breathing was loud. I also realised I was starting to get cold, so I gave a little shake of my coat to get all the seawater from it.

It was so dark. There was a strange smell, like when something's been wet for way too long.

This cave was definitely where I needed to be, but why?

Moving further into the damp, cold darkness, I could smell something else. What was it? A human. I could smell a human. Now I was nervous. Would the human be friendly? Was it the human who needed me? And if so, why?

Then in the darkness, I could just make out the figure of a man. As I got closer, he sat down and put his head in his hands. He seemed to be cross, not with me, just cross.

"I can't find it," he cried.

I sat down beside him and nuzzled his hand with my nose.

"Well, hello you. Are you here to help me find it?" asked the man.

He looked so sad there by himself, but I didn't know how I could help him, and certainly didn't know what I was searching for.

"I came into this cave to find peace from the crowds and escape the heat of the midday sun," he began. "I knew it was getting past lunchtime, and I needed to take some insulin. But just as I got the syringe out of my rucksack, I dropped it, and I can't find it anywhere."

We both sat together, looking around the cave. The man knew what he was looking for, but I was just searching for anything, trying to think what a syringe might be.

Then he became quiet, and I could feel him leaning against me like he was getting sleepy. Around us, I could feel the water starting to flow into the cave, and my paws were getting wet again. I wondered how far the water would come into the cave. Surely, we shouldn't be in here if the water was going to keep coming in.

"I'll just have a lie-down and a little sleep," he said, and, with that, the man lay down.

This is not good, I thought. This is not good at all.

"Wake up, wake up," I cried, nuzzling his face.

I walked around the cave to find what the man had lost. There were so many little pebbles, stones, and pretty shells, but I tried not to let myself be distracted - I was on an important mission.

Then right in front of me, I saw something glistening. It was like a plastic tube thing. I'd seen one of these before. But where? Think Beatrix, think.

I knew this was what the man had been frantically hunting for. I grabbed the tube in my mouth and took it over to him. I nudged him to get him to see that I'd found it for him, but he didn't even open his eyes.

Licking his hand, I felt something cold on his arm. My mind was working overtime. Was that one of those metal things that Mum's friend, Salena, wears? That's it. Salena wears one of these metal things, and she's always pushing one of those plastic tube things into her tummy when she's eaten too many of Mum's cakes, which seems to be each time she comes to our house.

Instinct told me this man desperately needed whatever was inside this plastic tube, which was why I couldn't wake him up. But what would happen if the water kept coming into the cave and he stayed asleep?

The sea was slowly creeping further up the cave, and even the man's boots started to get wet.

I needed to get help for him, and quickly. But what could I do? Who could help? What about that nice family? That mum who gave me the water was friendly. Perhaps she'd help me.

Putting the plastic tube down on the ground away from the water, I nuzzled the man's face with my cheek and licked his nose, but he moved his face away. I felt terrible doing it, but I grabbed hold of the metal thing on his arm with my teeth, and pulled at it until it broke away. I started to make my way out of the cave, taking a final glance back at the man, praying he'd be OK until I could fetch help, and left him there in the cold, wet cave. I held the metal thing carefully between my teeth.

Making my way back across the rocks was tricky, with more pools of water than rock to jump on. I needed to make sure I didn't stumble now that I had this important metal thing in my mouth. Carefully I jumped across the pools, slipping and sliding on the seaweed, but was relieved to then find myself back on the sandy beach.

The humans had started to pack up their chairs, umbrellas, and tents as the sea made its way up the beach.

Oh no, I thought. How am I going to find that nice family now?

I started running around all the humans. The sand was blowing everywhere, and humans were screaming at me to stop.

"Look, that dog has something in its mouth. Stop it before it gets hurt," cried a lady.

But I needed to keep running and find that family. They were good humans. Then I saw them going up the steps away from the beach. I ran faster and faster to reach them. I knew I'd never get to them once they'd left the beach.

"Look, Mummy. There's that black and white dog running towards us. The dog must need us," cried one of the children.

The lady put down all her things, knelt on the ground and stretched out her arms to me. I ran to her, sat beside her, and allowed her to take the metal thing from my mouth.

By now, there were lots of other humans around us, all wanting to know what was going on.

The lady said, "I'm a nurse. This is a diabetic medical emergency bracelet. The dog must have found it somewhere. Maybe there's somebody in need of their insulin."

I needed to get the lady to come with me back to the cave. I got up and ran a little way from her, then stopped, ran back to her, and nuzzled her hand, before running away from her again.

"The dog's trying to get you to follow it," said one of the children.

Then it seemed that everyone wanted to follow me. The lady left the children with another human and started coming towards me, calling out for other people to help her.

I began to run, turning back to see if the lady was following me. She was, along with some other humans. There was a man in a red and yellow uniform carrying a red float thing, and another man dressed in smart black clothes with a white shirt and yellow waistcoat.

I started to run faster and faster, with all the humans following behind me, back along the sandy beach and towards the cliffs and the caves. It must have been a remarkable sight indeed.

The sea was starting to cover the rocks. Some of the pools were much deeper now, so I had to paddle across them. The water was so cold!

It's a good job that I'm a Border Collie because I have an innate ability to find a place even if I've only been there once. This skill has undoubtedly helped me on a few adventures with my mum when she's got us lost, and I've had to find the right path for us.

However, I did have to concentrate on finding the actual cave as they all looked and smelt the same.

At last, I came across the large cave where I'd left the man. I ran straight in and up to him.

The seawater was getting deeper, now reaching halfway up my legs. And it was cold. The man was still asleep on the ground, with the sea creeping further up his ankles. I nuzzled up to his face and licked him to tell him I was back.

The lady knelt beside the man, talking to him, and checking his breathing. She pulled out a card from his pocket.

"This is him," she said. "The medical bracelet belongs to this man. But where's his insulin?"

It's the plastic tube! The lady wants the plastic tube, I thought.

I went to the spot where I'd put it earlier, picked it up and put it by the lady.

"You clever dog," she said, stroking my head.

Then she lifted the man's shirt, and I saw her stick the plastic tube thing into his skin, just like Salena does to her tummy at our house after a cake feast.

The next few minutes were a blur. There seemed to be humans everywhere, and they had a long bed. In no time at all, the humans had the poorly man on the bed thing, and they were all working together to get him out of the dark, wet, cold cave. Humans can be kind to each other sometimes.

The lady knelt beside me.

"This dog is amazing," she said to the other humans. "Without getting his insulin and taken out of the freezing water, this man would not have survived. This dog undoubtedly saved his life."

What a feeling it was to know that I'd saved a human. I felt as tall as the Tibetan Mastiffs back at the B&B in Scotland.

Then, in the back of the cave, I could see a bright light and hear a gentle humming.

I went to the man on the bed thing and gave him one last nuzzle. Walking towards the light, I glanced back at the lady, and she waved, smiling at me. Was that a tear I saw rolling down her face?

As the light fell upon me, I started to spin, listening to the humming. Then, as quickly as the spinning had started, it stopped, and I was back on the riverbank at Glenfinnan with Mum and Dad.

I flopped onto the ground next to Mum, and from my mouth fell a strange stone.

"Thank goodness! You've come back," said Mum. "And you've brought us a fossil. Have you been to the coast at Filey?" she asked.

Chapter 22

Six Little Kittens

It was 7 o'clock on a chilly winter's night, but that didn't worry me, living in a warm and snug home. The central heating was on, the curtains drawn, and scented candles lit. Don't panic! Only the finest soy candles get used in my home. They're only lit for a brief time in the evening during the dark winter months, and of course they are high up on the unit, way out of reach of any paws, wagging tails or little human hands.

Perhaps it's how dogs have been brought up and the lifestyle that their humans live as to whether they know that feeling of hygge. I live in a home with no noisy television, where my humans talk to each other, hand-crocheted blankets are always ready to curl up with, and soft, gentle music plays in the background (except for the occasions Mum plays Bruce Springsteen's Thunder Road at full blast) - none of the bang, bang music that I've heard about, and no noisy distracting TV programmes. So yes, I enjoy that feeling of hygge and was certainly feeling it that chilly January night.

Just as I was dreaming about what delights I'd have for supper; I could hear a gentle humming. "No! Not tonight," I sighed.

But there was no escaping it. The now familiar humming had started, along with the gut feeling that somebody somewhere needed me.

I got up, had a stretch, and started to pace slowly in small circles. Mum looked up from her cross-stitching, probably recognising the tell-tale signs that I was once again leaving her, and she gave me a weak, sad smile.

My spinning quickened, with a mist developing around me, and I heard a familiar gentle humming sound. A bright light shone in the distance, and I knew I had to follow it. Finally catching my tail, I gave a little yelp and let go of it. The spinning stopped, the mist cleared, the humming faded, and I found myself once again running into the bright light. As I ran, I looked around me, wondering where I could be, and who or what I'd be helping.

It was cold. Very, very cold. Crisp, white, virgin snow lay deeply everywhere, and a bitterness crept through the darkness. Even with my double-natural coat, the biting wind was cutting through me. I hoped my work on this adventure would be inside somewhere nice and warm. The guiding light led me to a small cottage just beyond the village name sign of Asdel.

I began to edge my way towards the light source, fighting through the howling wind. Crisp snow crunched under my paws, cutting into my pads. A layer of ice was already forming on my coat. Despite the winter's night trying to defeat me, I knew I had to go on.

Approaching the cottage, I looked around for any sign of life, but there was nothing. No humans, animals, or even stray rats were out that night.

Following the light, I found myself on a small porch. Although still open to the elements, I was relieved to be out of the full effect of the wild conditions of that winter's evening.

I listened, sniffed the bitter freezing air, feeling it nip at my nostrils. But even with the wind howling around the porch, I could hear faint squeaks.

What was that? It sounded like babies. Frightened little babies.

In the corner was an old woollen blanket. It was beginning to freeze, with a layer of snow settling on it. I nuzzled my face underneath the blanket, and huddled together were some of the tiniest kittens I'd ever seen.

"Oh please," I cried into the freezing air. "Please don't tell me I'm here to save some cats."

But then, my heart melted, despite my innate distrust and dislike of felines with their sharp claws, frightening hisses, and aloof, antisocial personalities.

"Oh, would you look at them. So tiny, and they are so scared. They can't be more than a few hours old," I whispered into the night air.

I counted them. One, two, three, four, five, six. Six little kittens.

I shuddered as it brought back memories of being a puppy all those years ago. I remembered being cold and scared, unable to see anything. Fortunately for me, my mum was always there to snuggle up to and provide a never-ending supply of sweet, warm milk. On that cold, wintry night, I could still feel my mum's love warming me.

"Mummy, Mummy," cried the little kittens.

It was such a harrowing sound to hear. I looked around for their cat mum, but there was nobody to be seen. No large cats and no humans. What was I to do? The kittens needed warmth and food from their mum. I knew I could provide them with warmth, but there was no way I could give them food. Surely somebody should be searching for these little bundles, even if they are only cats?

I crept back out of the porch into the wintry night and could see the light on in one of the cottage windows. I knew there'd be somebody in there and that I had to let them know about the kittens.

I began to bark, quietly at first, but then I started my deep, loud barking. Despite the howling wind, I thought my barking was enough to awaken the dead - that's what Mum's always telling me. That should get somebody's attention, I thought, hoping it would happen quickly, as the freezing air cut into my throat as I barked.

"Who's there?" cried a voice from inside the cottage.

The door flew open, and in front of me towered an old man, shining a torch with one hand and holding a wooden stick with the other. He looked down at me. I was already covered in snow.

I don't mind telling you, I cowered on the step, fearing that I'd feel that wooden stick upon me. But no, the old man reached down and gently touched me as though he needed to believe I was really at his door.

"Come in," said the old man softly as he stepped to one side and encouraged me to go into the warmth of the cottage. But I knew I had to get him to see the kittens under the blanket. They needed food before it was too late and before they succumbed to the cold and hunger of this winter's night.

I nuzzled at the blanket, looked up at the old man, looked at the blanket again, then at the old man and back to the blanket - the trick I learned long ago to get humans to look at something.

"Hvad er der galt," cried the old man. "What is it?"

Seeing the kittens, he bent down, scooped them all up in his arms, and went inside the cottage, with me following closely behind him.

The warmth of the log fire pulled me closer inside, but I thought I'd be leaving now. Surely my work was done. The kittens were now safe in the warmth and security of the old man's cottage.

But no. The light wasn't shining. I must still be needed here.

The old man found a wicker basket and lined it with a soft, clean blanket.

"Really!" I said under my breath. "How is it cats always get a clean blanket in front of a lovely log fire, and dogs just get an outdoor kennel?"

I climbed gently over the kittens and lay beside them. Obviously feeling the heat from me, they all curled up into my thick, warm coat. Some of them even tried to hunt for milk from me. It was heart-breaking to watch. I had to brush a tear away from my face, and I was sure I could see a tear in the old man's eyes too.

Over the next few hours, I allowed the kittens to feel my warmth and love, and the old man found some little bottles and filled them with milk. The pitiful cries of the kittens gradually eased, and before long, they fell asleep against me.

The old man looked for the kittens' mum outside but never found her.

"Where did the kittens come from? Who put them on the porch? Where did the black and white Border Collie come from?" he said, as though talking to the flames in the fire.

"This is going to be a long job," I sighed.

So that night, I became a surrogate mum to the kittens. I'm sure the old man didn't understand where the kittens had come from but seemed to have taken it upon himself to care for them.

Over the next few weeks, as my mum had done with her children all those years ago, I began to teach the kittens how to behave, to feed, to show good manners to each other, and how to keep their sleeping area clean and tidy. I taught them how to clean themselves, play, and stay safe.

The old man provided milk for the kittens and the most amazing food for me.

As the days and weeks passed, the weather improved, and the snow began to thaw.

I couldn't believe how much love I felt for those little kittens. But I swear I'd never admit to this, even in a court of law.

I knew in my heart that the kittens would soon, one by one, be leaving the cottage, just as I'd watched my brothers go, and I remembered how I too, had to leave my own farmyard barn when I became a human dog.

As the kittens found their feet, their personalities, their cheek, and of course, their agility, I noticed a change in the old man. He seemed to spend longer each day stroking the kittens and even started to allow them to sit on his knee.

I would lie at his feet, toasting in front of the open fire. I was missing my mum and dad, but life wasn't all that bad now, even if I did have to share my new home with some cats.

Then the old man began talking to the kittens and me.

"I've been so lonely these last few months since my darling wife of thirty years died. I'm so angry with her for leaving me alone in this cottage in the middle of nowhere. The house has felt so empty, lonely, and cold, despite the open fire," he told us through tears.

But slowly, over the weeks, the old man began to talk about his wife, the things they used to do and how they loved the cosy feeling of their cottage, especially in the dark winter evenings.

All this time, I remained by his feet, and the kittens would snuggle up in his arms.

He spoke about the love he and his wife shared, and the wonderful life they had together.

Then one day, he rose from his chair. Slowly, but with purpose, he walked towards the large oak dresser, resting his hand on the drawer handle. After what seemed an eternity, he pulled open the drawer and lifted out a photo in a picture frame.

"She's still here, isn't she? Her love still fills this cottage, but I couldn't feel it. I feel it now. It's taken an unknown dog and six kittens for me to realise it," he sobbed, holding the photo close to his chest.

"Shall I tell you something?" the old man said to the kittens. "We belong together. This is your home now, and I love each of you."

And he smiled for the first time in months.

With this, I could see the light in the corner of the room and hear the gentle humming. I stood up and gave the old man one last nuzzle with my nose.

"I know. It's time for you to go," whispered the old man, looking deep into my eyes. "It's OK. I'm OK. Safe journey my friend. And thank you."

A tear ran down the old man's cheek.

The light fell upon me, and I felt myself spinning as I listened to the soothing humming.

A moment later, I landed back on my lounge floor, dropping a Danish krone at Mum's feet.

"Well, hello you. So, you've been to Denmark, have you?" said Mum, looking up from her cross-stitching.

Chapter 23

Grasmere, The Lake District

Life with my amazing mum and dad is just the best. I must be the luckiest dog ever, but I also know that Mum and Dad are fortunate to have me.

My human parents are quite different to each other, a bit like chalk and cheese. Dad likes to watch football and going to the horse racing. He's got such bad knees now, and Mum's very naughty when she laughs at him, telling him it looks like he's lost his horse. Of course, I don't laugh at this (well, not so that he can hear me).

Mum is a character, to say the least. I've already told you she's from Yorkshire and has a lovely, soothing voice. Mum always says she's a tough Yorkshire bird, but that's not true. Yes, she's brave and keeps on keeping on sometimes, but I don't think she's tough. I've seen her crying at films on the big movie screen we have at home instead of a television. But I've also seen her cry because she's laughing so much. It doesn't take much to make her giggle, and she often giggles at things that are not funny - like laughing at Dad's wonky knees. And I don't think she's much like a bird either if I'm honest?

She loves to be out on the hills walking with me but has one bad habit that I hate - she loves cycling. When I see her with her cycling helmet and biking clothes on, I sulk in the front room because I know she's going out without me. I try to sulk when she comes back and not talk to her, but I can't help it as I've missed her so much. I sit on the window box, waiting for her to come back and then rush into the back garden to get a stone for her to play with me. I'm always relieved when she gets home from a cycling trip as I've not been there to look after her and keep her safe. I wonder who looks out for her when I'm not there?

Then there's the baking. Mum loves baking. There is always something wonderful cooking in the kitchen. I know I'm not allowed in the kitchen when she wears her white jacket and hat. I lie at the door, just watching her. You can tell she loves being in the kitchen and making cakes. I'm not sure which she likes best, baking the cakes or eating them. Of course, I usually get to sample the bakes unless they have some ingredients that dogs can't eat.

When she's not walking, cycling, or baking, she loves to do something called crochet. Sometimes she can sit for hours twisting wool around a stick. It's like magic. The big ball of wool gets smaller as she winds the wool around her fingers and the stick. I'm not always sure what she makes, but I know she makes lovely blankets. I love watching her. It's so relaxing that sometimes I fall asleep. Dad doesn't like to do this crochet thing. I often hear him saying to Mum that she doesn't need any more wool, but Mum says you can never have enough wool.

If wool makes Mum so happy and relaxed, I agree with her. You can never have enough of that.

As the years passed and I settled into my life as a human dog, I also became familiar with that inner feeling of being needed somewhere. It always fills me with trepidation about where I'll go and why. As I live in a home filled with love and security, there's also an element of sadness. Would the journey be a one-way trip? Would I become lost along the way and not find my way home to Mum and Dad?

One blissful afternoon, as I watched Mum create something with her wool and stick, I got that feeling deep in my tummy again. I had to go. Somebody needed me. Taking a last look at Mum sitting crocheting in the lounge, I began to chase my tail. Slowly at first, but then gathering speed as I ran in small circles. The rug ruffled beneath me as my paws struggled to keep a firm grip on it. I must remember to step off the rug before the next trip.

As the rug got pushed to one side and I was about to catch my tail, I caught a glimpse of Mum, who, looking up from her crochet, gave me a sad smile. Every time I head out for another adventure, I wonder if the sight of my tail-chasing fills Mum with pride, knowing that I'm going to help somebody, or with sadness, because she doesn't know what I'm heading into or know for sure I'll return safely to her once again.

For me, everything became blurred as a mist developed around me, accompanied by a gentle humming. A bright light shone in the distance. As I finally caught my tail, I gave a little yelp and let go. The spinning stopped, the mist cleared, the humming ceased, and I was running into the bright light.

I looked around and sniffed the air. Where was I? It smelt familiar. Clean country smells and a hint of ginger wafted in the air. Slate buildings were everywhere, and I was in a garden raised up from the road. I'd been here before; I was sure of it. Sitting down, I allowed the smells and sounds to register. That's it, I realised. This was April Cottage in Mum's favourite place, Grasmere, in the Lake District. I'd been here many times before with Mum and Dad.

The small garden felt safe and familiar, even with the small slate pebbles digging into my paws, exaggerated by the heat of the midday sun.

Over the low drystone wall, I jumped out onto the lane. The lane had a familiar smell, and I recognised the wild raspberry bushes in the hedges and the metal gate. Yes, the metal gate. I had to go through the gate but couldn't open it myself. I stood there for a few moments as some walkers came down the road towards me. Using the trick my dog mum had taught me all those years ago, I tilted my head to one side and did the puppy-dog eye trick. That did it. I'm so cute when I do that, even if I say so myself.

"Oh, you want to come through the gate, do you?" asked one walker.

Taking my opportunity, I slipped past the walkers through the open gate, running along the little track past more raspberries on the left and the wild meadow on my right. I pushed my way through another swing gate into a small pasture. Giant Herdwick sheep were grazing alongside the track and gave me a cursory glance as I sped towards them.

Ignore the sheep; I told myself over and over again as I ran along the track, jumping over the cattle grid and finally reaching the road.

I ran and ran, ignoring the gasps of the humans walking by.

"Oh, look. That dog must be lost. We need to catch that dog and find its owner," cried one of them.

But I kept running. You might not believe this, but I can run as fast as a car, at about 20 to 30 miles an hour. I followed the road, keeping close to the wall that had a small trickle of water running alongside it. The sun never seems to warm that side of the road. I stopped a couple of times to drink the water and to relieve myself. I wondered who would pick up my poop now that Mum wasn't here, but I did make sure it was on the edge of the road and not where humans would be stepping.

As the road started going uphill, I began to get an inclination of where I was going - the lake. I had to go to the lake. I'd been there many times before. There should be another gate to take me down to it. Where was it? Had I missed it? Was I lost?

Calm down, Beatrix, I told myself. Breathe. Smell. Can you smell the gate? Yes, that's it. I can smell that gate. It's up here.

And there it was, nestling on the other side of the road at the top of the hill, and it was open. When will humans ever learn that gates should be closed? I'm not that great at reading, but I was sure that's what the sign on the gate said. But that day, I was so glad that many humans never follow the country code.

I ran through the gate and down the track, with my feet hurting on the sharp slate slivers covering the path. The sun's heat was so intense now, and a white dust rose around me as I ran towards the lake.

As I reached the lake, I ran straight into the water. The cold, fresh water lapped around my paws, and I felt it clearing the dust from my coat. Bliss.

But wait, this was not the spot. This wasn't where I was needed. I had to go on.

Leaping out of the water, I continued along the track running alongside the lake. The geese in the opposite field were startled and took flight, honking and moaning.

"Steady on there, Collie. What's all the rush?" the leader of the gaggle cried out.

"Sorry, Mrs Goose, I didn't mean to startle you. I'm needed at the lake; I must rush," I shouted apologetically as I continued to run.

When I got further along the lakeside, I recognised the area I'd played in during trips with Mum and Dad. A pebbly beach area leads onto the lake's deep, clear water. What a lovely place this is.

I took a few steps into the water, and, feeling a rush of adrenaline I looked around. There were lots of humans, either in the water or walking alongside the lake. But who needed me? I didn't know.

I continued to look around. Then, standing still in the water, ignoring the crowds and the noises, I listened to the voice in my head.

"Look out further," it whispered.

I could see a man on a paddle board out on the lake, with two young children sitting behind him. All wearing red life jackets, they certainly seemed to be enjoying themselves.

I needed to get out to that paddle board, I thought, and started swimming towards them quickly, trying not to panic myself or others.

Humans at the side of the lake started to shout and laugh.

"That dog is trying to rescue those people. The dog thinks they're drowning."

As I got closer to the paddle board, the little children started to scream. "Daddy, Daddy! That dog's coming to get us. It will knock us off the board, and we'll fall in the water."

The man started to shout at me. "Get away, you silly dog. Get away. We don't need you."

"Don't worry, little ones," I told them. "I'm not coming anywhere near you."

Ignoring all the shouting and commotion, I swam past the paddle board until I reached a young lady who was silently going under the water for yet another time.

I approached the struggling human; she reached out and put her hand on my back.

"Gosh, you feel so heavy," I gasped. "You're nearly pulling me under the water. Just hold on to me, and I'll swim towards the shore with you."

By now, the other humans had noticed what I was trying to do. Another man on a board quickly paddled to the lady I was helping and grabbed hold of her.

Within seconds, other humans scrambled into the water. They pulled the young lady from the water and onto the lakeside, wrapped her in blankets, and sat her on the grass away from the water. I got myself out of the water without any trouble and lay beside her.

The humans were talking to each other, "That dog's amazing. The dog noticed the drowning lady when nobody else had."

"We need to get you to the hospital," one man said to the lady who was shivering now.

But she shook her head and said, "No, it's OK. I'm perfectly fine now, just a bit shaken. I need to phone my sister. I'm staying with her in her cottage in Grasmere village.

A few of the humans from the lake (and myself) stayed with her and listened to her ramblings.

"My name's Gertrude. I'm trying to build up my wild swimming experiences. I'm so embarrassed that I allowed myself to get out of my depth," she said, cuddling me. "I'm indebted to you for saving my life."

Before long, Gertrude's sister came flying along the track and fell upon her sister, hugging and kissing her.

"Thank you so much. I'll take Gertrude to my house to take care of her. If there's any sign that she's not well, I'll take her straight to the hospital," she told everyone with a sob.

The humans all sat together in the warm evening sunshine, discussing the incident.

"I can't believe that nobody noticed you were in trouble, even though there were loads of people around you," said one man.

But one of the rescuers started to explain, "Recognising a drowning person isn't always as easy as you think, and drowning often happens silently and unnoticed with no shouts, exclamations, or arm waving. Often, cases of drowning happen when others are nearby and simply don't recognise that something is wrong."

"That's so true. That's exactly what happened here today," said another man.

By now, it was late, and most of the humans had left the lakeside, leaving Gertrude, her sister, myself, and a couple of the rescuers. They were concerned about Gertrude, of course, but by now, they also seemed worried about me because there didn't appear to be anybody looking after me.

"We'll go to my sister's house and take the dog with us. We'll come back to the lake in the morning with the dog and see if anyone is searching for her. I'll put a post on Facebook too, to see if anyone knows who she belongs to," Gertrude announced, getting to her feet, still appearing a little bit wobbly, but she said she felt well enough for the short walk back to Grasmere.

If truth be known, I was a little confused now. I couldn't understand why I was still there and not back with Mum and Dad. I looked for the bright light and listened for the humming, but nothing.

Why am I still here? I've saved Gertrude. What's stopping me from returning home? I wondered, looking around me for any clues to what I should do.

As promised, Gertrude and her sister took me back to the lakeside the following day. There had been no reports on social media or the local radio of anyone searching for a lost Border Collie. The lakeside was busy, but nobody was looking for, or shouting for their dog. I could have told them that if they'd asked me.

I stayed close to Gertrude constantly. There's a saying about getting back on the horse before you're too scared to do so, and Gertrude had decided she'd be doing this by getting back into the water today. Of course, her sister would be there to keep an eye on her, and her new best friend, me, the Collie, would be on-hand too.

Gertrude gingerly entered the water and allowed herself to float a little. She didn't go out of her depth and stayed in for only a few minutes. The grin on her face as she walked out of the water told us that she was OK and glad to be back doing what she loved.

But still, nobody came looking for me.

For three days, the two sisters followed the same pattern, checking social media and local press for reports of a lost dog, and taking me back to the lake to see if my owners were there searching for me. Nothing.

"Where did she come from?" Gertrude asked her sister.

They were good days though. There was always a picnic, not as good as the one Dad makes, but I wasn't complaining. We enjoyed the fantastic views along the lakeside. Looking towards and beyond the village of Grasmere, the hills of Helm Cragg make an impressive backdrop. Mum once told me that the tops of those hills are called The Lion and The Lamb, but I've been there, and

I've only ever seen rocks at the top. The sunshine made the whole valley light up in colour like an artist's palette. Greens, yellows, and purples blended with the deep blue summer sky were a sight to behold. It's no wonder the poet William Wordsworth said of Grasmere, *"This is the loveliest spot that man hath ever found."*

On the fourth day, I ran ahead of the two sisters and headed straight for the lakeside. High up on the grassy hillside, something orange caught my attention. I grabbed hold of it and pulled it down to Gertrude.

"Wow! This is a brand-new, top-of-the-range flotation aid," gasped Gertrude. "I was always going to get one of these but didn't feel there was any need for it. You know, I think this was meant to be. I was foolish to go swimming out of my depth alone, without telling you where I was going and without a flotation aid. I'm never going to do that again. I promise you I will always take this with me, and if I ever get into difficulty again, it could save my life."

She hugged her sister, cuddled me, fastened the flotation aid to herself and walked into the water.

I watched her go, but in the distance, I could see a bright light and hear a faint humming. The humming became louder, and the light fell upon me. I knew then that I'd finally finished the task I'd been sent for.

Once again, I felt myself spinning into the bright light as I listened to the soothing humming. A moment later, I landed back on our lounge floor at home and dropped a tin of Grasmere Gingerbread at Mum's feet.

"Well, hello you. So, you've been to the Lake District without us, have you?" said Mum looking up from her crocheting.

Chapter 24

Rustling in the Leaves

I thought things would start to get back to normal after the horrible things that happened in 2020 and 2021 because of that Covid thing, but 2022 was turning into another strange year. That Covid thing was still hanging around, and some humans, including Mum and Dad, continued to wear strange face coverings.

The weather had been really rubbish for most of the summer, and even I was fed up of the rain. My human brother and sister down in Yorkshire had some lovely weather, but up here in Scotland, it was like summer had forgotten us.

I was used to Dad having a moan about everything, but it seemed that now Mum was becoming grumpy too. Mum and Dad had been talking about the cost of fuel and how they shouldn't need to put the central heating on in July. It seemed that humans were now worried about everything – the cost of fuel and food, the war in Ukraine, and whether Covid was still a danger to society.

Every day, Dad would read unwelcome news from his computer. I wondered if he could get a different computer with some good news on it. Mum obviously felt the same.

"Did I ask you to read all the sad, depressing news to me?" snapped Mum. "Enough. Put that computer away. We're going to the seaside for the day. I don't care if the train fares are expensive. We're going out. Now!"

Dad looked at me, and we both looked at Mum. When she's in this mood, we both know that we have to do something to make her happy again.

"Where shall we go to, my love?" asked Dad.

Oh, wrong voice. Careful Dad, I thought to myself.

"Don't use that tone with me!" shouted Mum. "Let's make a picnic and get the train out to the seaside at Largs. We can have a lovely day on the beach, let Beatrix play in the sea, and get a coffee before coming home."

"A coffee from the seaside will cost us an arm and a leg," moaned Dad.

I secretly hoped we could do everything Mum suggested, except the coffee thing. I'd hate for Mum or Dad to lose one of their limbs to pay for a drink. And it would probably be Mum because Dad says she has that touch bank card to pay for things. How would she take me on adventures if she lost an arm and a leg? But my panic was short-lived when I saw Dad making a flask of tea for them so they wouldn't need to buy some coffees.

And then we were off. We left the car at Croy Station, and we had the short train journey to Glasgow Queen Street, a walk through Glasgow city centre to Central Station, avoiding all the humans, and then we were on the train to Largs. Of course, the picnic came out shortly after leaving Glasgow Central station, but Mum told Dad and me that we could only have a snack because the main picnic was for the beach. We didn't argue.

Dad didn't tell us any more bad news, and Mum was in a much better mood now that we were out of the house.

I had a wonderful time when we got to Largs. Lots of humans were on the beach, who all wanted to play with me and throw sticks and stones for me to chase. I know I should only play with a ball, but sticks and stones are much more fun. They feel lovely in your mouth, and they all have different tastes and smells. I like to imagine who else has been playing with them.

Once we'd had our picnic, Mum said we should be making our way home before Glasgow Central became too busy with people going to a festival. I didn't know what a festival was, but I was all for missing the crowds.

"Shall I stop at this Costa Coffee and get us a couple of takeaway drinks for the train?" asked Dad.

I was alarmed at this. I hoped Dad wouldn't have to pay with any of his body parts.

"I've got enough beans on my Costa app to get a free drink for us both," Dad continued, smiling. Phew!

The return journey to Glasgow Central on the train was an experience. Millions of humans, who didn't seem old enough to be out without their parents, were packed into the train. I know it was a sweltering hot day, but some of the outfits were a bit brief. I've never seen so much human flesh in my life. The humans were so noisy too - laughing, shouting and being silly. I was a bit nervous and hid out of the way under the table alongside Mum and Dad.

I thought it would be better once we got to Glasgow Central, but it was even worse. I know they were having fun, but the number of humans and their noises and smells were too much for my delicate Collie senses.

"Oh dear," said Mum. "There'll be some drunk teenagers later. I hope there's someone to look out for them and nobody ends up being left alone in the middle of the night, unable to look after themselves."

Walking through the station, praying we'd get to the outside door and fresh air soon, I could hear that familiar gentle humming above all the noisy humans. I looked around, and above the crowds, I could see a bright light moving towards me.

"I need to go, Mum. The light's shining again."

Mum bent down and unclipped my lead.

"Off you go Beatrix. Stay safe and return to us when you've given your help."

I began the usual chasing of my tail, faster and faster. The humming became louder and the light brighter, with a mist surrounding me. Catching my tail, I yelped with the pain, let go of my tail, and the spinning stopped, the light disappeared, and the humming faded.

The sun was beginning to set, and the air felt chilly but not cold. I took a moment to gather myself, sniffing the air. Well, at least I'm not in a busy train station, I thought, taking in the fresh country air.

I could see nothing but fields of purple lavender. The smell was amazing. We've got some lavender in the back garden at home, but its colour and smell are nothing compared to this. Humans should bottle this and sell it, I thought to myself.

But I didn't know why I was in a field of lavender. I couldn't see or hear anybody needing my help. Wandering through the field was so calming. I could sense my heartbeat getting slower as I took in some deep, long breaths. The lavender was rubbing against me and sticking to my coat. I felt I could lie down and sleep; I was so relaxed.

Enough Beatrix, I told myself. There's a reason you're here.

Reaching the end of the field, I squeezed through an old wooden fence. As I headed towards a wood, darkness fell quickly, and the temperature dropped.

The wood was amazing, with millions of sticks to play with, and so many different grasses to smell and taste. There were lots of crisp leaves on the ground too. I don't know about you, but I can't resist rolling about in piles of leaves. It's so much fun. I knew deep down that I should be trying to work out where my help was needed, but the leaves were too tempting. I started to jump and roll in them. But then, suddenly, I could hear a strange crunching noise, as though somebody or something was rustling through the leaves.

Taking me by surprise, from amongst the leaves crawled this little spiky thing with such short legs. I'd never seen anything like it in my life. I reached out a paw to touch it but was surprised it was so prickly and sharp.

"Aileee, dégage! Que'st-ce-que vous faite?" the creature shouted.

"I'm so sorry," I said, apologising. "I didn't mean to be rude, but you surprised me."

"Ah, you are not a French dog?" said the creature.

"Erm, no. I'm from Scotland. My name's Beatrix."

"Enchantée, Beatrix. My name's Russell. Have you really never seen a hedgehog?"

"Never," I replied, standing back from the prickly hedgehog.

It was at that point that I realised not only could I understand both my Scottish dad and my Yorkshire mum's accents, but I could obviously speak many different languages. I'd already been speaking Danish to the old man with the six kittens, but now I was speaking French to a hedgehog. Wow, it's true. I'm a really clever Border Collie.

"Don't worry about my spikes," said Russell. "I have about 5,000 quills on my body that are there to protect me should anything decide to try to eat me."

I noticed with some alarm that he was now making his quills stand up like thousands of sharp pins.

"I'm harmless so long as you're not hungry. So, what brings you to the Dordogne on this chilly autumn evening?" asked Russell.

"I'm not sure. I'm here to help somebody or something, but I don't know what I need to do yet," I replied, relaxing a little now I knew I was not going to get all those pins fired at me.

Sitting down next to Russell, I told him about my adventures, how I always get whisked into the bright light but never know where I'm going or why I'm needed.

It was lovely chatting with him. I've already told you that Mum has a gentle voice I could listen to all day. Don't tell Mum I've said this, but Russell's voice made me melt inside.

"I wonder, Beatrix," said Russell. "Earlier this evening, there was a group of humans who'd obviously had way too much of that falling-down water they drink. Some of them looked like they should be already tucked up in bed at home, with their parents looking after them. I did see one of those humans fall into the lavender field. Now I think about it; I'm not sure I saw her get back up."

"That's it," I gasped, jumping up onto my feet. "I'm here to find the human in the lavender."

Then I thought about the task ahead of me.

"Oh no! I'll never manage to find her. I usually sniff the air to find humans, but I'll only be able to smell that wonderful lavender."

"Don't worry Beatrix. I'll help you. Come on," offered Russell.

So together, we started to hunt through the lavender field. My nose was itching, and I was constantly sneezing.

Russell laughed. "You're not used to our strong odours, young Beatrix."

We wandered up and down the lavender field for what seemed like hours, hunting for the human. Was she even in this field? I wondered. Was Russell mistaken?

Russell suddenly stopped, and I almost stepped on top of him.

"What is that awful smell?" he cried.

"I know that smell," I said, racking my brain and trying to remember. "I know. Sick. It's that sick stuff that comes out of me when I've been in a bumpy car or eaten too many treats."

I ran towards the smell. And there, in the corner of the lavender field, was a young human.

"Oh no! She's been sick all over herself, and she's fast asleep."

I tried to wake her up, but she kept groaning and doing that sick thing. She felt so cold too, which was hardly surprising as she was wearing no outdoor clothing.

"Russell, we must make sure she's safe until she wakes up. She's too young to be out by herself, and anything could happen to her. I'll lie next to her to keep her warm."

Ignoring the pile of nasty stuff by her and the terrible smell, I cuddled up to the young girl, hoping that my body heat and fur coat would help to keep her warm.

During the night, as the young girl slept, I listened to Russell telling me beautiful stories about his life in France. He told me about his favourite foods that grow so abundantly in France, like apples, berries, and the sweetest tomatoes you could imagine. Russell told me about dishes he thought I'd love, like boeuf bourguignon, salmon, duck, and amazing-sounding cheeses. My mouth was watering as he spoke.

After what seemed like hours, the sun began to rise, lighting up the sky. Gradually the darkness lifted, and the chilly air was gently warmed by the heat of the morning sun.

Before too long, the girl began to move. Obviously alarmed by the sight of a black and white Border Collie and a hedgehog staring at her, she sat up with a start.

Then she started to cry. Big, noisy sobs. Her hair was a right mess, and dried sick stuff was all down her face and clothes.

"What am I going to do?" she cried. "I was at a festival with my friends. I knew my mum and dad wouldn't let me go, so I told them I was having a sleepover at a friend's house. Now I don't know where my friends are, and my parents don't even know that I'm lost. I can't go home like this, or they'll know I've been drunk."

"Don't worry, mademoiselle," said Russell in his wonderful soothing French accent.

The girl was alarmed.

"A talking hedgehog!" she cried.

"Of course, he can talk," I laughed.

"And a talking dog," she gasped.

With that, the three of us all fell about laughing with each other. What a sight it must have made!

"Russell, you know the area. Where can we take this young girl to get some help?" I asked.

"Ah, I know there is an old chateau at the other end of this wood. I go there regularly as it has an amazing vegetable garden, and the lady who lives there is lovely. She never chases me away. I bet she'll let you have a wash in her huge water pool. She goes to wash herself in it every morning.

When she gets out, she puts on clean clothes and sits with a cup of tea, lemon drizzle cake, or a sultana scone. She is the friendliest person ever, and I'm sure she'll know how to get you home."

"I can't thank you enough," said the young girl, cuddling me and giving Russell a gentle pat on his back.

New friends together, the three of us walked through the wood, and, just as Russell had promised, there was a lovely chateau. The sun was shining on the blue water pool, and a lady with light-coloured hair was about to jump into the water. She didn't have on many clothes either.

Catching sight of us walking towards her, the lady looked shocked, or was she amazed, or just astonished? The young girl burst into tears again, telling this lady all about her ordeal.

"My name's Sue," the lady said gently. "Don't cry. I'll contact your parents. Let's get you washed and into clean clothes to spruce you up a bit to make you feel much better. Then I think we could do with a cup of tea, a piece of lemon drizzle cake, and perhaps a sultana scone."

Russell and I looked at each other and smiled.

Sue glanced over at me and rubbed her chin with her hand.

"It can't be. Surely not! Is that you Beatrix, the famous black and white Collie who lives in Scotland with the Yorkshire girl who bakes cakes?"

With that, the bright light appeared above me, and I gave Sue one of my cute Collie smiles.

"Thank you Sue, and Russell. Au revoir," I shouted as I felt myself being drawn into the light, with a gentle humming sounding around me. I was disappointed not to have any of the lady's cake but was very pleased to be going home once more.

Then as quickly as it began, the light vanished, the humming stopped, and with a thump, I landed back at Glasgow Central Station, dropping a large piece of Camembert cheese at Mum's feet.

"Well, hello you. Welcome back. So, you've been to France this time, have you?" said Mum.

Chapter 25

Friendship is a Two-Way Thing

My life as a human dog has been amazing. I remember my dog mummy telling me that if I showed enough love to my new human mummy and daddy, they'd grow to love me as much as she loved me. I hope I've made my dog mummy proud because I've shown plenty of love to my human parents, and I am living a perfect life. I have a lovely, warm, and cosy home. I have food and water that I don't need to share with anyone. Mum and Dad often share their food with me, but don't expect any of mine. I have plenty of exercise and walks, and I even have my bed high enough to see out of the front-room window to keep an eye on what's happening in the outside world.

I've never been frightened by my human parents, although Mum does do some scary things when we're out on our adventures. But we always seem to survive her antics, and I know for sure she never actually means any harm.

Last year we got one of those campervan things. You know what I mean – a tiny home on wheels. Ours even has a name, Evie. I think I've already told you about her. Mum says she named her after the singer, Eva Cassidy.

When we first saw Evie, I was a little unsure. It was all strange to me, and I was concerned when Mum was driving this new campervan for the first time. It's bigger than our car. But she's getting much better at driving Evie now, and there's not as much tension in the air when we go anywhere. She's even started singing along to the radio as she drives, though I prefer the tension in the air rather than Mum's singing, but don't tell her I've told you that.

We've already had some great times in Evie, and our trips always seem to involve hills, rivers, lochs, and lots of peace and quiet.

I love it. I can see Mum loves it too, as she always smiles when we're out in Evie. As Evie is so small inside, I'm never far away from the cooker, and there was even a time when Mum dropped a whole sausage on the floor as she moved it from the oven to the table. Well, not surprisingly, that sausage quickly became my sausage. Most of all, I love sitting outside Evie under the canopy and watching the world go by.

Now Mum and Dad are chatty humans and always talk to lots of different people when we go on walks and to cafés. The humans we meet are similar in many ways to Mum and Dad. Everyone enjoys getting to know each other and spending time chatting. Of course, I was certainly glad of that when I had to get help for Mum when she fell ill on the mountain. Like-minded humans are quick to help each other and make each other feel good about themselves.

Well, the humans we meet on the campsites when we go away in Evie are the same. Sometimes, Mum hardly has time to turn the engine off before new humans are chatting away with us. It's like they want to be friends with everyone. They don't care who the humans are, where they're from or how much money people have; they just want to be friends. Lots of dogs are like that too. That's how it should be if you ask me.

There's a saying that humans often start to look like their dogs. I'm not sure Mum and Dad look like me, but we are all kindred spirits. We just like seeing humans happy. When we're about, nobody needs to be lonely. We chat away with everybody. We make friends wherever we go.

Maybe it's coming from a human family like mine that has helped me to understand why I was sent to help somebody on my secret adventures. Don't get me wrong, sometimes I think I know my purpose of the adventure, but then I'd find myself still on the trip, and I realise there's somebody else I need to help too. This was certainly the case in this next story.

We were enjoying the evening sunshine at the campsite in Strathyre. Mum was at the camping table outside next to Evie, enjoying a cup of tea and a piece of cake and doing some crocheting. Mum's always drinking tea and doing some sort of crafting. I sometimes wonder if Mum will turn into a cup of tea. She says that all problems can be solved with a cup of tea, a cake, and some crochet.

Lying under the awning and enjoying the peace, I could hear that familiar humming telling me somebody needed my help. As I stood up, I could see a bright light shining above Evie the campervan.

"It's time to go," I sighed.

I stood up and gave Mum one of my knowing looks.

Mum peered over at me, smiling, and whispered,

"Take care Beatrix and come back safe and sound."

I started to run around in circles to chase my tail, faster and faster. A mist began to surround me, and the humming became louder, and I could now see the familiar white light shining brightly above me. After what seemed an eternity, I finally caught my tail, gave a little yelp, let go of my tail, and I fell to the ground.

Landing with a bump, I looked around. I don't know about you, but I'm always a bit embarrassed when I've taken a tumble and hope nobody's seen me and is laughing at me. I know Mum does that glancing around thing when she falls on the ice and snow. She doesn't realise that I know she is embarrassed, and I have a little smirk to myself.

Right in front of me was a large metal school gate, and through it I could see lots of little children playing. Not just seeing, I could hear them too. Screams and shouts of happiness filled the air as they all ran around the playground together, having fun.

At least this time, it's a warm adventure. So many of my tasks have taken me to cold, dark, and snowy places. I don't feel so bad about leaving the evening sunshine of Strathyre now. The sun was beaming down and shining nearly as brightly as the children's smiles.

I wondered what my job was here. I couldn't see anything wrong. The children all looked safe and happy. What could possibly be wrong?

Finding myself a shady place beside the stone school wall, I watched this happy scene. I quite like children when they're at arm's length. When they get too close, I'm not as keen on them as they can get a bit too excited – pulling my ears and sticking their fingers in my eyes and nose. Well, that's what happens when that little Minnie the Minx is near me.

As I watched, something caught my eye from the corner of the playground. A little boy was sitting on a swing alone.

He didn't seem to be having as good a time as the others. Perhaps he was tired and having a rest, I thought to myself.

Suddenly, a loud bell rang from inside the building. The big red doors opened, and from behind them appeared a lady.

Wow, I thought. That's a stern-looking human. She had her hair tied up on top of her head in a bun thing and wore a long woollen skirt and matching jacket with a crisp white shirt peeping from under it. She was stern, but not scary.

The children all stopped playing and running around. Then as quickly as anything, they ran towards the stern lady, forming four lines of silent children in front of her. I was amazed that children who were once so playful could suddenly be quiet and orderly.

As I watched, I noticed that the little boy on the swing stood up and walked slowly to join the back of one of the rows of children. He never looked up, but just walked head down with his hands in his pockets.

Oh, he is such a sad little boy, I thought to myself.

Before I could wonder further about him, all the children had disappeared into the school, and the doors closed behind them.

"Now what?" I said aloud.

I had a feeling I was there to help this little boy. He needed to have something to smile about. I guess I'll have to wait here until the doors open again.

I lay down with the warm sun shining on my back, and before too long, I found myself dozing. Collies never fall sound asleep because we're always on guard. Mum's always saying I sleep with one eye open. Well, I'll let you into a secret; I also sleep with one ear open.

Before too long, I heard the bell again from inside the school. The big doors flew open, and the children came thundering out. Happy screams and shouts could be heard once more.

Looking around, I noticed a few grown-ups waiting by the school gate. A couple of them gave me a stroke, but most of them were too busy watching for the children to bother with me.

As I watched, one by one the children came through the gate and into the arms of their waiting mum or dad. It was a heart-warming scene. Such happiness. These children were genuinely happy and loved.

Gradually, the children and grown-ups all drifted away, some children running together down the pavement, clearly the best of friends.

Then, last to leave the schoolyard was the little boy from earlier. He still looked sad. Oh my.

"See you tomorrow Tommy. Take care on your way home," said the teacher, locking the school gates as Tommy walked out onto the pavement.

"Goodbye Miss. See you tomorrow," Tommy replied.

I stood up and walked over to him.

"Hello doggy," said Tommy smiling. He gave me a little pat before beginning his sad, lonely walk along the pavement.

"No! Wait. I'm here to help you," I cried after him.

Tommy didn't understand me yet, but he turned around.

"Go home doggy. Your mummy will be looking for you."

Not deterred, I began to follow Tommy, and we walked together.

"You can walk with me for a little while," Tommy said, and we walked along the pavement.

"I must cross the road now. Goodbye," shouted Tommy, waving to me.

I was horrified and ran up to him, grabbing hold of his coat so he couldn't run into the busy road. I couldn't understand why he was trying to cross the road here. He needed to get to the bleeping green man thing that Mum always insists we use.

Mind you, I don't understand what humans are thinking about sometimes. Mum calls it a pelican crossing and says we must wait for the green man to flash. Well, every time I'm at one of these crossings, I look all around for a pelican crossing the road, but I never see one. Even more alarming is the idea that there'll be a green man at the side of the road, but thankfully all I ever see when Mum presses the button is a flashing green light. Sometimes, it also makes a bleeping noise. Then it's like magic. All the noisy, fast cars stop, and we can just stroll across the road. I always try to run, but Mum says we must walk so we don't trip and fall. She always says that teaching me to cross at the green man might save my life one day.

Oh, and another thing while I remember. Mum sometimes gets us to cross the road at something called a zebra crossing. The first time she told me we would go to the zebra crossing I was beside myself. I'd never seen a zebra, so I didn't know what to expect. It was a bit of a disappointment to find that it was just a few white stripes painted on the road. It seems to be magic though, just like the pelican crossing, because when we stand at the side of the road next to the zebra, all the traffic stops for us to cross the road safely.

Still holding onto Tommy's coat, I pulled him towards the crossing.

"Oh, you're right," said Tommy. "Mummy always tells me to use the pelican crossing. I was feeling so miserable I completely forgot. Thanks for reminding me."

Tommy pressed the button, and the two of us watched for the green man to flash. We waited for the cars to stop, and then we carefully crossed the busy road, Tommy giving a thank-you wave to the drivers in the cars who'd stopped for us.

I wanted to ask Tommy why he was sad. Why didn't he seem happy like the other children? Why didn't the other children walk with him, and more importantly, why didn't any grown-up humans come to meet Tommy at the school gates?

Do you know that all you humans can talk to dogs, but only if you open your ears, listen to us, and genuinely want to hear what we have to say? Too many humans think that they're too clever for us dogs, and that we are silly animals. It's actually the other way around.

Tommy was a lovely little boy, and as he walked, he started to talk and listen to me. Perhaps it was because he needed a friend.

"Do you want to come home with me?" asked Tommy. "Are you here to be my friend?"

"Yes," I replied, and if I was not mistaken, Tommy's chin lifted a little, and a hint of a smile appeared on his lips.

As we walked through the streets, Tommy began to talk about his life.

"I don't have any friends at school or home. Nobody likes me."

I listened, and Tommy continued.

"Me and my mum moved here after my daddy died. By the time I started at the school, all the other children had already been there a couple of months, getting to know each other and forming friendships and gangs. It's not that they were exactly horrible to me, just that they never made any attempt to make friends with me because they all spoke differently to me, and they couldn't understand me when I was talking.

"It takes time to make friends Tommy. And the effort must come from both you and the other children. Did you try to talk to them and ask if you could join in with their games, and laugh at their jokes, even if you thought they are terrible jokes, or you've heard them many times before?" I asked him.

Tommy shook his head.

Before long, we reached Tommy's house.

"Do you want to come in? I'm sure Mummy would like to see you. She'll be glad I have a new friend."

Going into the house, Tommy dropped his bag on the hall floor, kicked off his shoes and hung his coat up on a hook behind the door.

I looked down at the polished floor of the hall and then at my dusty paws. I wished then I could take my outsides shoes off too. It's not our fault, but we dogs feel guilty about trailing mud and dust into the house. Mum's always telling me she wished I'd learn to wipe my feet on the way into our home. But she doesn't seem to like me wiping my wet face on the carpet. There's no pleasing her sometimes.

Walking behind Tommy into the kitchen, I caught a delicious smell of something cooking.

"Hi Mummy. I've made a friend. This dog followed me home. Can we keep her until we find her owners? Please, please," begged Tommy.

"Let's see what happens shall we," Tommy's mummy answered, smiling. "The dog will want to go home, and she will know how to get back there on her own. Perhaps she wanted a little holiday. We're having stew for tea, and I'll put a little bit in a bowl for your new friend."

The lady smiled at me. But I noticed the smile didn't quite reach her eyes.

I was too polite to sit under the table asking for food that first night, so I lay by the kitchen door, but Tommy's mum put some meat and potatoes down in a bowl for me. Then we had a lovely evening. I sat next to Tommy as he watched the TV, and then I was even allowed to sleep next to Tommy's bed.

The following day, we were up early, and Tommy's mum made us both hot buttered toast.

"I bet you're a dog who gets spoiled at home," she smiled, as she passed some toast to me.

"Are you going out anywhere today?" Tommy asked his mum as he munched on his toast. Some butter ran down his chin, but I didn't say anything.

"Not today. Maybe tomorrow. I've got the shopping being delivered by Tesco today. I thought I'd make your favourite lasagne for tea tonight."

Then we set off for school. I was so pleased that Tommy remembered to use the pelican crossing this morning.

When we got to the school gates, Tommy gave me a little cuddle and whispered, "See you later. I do hope you'll still be here when school's finished."

Another little boy shouted across the school playground, "Nice dog Tommy."

Tommy nodded his head.

"Say something back," I nudged Tommy.

Tommy looked sheepishly over to the little boy and replied, "Thanks. What's your name?

"My name's Jack," replied the little boy.

"Do you want to say hello to her? She's friendly," continued Tommy."

Jack came over and patted my head, asking Tommy, "Are you coming to join the line? The bell's about to go."

With that, Tommy and Jack walked into the playground. Tommy glanced back at me. I winked at him.

"I think you have a new friend," I whispered.

I knew then that Tommy would no longer be the sad boy with no friends at school, but I also knew that my job here was not finished yet.

I lay down at the side of the school wall, waiting for the end-of-day bell to sound.

It was a long day, but I could doze, stretch, and walk up and down the pavement outside the schoolyard.

A few humans came past and patted my head.

"Aw, how cute is that! The dog is waiting outside the school gates for its owner to come," one of them said.

Eventually, the bell sounded, the doors flew open and out rushed all the screaming, shouting, happy children. I waited nervously, praying that Tommy was in the crowd of children and not alone behind them.

Yes, there he was, laughing and playing with some of the children.

When Tommy saw me, he ran straight over to me, a smile beaming across his face.

"I've made so many friends. They said they had never seen such a beautiful dog as you, and that if you were happy to be my friend, then they had been wrong about me. They said they were sorry it's taken us so long to get to know one another. Thank you."

One of Tommy's new friends was now by my side, cuddling me.

"See you tomorrow Tommy," this little boy shouted as he ran over to join his mum.

I nudged Tommy again.

"Why not ask him to come over to your house to play? His mum will be able to say if it's OK."

"You're right. It would be nice to have a friend to play with at home. I have loads of toys, and it's boring playing with them by myself all the time," said Tommy.

After a bit of discussion, the little boy's mum said it would be OK, but that she'd walk with us back to Tommy's house to see if it was all right with his mum.

What a different little boy Tommy was today. No more walking with his head down, dragging his feet, and bowing his shoulders. Tommy was a happy little boy. I felt a surge of pride, knowing I'd played a part in this change.

With Tommy now happy, I wondered why I was still here.

Tommy's mum was a bit surprised when the door opened, and she saw not just a smiling Tommy but another smiling little boy and his mum.

The two mums agreed that the little boy could stay at Tommy's to play and have tea, and his mum would come back later for him.

As the boys played upstairs, Tommy's mum sat at the kitchen table drinking tea. I looked at her, and she smiled, rubbing my head. I noticed again that her smile didn't reach her eyes. She was cuddling her cup of tea like my mum does when she's sad.

It's strange, but humans often start talking to me. It's the same with Mum. Humans seem to feel safe with us and share all their problems even before they get to know us.

"You don't know how grateful I am to you for helping Tommy to make friends," Tommy's mum began. "It's been so hard since his dad died last year. My husband, William, was the love of my life, and Tommy was the apple of his dad's eye. I found it hard being in the house without him and decided that if I had to create a new life for Tommy and myself, I couldn't do it in the house I'd shared with William. It was too hard reliving the memories and expecting William to come through the door every night after work. It was breaking Tommy's heart too."

"So, I sold the house," she continued, "and moved here. It's a lovely quiet village, and the school is small. I thought we could fit in nicely here, and Tommy would easily make new friends. It's been tough for the both of us, and I'm so lonely. I don't know anyone, and I can't seem to get myself out of the house to make new friends, even though I know I need to. I feel guilty because I know I should get out of the house, which would help Tommy make friends. I can't even bring myself to take him to school. What sort of terrible Mum leaves their young child to walk to school alone?"

And she started to sob.

It was so sad listening to her talk. She really was baring her soul to me. She seemed such a lovely person and deserves to be happy. I'm sure her husband, William, would have wanted her and Tommy to be happy in their new life.

Before long, the doorbell rang. Tommy's mum opened it, and there was the little boy's mum.

I looked at this lady on the doorstep, smiling at Tommy's mum. I wonder, I thought to myself. I grabbed the lady's bag that was hanging over her shoulder and pulled her towards the hall.

"Oh, what's wrong," cried Tommy's mum.

The little boy's mum smiled.

"I think the dog wants me to come in. I have time for a cup of tea if you'd like that," she said to Tommy's mum.

Soon, the two mums were sitting around the table drinking tea, eating biscuits, and chatting away like long-lost friends.

I lay under the table, hoping some biscuit crumbs might be dropped.

Then, there it was - that familiar humming sound. I came out from under the table and saw a bright light shining in the hall, waiting for me to step into it.

Tommy's mum looked over at me.

"I don't know where you came from or how you knew we needed you, but you have finished your job now. Tommy and I are going to be simply fine. Thank you."

I walked over to her and nuzzled up to her before stepping out into the hall. The humming became louder, and the light fell upon me.

Once again, I felt myself spinning in the bright light as I listened to the soothing humming sound. A moment later, I landed back on the ground outside the Evie the campervan and dropped a box of Cornish fairings at Mum's feet.

"Well, hello you. So, you've been to Cornwall, have you?" said Mum looking up from her crocheting.

Chapter 26

The Pink Coat

Winter was still making its mark across the country, with temperatures dipping well below freezing for the last seven days. But I have my thick Collie double coat to keep me warm; I love the winter, and fortunately, so does my mum. We walk in all weathers, laughing together, especially when there's snow and wind on the hills and mountains. Dad's not so keen on the wintry weather and stays at home to get the tea ready for our return.

This particular winter, I did feel rather posh because I had got a smashing pink waterproof coat to wear. Mum had been worried that as I got older, I might start to feel the cold more, especially after an operation where all my lovely coat had to be shaved off my hip at one side. I was so embarrassed at my bald patch.

Mum and I have been lost in the Scottish mountains on several occasions. Well, Mum thinks we've been lost, but I knew where we were all the time. The time the weather turned very quickly when we were up Ben Ledi was quite funny. I was like a polar bear, and Mum looked like a walking ice human. I was always OK and never felt too cold, but I was glad to get back into the car that day.

But Mum, bless her, wanted to be sure that if anything happened again, I'd always be warm and dry, so she bought me this fancy new coat. I was sceptical when I first saw it, but as soon as I tried it on, I loved it. I must admit that it's nice not to get soaked in the rain or have the snow build up on my own coat, and it keeps the biting wind off me too. It's a lovely-fitting coat with a collar that makes me feel regal. It fastens easily with Velcro straps and has a little loop to go over my tail, so the coat doesn't restrict my legs and tail. It has some reflective silver bits too, so I can be seen in the dark by car drivers or when a torch shines on me. What more could you ask for? A coat to keep you warm and dry, that still allows you the freedom to run up and down the hills and moors - and to do other things that a dog needs to do.

It was just after Mum and I had finished our last walk of the day through the local wood, when I heard the gentle humming again, and that feeling was building up in my tummy. Somebody somewhere needed me.

I had a scuffle with Mum as she tried to take my coat off me in the porch at home. But I knew I had to go. Something inside me told me that my fancy pink coat would be a godsend during this adventure, so I did something I wouldn't usually do. As Mum unclipped the lead from my coat, I ran back out into the middle of the garden before she could remove my coat.

"Come back Beatrix. Come in out of the cold. We need to get inside," Mum cried.

But I gave Mum a little smile and began to run around in circles in the snow to catch my tail.

She must have recognised the signs because Mum sighed, "Stay safe in this frosty winter weather. Stay safe, give your help where it's needed, and then return to the warmth of our house. Please, please be careful."

I ran around in circles, faster and faster. As the humming became louder, a mist surrounded me, and I could see the familiar white light shining brightly in the distance. At last, managing to catch my tail, giving a little yelp, and letting go, I fell to the ground.

It was dark, very dark, with snow all around, and it was bitterly cold. I was certainly glad I still had my pink coat on.

"It's time I had more summer adventures," I cried out to anyone who might be listening, wondering where I was and what my job here would be this time.

The bright light was shining over a run-down barn.

"Here goes," I said. "I'm getting too old for this."

I squeezed myself through a small hole in the wooden barn wall. At least it's a bit warmer here, I thought to myself. I stood for a while, looking around, listening, and sniffing the air. Why was I here?

From the back of the barn, I could hear crying - a sad, heart-breaking, quiet whimpering. I've never been a mother, but deep inside me, my mothering instinct took over, and my heart melted. I edged slowly towards the sound of the crying; not yet sure if I was safe there.

The crying stopped.

In the darkness, I could just make out the shape of a crate. I recalled my crate as a safe place that provided comfort and security as I found my feet and confidence in my new life as a human dog.

Reaching the crate, I found it odd that the door had been jammed shut with a big stick.

"Oh! What's this? The door on my crate was never locked. I could always get out if I wanted to," I said quietly.

There, in the locked crate, I saw a shivering little black and white Border Collie puppy. Tears were rolling down the puppy's face, and it was giving little sobs, peering into the darkness to see who was approaching. What a sad sight it was.

"It's OK, little one," I whispered. "I'm here now. My name's Beatrix. Don't cry."

But I didn't know what to do.

At a loss, I sat by the crate and began to talk to the puppy. As my eyes became more accustomed to the darkness in the barn, I noticed how similar the puppy was to me. A girl, she had black and white markings almost identical to mine. The puppy had two white front legs making it seem like she had long white socks on, whilst her back two legs were black. I glanced down at my legs. How odd.

Trying to soothe the little puppy, I whispered and said, "You're just like me. Oh, and would you look. You have a white tip to your tail, just like mine."

I gave a little wag of my tail just to show the puppy.

The puppy wiped her tiny face with her paw and stopped crying.

"And you have a pink patch above your nose just like mine. But tell me, little one, what's the matter? Why are you so sad?"

"I was taken away from the lovely place where I lived with a farmer and his wife, and my dog mummy, brothers, and sisters. Now I'm being kept in this crate by a nasty human with a large stick," the puppy began to tell me.

"But the farmer's wife wouldn't have let the man take you away if she didn't think you'd be safe," I gasped.

"When the man and lady came to the farm, they did seem lovely," the puppy continued. "They were laughing, smiling, and cuddling all the puppies. They told the farmer's wife they wanted a female Collie and would love her with all their hearts. They said they had a new bed for the dog in their kitchen and were desperate to find a perfect dog to become part of their family and who could go on walks with them every day. They promised that if they could have the black and white puppy, she'd be cherished as though she were made of gold."

I smiled, remembering how Mum had been when she came to see me at the farmhouse all those years ago.

"That sounds like my humans," I said to the puppy.

The puppy started to cry again.

"But it was all a lie. As soon as we arrived here, they put me into this crate, and I've been in here ever since. The humans won't let me out. I never see the light of day and can't even remember what the warmth of the sun feels like. I have a little bit of food and water every other day. But the worst thing is," and she began to give big sobs again, "I'm so ashamed because they don't let me out of the crate, and I have to go to the toilet in my sleeping area. My mummy told me I should be respectful to my owners and always keep my home clean and tidy. What would my mummy think of me?" sobbed the puppy.

"The man has a horrible, wicked voice and said something about it not being long before I would be old enough to have puppies. He has a nasty laugh and always tells me I will be his little gold mine. What does he mean?" asked the frightened puppy.

I put my paw through the crate and let the puppy cuddle up to me. I knew then that my job here was to rescue this sad, mistreated puppy. But what would I do? Where could I take her? And, more importantly, how would I get her out of the crate?

From outside of the barn came the sound of footsteps and a hacking cough. I crept away from the crate, slipping quietly into the dark corner of the barn, hiding behind a hay bale, hoping the puppy would keep quiet and not look at me to let the man know I was there.

The evil man marched through the barn and over to the crate. He had a cigarette hanging from the corner of his mouth and a large brush in one hand.

"All right you. Stop that whining."

I watched with horror, anger building up inside me, as the man pulled the stick away from the crate, allowing the door to swing open. Pushing the puppy to the back of the crate with the brush, he swept all the puppy's waste into a pile next to the crate and threw a handful of dried food into a dirty, rusty bowl.

"Don't say I don't treat you well," shouted the man. "I'm even cleaning your mess up for you. There's some more food for you, and there's still water in your bowl. A few more weeks, and you'll be old enough to start earning me some money."

Pushing the stick back through the door to lock the crate once again, he walked away, whistling to himself, leaving behind a nasty smell of stale tobacco, and sweat.

Silence returned to the barn. Sitting close to the puppy as near as I could get, resting my head on the wire frame of the crate, I tried to reassure her everything would be OK. I told her I'd find a way to get her out of this prison.

"I think I should give you a name. I can't keep calling you puppy." Sitting down, I thought about a suitable name. "I know. I'm going to call you Trisha. I have a dog walker called Trisha, and, other than my human mum and dad; I'd trust Trisha over anybody. She's amazing, caring, gentle, and so much fun. Trisha is a perfect name for you. Of course, once I've worked out how to get you away from here and to some nice humans, they'll probably give you another name."

I explained to the puppy how I had been born Beinn Fhada, but my new mum had given me a new name, Beatrix.

"Mum named me after the famous writer Beatrix Potter," I said proudly.

Over the next few days, I stayed beside the puppy, hiding in the back of the barn every time the wicked man came in. Wondering how I would feed myself as I worked out an escape plan, I chuckled when I spotted the giant bag of dried dog food in the corner of the barn.

"Well, that's going to keep me going, and I'll be able to give a few more bits to the puppy to strengthen her up," I chuckled.

I think of myself as a clever dog, and I realised I had to be careful not to raise the suspicion of this man by eating too much of the food too quickly. Each time the man had been in, I went to the bag of dried food, ate a little bit myself, and carefully carried extra pieces over to Trisha.

"Eat this up, and you'll start to feel stronger," I told Trisha.

Of course, this was a shock to my system as I was used to having good quality meals at home and lots of little treats throughout the day. I always had clean water and lots of fresh air and exercise. I knew the little bit of food I was getting was not enough for me, and I'd quickly become weak on these tiny rations.

I also knew that if I was to get Trisha away from here, she needed to be fit enough to run. As it was, Trisha was just sitting in the corner of the crate, hardly moving. I had to act fast and began to put a rescue plan into place.

"First things first. We need to get you fit," I said to Trisha. "You need to be able to run as fast as you can. Get up off your bottom and start walking around the crate. Good. Now, let's see how fast you can run around the crate."

Trisha, eager to please me, got up and began to run. She ran and ran around that crate until she was out of breath.

For the next few days, Trisha and I ran together - her inside the crate and me around the outside of the crate. Day by day, Trisha was becoming fitter and stronger with the new exercise regime and the little bit of extra food I was slipping into her crate.

I began to plan.

Under the cover of darkness, I'd creep out of the barn to explore the area. I didn't know where I was, but soon found a road beyond the barn. It was a narrow road, but there were a few vehicles using it. That's good, I thought to myself. It must be a road going somewhere, not a dead end.

Each day I talked to Trisha about my plan.

"I'm going to get you away from here to safety. You need to trust me. First, I must find out where that road leads to. I need to make sure I can get you to safety and not put you in more danger. If I don't get back here before it's light, I'll not be able to come into the barn until night falls again. Don't worry. I will come back. I promise."

As darkness fell, I waited for the nasty man to come back into the barn and then leave again. It was time.

I held my paw out to Trisha to stroke her face.

"Hush. Everything's going to work out fine."

I crept silently out of the barn and began to run down the road. I knew I had to get a long way down the road before anybody saw me. My pink coat had fluorescent bits on it, so if any lights shone on me, it would light up. As I ran, whenever I saw a vehicle, I hid in the bushes to make sure I couldn't be seen. All the time, I was hoping that I wouldn't tear my lovely coat on the sharp bushes and branches. Mum would be so disappointed in me.

Before long, I came upon a gate blocking the road. The gate had red lights lighting it up.

I know what that is, I gasped to myself. That's to let the train through. Yes, there's the train line. There must be a station near here. I told myself I could follow the railway line and find a station.

I was scared. Trains are big, noisy, and extremely fast. But if I could find a station, I could creep onto a train with Trisha. But is it OK to run down the train line, and can I keep Trisha safe? Mum always told me I had to stay away from the train lines and sit nicely on the platform behind the yellow line until the train arrived.

First, I need to find the station.

Thankfully, the railway line had a ditch by the side of it. I sighed with relief, knowing that if a train did come, I could lie down in the ditch until it passed. I also knew that even though my sight wasn't the best, especially in the darkness, I had good hearing, so I'd be able to hear the train coming from a long way off.

I ran down the railway line and, before too long, saw the dim lights of the station in the distance. I knew I'd be safe there, away from the train track and well-hidden so nobody would see me. I pushed my way into the shelter of the bushes next to the station.

There I stayed until it was almost daylight, and I counted only one train. I was certainly thankful for my pink coat. I wasn't used to sleeping outside, and it was so cold. But a plan was starting to develop in my head.

I hid in the bushes by the train station all day, just watching. There were quite a few trains, with lots of humans getting on and off.

I waited for the stillness of darkness before running back along the train track, re-joining the road at the railway gate. I ran quietly up the road, hiding in the bushes to avoid the lights of the vehicles illuminating my coat. Eventually, I arrived back at the barn.

Everything was quiet, and I crept silently into the dark, damp, miserable barn. Trisha heard me straight away and started jumping around the crate.

"Quiet!" I hissed. "Don't create a commotion, or the man will hear you."

"I was so scared you wouldn't come back or that something had happened to you, and I'd never be rescued," whimpered Trisha. "The man was cross today. He said he couldn't understand how the food was going down so quickly and that he'd have to start giving me less to eat. He was so nasty. He hit me with the brush, then kicked me with his hard boots as he locked the crate again. My side is so sore now."

Trisha started to cry once more.

"Can you still run around your crate?" I asked, alarmed at what Trisha had told me.

Trisha got to her feet and tried her best to run but couldn't put the weight down on one of her back legs.

"OK," I said. "So, we will have to wait until you can run again. We need to get you strong once more. Now listen to me. I know you've only been having this dried food, but did you know that dogs can eat just about anything? We're not simply meat-eating carnivores. Far from it, we enjoy vegetables and some fruits. Sometimes, these can be as nice, even nicer, than our dried food. Of course, we must avoid those nasty avocados and oranges and lemons. And we can't eat grapes either," I told Trisha.

"Outside the barn, I'd seen lots of trees and bushes with bits of fruit and grasses to eat. I'll bring some to give you extra goodness besides this awful food, but the man will not know anything about it. You need to rest your leg for a couple of days to allow it to get better before we have you running again."

For the next few days and nights, I scavenged for any food I could find, including rotten fruit, grass and even a couple of field mice. I shared my pickings with Trisha and watched eagerly as she slowly regained strength in her injured hind leg.

During the nights, I told Trisha about my wonderful life with my human parents and all our adventures.

"You know, Mum is a great person. She loves me to bits, but she must be the clumsiest of all the humans I've ever met. She's always getting us lost, falling, or doing something foolish on our adventures. But I know she'd never hurt me. I'm going to take you to her. You'll be safe there. Mum will know what to do."

My mind started to wander. This puppy was exactly like me. Same colour and markings, and I smiled to myself, the same cheeky personality and perfect puppy eyes. This puppy had excellent manners and knew how to keep herself clean despite her terrible living conditions. She never gobbled her food up and always offered me the last bit. I had a feeling. This was a very special puppy.

I recalled conversations I'd had with my dog mum all those years ago and remembered her saying,

"There will be a time as you grow older when it is time for you to talk of this with another chosen Border Collie puppy."

I wonder?

"Trisha, did you ever chase your tail while still on the farm with your dog family?" I casually asked.

Trisha sat bold upright and went silent.

"What's wrong," I asked.

"I can't say. I'm not allowed to tell you," Tricia said quietly.

"Did your mummy tell you that you couldn't chase your own tail because you're a very special Border Collie?

"Yes," whispered Trisha, looking puzzled.

I knew then that this was the chosen Border Collie puppy, but this was not the time for her own magical adventures to begin. I had to get Trisha to the safety of my home and my human mum.

"You need to listen to everything I tell you. I've been watching what that man does. The crate is only locked with the stick. I'm sure I can pull it out of the latch, and you'll be able to open the door. Sticks are good, you know. They taste delicious and are just the best thing to chase, but this stick will help you run away with me. Once I've dragged the stick out, I'll hold one end in my mouth. I need you to hold onto the other end of the stick in your mouth and not let go. Do you think you could do that?"

Trisha's eyes were wide like saucers as she listened to me, but she nodded.

"Then we're going to run out onto the road towards the railway line to follow the track until we come to the station. We shouldn't go onto the train line, but there's a ditch at the side where we'll be safe if a train does come."

"Now listen to me carefully. When we get onto the road, you must stay beside me and keep hold of the stick. Don't look back. Keep running. Some big noisy vehicles with bright lights will come along the road. You need to ignore them. I know you'll want to chase them just as I did when I was a young puppy. But you must pretend they are not there. Hold onto the stick and do as I do. Promise me, Trisha?"

Trisha was frightened and started to whimper but promised to do exactly as I told her.

I tried to reassure Trisha, telling her, "I've been on loads of trains with my human parents, and they're great fun. We could sneak onto the train with the humans and, once onboard, hide under one of the seats. There's always food on the floor under the seats too."

I was scared but felt sure if I could get Trisha away from the farm and travel on the train to the end of its journey, I could work out how to get us back to my home, where the wicked man wouldn't be able to find us. Not all humans are cruel, so there would surely be somebody to help us.

That night, sure as anything, the smelly, nasty man came into the barn. Pulling the stick from the crate door, he threw a few scraps of food to Trisha and re-locked the door before staggering back out of the barn. I watched him from the darkness of the barn corner, praying that he'd not pushed the stick into the crate too hard for me to pull back out.

"Eat up your dinner, Trisha," I said. "I know you won't feel like it now, but you'll need it, little as it is."

We waited patiently, listening to the different sounds outside die down, telling us that it was safe for us to make our escape.

I set about freeing the stick that was jamming the crate closed. Gripping the stick with my teeth, I pulled and pulled. I was grateful for the many times I'd played tug-of-war with my mum at home, which had given me the strength in my jaws to do this.

At first, I thought the man had pushed the stick too tightly into the crate door for me to shift it, but then slowly but surely, it began to move. Trisha, bless her, was trying to push the stick out from the other side too.

Finally, with one last almighty tug, the stick flew out of the crate door, I landed on my bottom, and the entrance to the crate creaked open.

In the silence of the dark night, the creaking of the crate door sounded so loud I was sure it would wake up the evil man. Getting Trisha out of the crate, I found a few stones to push up against the crate door to hold it closed. That way, if the man looked into the barn, he'd think the crate was still locked and only notice Trisha was missing if he came into the barn right up to the crate.

"Ready?" I whispered.

Trisha nodded.

"Take hold of the stick and do not let go. You go on the left-hand side of me, so you're not next to the road. I'm used to the noise of the vehicles and won't be as frightened as you."

Together, we crept out of the barn and away from the horrors of that place. It was a cold, but thankfully dry, clear evening, and the moon was shining brightly, lighting up the road in front.

Trisha followed my instructions and held tightly to the stick as she ran beside me. I made sure that I didn't run too quickly, reminding myself she was only a tiny puppy with little legs and was still injured. Each time a car came past, I pushed Trisha into the side of the road out of sight, hoping that my coat would not be caught by the lights. At last, we reached the railway line. Trisha dropped the stick and started to cry.

"I'm scared, and I'm cold, and I'm tired. I can't go on any further," Trisha sobbed.

"Listen to me. Do you want to go back to the barn to the evil man? Do you want to know what he had in mind for you? Do you want to know how you would be his gold mine?" I shouted at Trisha.

It was heart-breaking. I knew I was harsh with her, but I had to get her to keep going. I couldn't go soft on her now. We were so close to safety.

Trisha looked at me with sad eyes, but she took the stick in her mouth once more, and we set off running again, this time along the railway line.

As we were running, I could hear a train rumbling in the distance. Quickly, I pushed Trisha into the ditch beside the railway line and lay on top of her. As though Trisha sensed the danger, she never struggled and lay still beneath me. The train sped along the line beside us, rumbling and shaking. I thought at one point that the wind the train was making was going to grab hold of my coat and pull me under the train. But then, as quickly as the train approached, it sped away into the distance.

"Wow," gasped Trisha. "Was that a train? I thought you said they were nice."

I laughed and told her I'd explain everything later once we were in a safer place. Grabbing hold of one end of the stick each, we jogged down the train line until we reached the station.

The station was all quiet, and there were no humans about. I found the quiet, hidden place I'd been using to watch the station, and we both lay down, glad of the rest.

"You have a little sleep now," I told Trisha. "We still have a long journey ahead of us."

Trisha quickly fell asleep, but I started to panic. How would I get her on the train, and how would I find my house? What if we were found and the humans took us somewhere else, maybe even more frightening than the barn we'd left behind?

"What's that bright light in the sky over there?" asked Trisha, stirring from her sleep.

I looked around, but I couldn't see anything.

"And listen to that lovely, gentle humming," she continued.

I realised then that it was time for Trisha to start her magical journey. She was indeed that special Border Collie. I also knew that this was the last secret adventure I'd be having.

"I can't see the light or hear the humming, but I know what it is. It's time for you to chase your tail. This is your light for you to follow. Trust it, and you'll be magically transported to a safe home. There you'll have a new mum and dad. They will give you a new name, but they will love you with all their hearts."

"It's been an absolute honour to see you at the start of your magical journey. Goodbye Trisha," I whispered.

Trisha began to chase her tail, faster and faster. As she built up speed, she looked at me, tears rolling down her face.

"Thank you Beatrix. I'll never forget you."

I saw Trisha finally catch her tail and let out a yelp. She was gone, but I knew she would be safe wherever she landed.

Then, I saw my own bright light in the sky, and I could hear the gentle humming. The bright light came nearer, and the humming louder. The light fell upon me. I felt myself spinning as I listened to the soothing humming.

A moment later, I landed on our lounge floor at home, dropping a half-eaten Bratwurst at Mum's feet.

"Well, hello you," said Mum, looking up from her jigsaw puzzle. "You've been to Germany, have you?"

Part 3

Beinn Fhada Once More

Chapter 27

I'm Not Dead Yet, Mum

August 2022

After the family holiday in Filey, life settled back into some sort of normality for me. The days were still long, and the sun shone brightly. I thought the days were a little too hot, and Mum felt the same. I'd lie in the shady corners of the garden, and Mum would go into the house declaring, "It's too hot," but Dad, who loves to be warm, would spend hours reading a book in the garden, basking in the heat of the sun. He even took his tee shirt and socks off, and his woolly gloves were nowhere to be seen.

But the good times always end, don't they?

A couple of weeks after the holiday, Mum was cleaning the front-room carpet with a huge noisy machine.

"Do you really have to use that thing?" I moaned. "It's spoiling the peace."

Mum stopped, turned the machine off, and looked at me with her scary eyes.

"Don't you dare complain," she hissed. "It's because of your hair and muddy paws that I have to do this. And don't even get me started on that disgusting habit of yours of wiping your face on the carpet after you've had a drink or eaten your dinner."

I realised Mum wasn't in the best of moods, so I decided to go and sunbathe in the garden.

A while ago, Mum had the idea of putting up a folding gate in the garden to stop me from escaping. Although, to be fair to me, I only ever run out of the garden when the postman comes to our door, or a cat passes by. Mum had obviously forgotten that I'm a clever Border Collie because that little obstacle wouldn't deter me. It was a poor attempt at a gate. I bet even one of my silly Afghan Hound friends could open it! When Mum's not looking, I simply push it to one side and sneak out to see what's happening in the big wide world of the front garden.

This particular day I was napping in the garden and caught the whiff of a cat. I was up in a flash at the wobbly gate and had it open in the flick of a tail.

The cat was sitting at the top of our driveway, pouting in that ridiculous way cats do. I laughed to myself at the cat seeing me open the gate. The look on its face was priceless.

The cat shot off down the road like a demon, with me in hot pursuit. We ran up and down the cul-de-sac for ten minutes, in and out of the neighbours' gardens; flowers and grass were being pulled up all around us.

Suddenly, I stopped. I was shaky, and everything seemed blurry. I didn't feel well at all.

I watched as the cat stuck its nose up in the air and sauntered away from me, like the cat who'd got the cream.

I needed to get home.

As I reached our front garden, everything started swimming around me. I felt like I couldn't stand up any longer. Then it all went black.

The next thing I remember was Mum kneeling by my side, stroking me, and Dad running towards me. Well, not exactly running, as Dad's running days are long gone. He walked quickly towards me.

Once Dad had helped me to stand up, I quickly came around. I didn't want to run back down the street, but I was OK.

For a few days I was a bit tired and wobbly when I got up. It was hard to explain, but I didn't feel well at all. It was as though I'd climbed ten mountains in a day without stopping, but I'd only walked from the front room to the garden.

Dad wanted me to play in the park with him and let me chase the ball, but I was too tired.

"It must be too warm for Beatrix out there. She just wanted to come home," Dad said to Mum as he flopped onto a chair in the garden.

Over the next couple of days, I began to feel odd. I didn't want to drink, and the thought of food made me feel quite poorly. There were a couple of times when I was sick at night-time like I had been on a bumpy car journey. When Dad came down and saw it, he told Mum I'd been as sick as a dog. What did he expect? For me to be as sick as an elephant?

Then Mum came and sat with me on the window box.

"What's wrong?" she asked, stroking my head, feeling me all over, and pressing my tummy.

I couldn't explain to her how I felt. I just knew I wasn't well. I looked Mum in the eyes, and we shared one of our moments.

"Beatrix is sad," Mum announced. "We need to take her to the vet. I don't know what it is, and she can't tell me."

I heard Mum on the phone organising a visit to the vet place. The vet is not my best friend, but I knew I needed to find out what was wrong with me. Dad had to lift me into the car because I was so weak, but we were soon at the vet place.

Getting down from the car, I didn't know if I'd be able to reach the door, but Dad took his time and allowed me to walk slowly.

"Leave her with us, Mr Murphy," said the vet lady. "We'll take her and get a scan done."

I glanced over my shoulder at Dad, and it took all my strength not to cry. Dad was crying.

After she had done a bit of prodding and poking and pulled out some of my blood with a tube she stuck in my leg, the vet lady led me back out of the room. Dad had hold of my lead again, and nothing much seemed to have happened.

"Beatrix is seriously ill. She's very anaemic, and the scan shows something in her tummy that we need to investigate further," the vet lady said to Dad. "Can you bring her back in tomorrow morning?"

Dad looked like he was going to cry again, with his bottom lip trembling. I've never seen Dad like this before. He was starting to worry me. What was wrong with me?

During the evening, I slept by the side of Dad's chair. He kept stroking me and saying, "There, there Beatrix." I didn't even have any supper, even though Dad tried to entice me with rich tea biscuits and quavers. Mum was away doing that working thing she does, so she wasn't here. I needed my mum. I needed to talk to her. Dad doesn't understand me like Mum does.

A Note from My Mummy

The following morning Beatrix was taken back to the vet but collapsed in the waiting room, so she doesn't know this bit of the story. Jim was distraught. The vet was amazing and quickly had Beatrix in the emergency room.

Jim was soon given the distressing choice of either allowing emergency surgery immediately (that she may or may not survive) or saying goodbye to Beatrix there and then.

I was still at work, but Jim made the decision to give permission for the surgery. He was warned that the cost would be in the thousands. Surgery was still the only choice for Jim, and he knew for sure that I would agree.

In the operating theatre, surgery revealed that Beatrix's spleen had burst due to numerous large masses. This had caused internal bleeding, and her stomach was full of blood, hence the severe anaemia. Beatrix's spleen was removed, the wound stitched, and samples were sent away for further investigations to determine whether the masses were malignant.

That same day, Beatrix was ready to be taken home to recover.

I don't know what happened today. One minute I was standing next to Dad with the vet lady; the next minute, I was lying with one of those ridiculous plastic cones around my head. I wasn't sore. I couldn't feel anything. I touched one paw with another. Nothing. Wow. Something serious must have happened.

The vet lady came towards me. "Come on Beatrix, time to go home," she said, holding the door open.

I could see Mum and Dad through the door, and I wanted to run to them but couldn't get my legs to work properly. I was a bit wobbly and felt a little bit queasy. Mum was on her knees, crying, giving me a gentle hug.

"Oh Beatrix. I'm so glad to see you. Let's get you home."

The next few minutes were tricky, with Mum and Dad trying to work out how to get me into our tiny red car. I knew I couldn't jump, so I stood there waiting for one of them to pick me up. I'd have been laughing if I hadn't felt so rubbish. It was like a scene out of a comedy show. Mum was at one door, reaching through to grab my lead, and Dad was at the other door, lifting me to get me on the back seat.

I know I said I couldn't feel anything in the vet place, but I could definitely feel something as Dad gently lifted me up. It was sore. I didn't struggle or try to help as I knew he was doing his best.

Lying there on the back seat as Dad drove us back home, I could only think that they would have to repeat this whole painful process to get me back out of the car and into the house.

Sure enough, with the car on the drive outside our home, the pantomime began.

"You lift her out this way," Dad advised Mum.

"No, I can't. I just can't. I don't want to hurt her," Mum sobbed.

What is it with her at the moment? I've never known her to cry so much. She's the one that's always telling people she's a tough Yorkshire bird who never cries, which I know is untrue. Firstly, she's not a bird, and secondly, I've seen her cry lots of times. But not usually so much in one day.

"Move out of the way, and I'll get her down," Dad said in his gruff voice.

Eventually, I was out of the car and on the drive. But this ridiculous performance had to be repeated once more to get me up the three steps into our back door of the house. At this moment, I'd have been happy to be a dog who lived outdoors in a kennel in the back garden.

The next few hours were a blur. I settled myself down as much as I could with my tummy feeling delicate and that plastic cone around my head blocking my vision. I managed to doze for a while, then I had a little drink. At least the plastic cone fits perfectly over my water and food bowls, so I won't die of thirst or starvation.

Mum tells me that the cone will stop me from scratching my stitches. I remember the last time I had to have one of these on. I had promised Mum that I wouldn't scratch if she took it off overnight. Mum was down those stairs like a little girl on Christmas morning when she heard me scratching. She didn't say anything but gave me one of her looks, and the cone was quickly fastened back in place. She must have good hearing, unlike Dad, as I thought I'd been scratching quietly. You must know how it is when you have a cut or stitches that need scratching. The more you can't do it, the more you want to, and the stronger the itch seems to get. I knew there'd be no overnight removal of the cone this time. I resigned myself to being demented with unscratched itches, but if Mum thinks it's for the best, then it must be.

If getting in and out of the car was a pantomime, wait until you hear about the administration of medicines. Mum says I must have antibiotics, painkillers, and anti-blood-clotting pills. It was that word that made my tired ears prick up. Pills. I hate pills. They always taste so terrible, and they seem to catch in the back of my throat. I wonder why they can't find something that tastes nice and that I can swallow easily.

Mum thinks she's clever and wraps up the pills in corned beef or cheese, then puts it in my dish with some food. She thinks she's so smart, but I always know.

"Come on Beatrix. There are some lovely treats for you in your bowl," she said with a silly grin.

I went to the bowl, and sure enough, some corned beef and cheese pieces were sitting there, but I could smell the tablets. I used my rough tongue to separate the treats from the pills.

"Thanks Mum, that was lovely," I said.

Mum looked at me and then at the bowl with the pills still there. I was surprised, but she never said anything. The next thing I knew, she was looking in the cold food cupboard.

"I know you're not feeling well, so how about a lovely cheese triangle? These are your favourites," said Mum.

I felt guilty now for not eating the pills.

"Wow, thank you so much. You're spoiling me," I said, gulping down the lovely soft cheese.

"Wait one minute! There were pills in that cheese triangle, weren't there," I said to Mum, who smiled at me like she'd won a million pounds.

And that game was repeated a couple more times that day. I was too tired to be bothered, and I guess I was poorly, so I probably needed the pills.

That night, I slept well. It must have been the stuff that vet lady had put in me, and the pills Mum had tricked me into eating. Perhaps it was also that whatever was in my tummy making me feel so rubbish now seemed to have been taken away.

There was one moment during the night when I was pleased Mum and Dad had gone upstairs. In the middle of the night, I felt like I needed a little trump to let out some of the gas the vet lady had pumped into me.

I was mortified!

Once I'd started to release it, it kept coming, like whistling from my bottom. And the smell! Oh, my goodness me. I have never smelt anything as bad as that in my whole life. I just hoped the smell would have disappeared before the morning.

Mum and Dad came down the stairs together the next day.

"Oh, flipping heck. You can't half smell the anaesthetic coming out of her," gasped Mum, covering her nose. "Don't worry Beatrix; it can't be helped. It happens to humans as well after they've been under anaesthetic."

I was still embarrassed, but as Mum rightly pointed out, there was nothing I could do about it.

"Are you sure you'll be OK by yourself with Beatrix today?" asked Dad, munching on his buttered toast. I was pleased to see that he gave me a piece too. I didn't feel like eating very much, but buttered toast is just the thing when you're a little under the weather.

"Go, you've been looking forward to going to the races with Danny for weeks. I don't need to be anywhere today. It will just be Beatrix and me. We'll be fine," replied Mum, giving me one of her beautiful smiles.

Once Dad had gone out to the races, the day with Mum began slowly. There was, of course, the palaver with the medication to go through again. I won this time.

"Beatrix, you need to take these tablets," sighed Mum. "We need to make sure you don't get an infection in your wound and that you're not in any pain."

"Next time Mum, I'll maybe take them for you," I whispered. She looked so worried.

We had a couple of walks to the grass at the bottom of the street for me to go to the toilet. I don't know how other dogs can go to the toilet on the pavement. I like my privacy and the comfort of grass to do my business. But the end of the street was far enough. Mum didn't try to encourage me to walk any further, and I didn't feel the need to do so.

The steps up to the back door were still a bit of a problem, but Mum allowed me to take my time, and she tried to help me, so I didn't have to stretch too much. I might not have been able to feel anything yesterday, but today my stomach is sore. It feels like I've got a massive cut along it. That must be why I've got the plastic collar on. It's starting to get painful now. Perhaps I'll take the pills next time Mum tries to give them to me.

In the kitchen, I could see Mum doing the usual hide-the-pill-in-the-cheese routine, but to be honest, I was so sore I'd have taken it straight from her hand. I gobbled up the cheese and the hidden pill, much to Mum's obvious delight, and she gave me a gentle cuddle and one of her smiles. I went to lie down by Dad's chair.

Well, I don't know what Mum had given me, but it was rather good. I wished I'd taken it in the morning. I felt a wave of warmth running through me, and the pain disappeared. And I was so tired. Before too long, I couldn't keep my eyes open any longer and drifted into a deep sleep.

"I can't wake her up. I think she's going. I don't know what to do."

Stirring from my deep slumber, I could hear Mum talking on her phone.

"Look at her," she sobbed.

What is it with Mum and this sobbing now? Through my glazed eyes, I could see Mum was not just talking on the phone; she was doing one of those video calls to my human sister Chlöe. Chlöe was crying too.

Mum was on the floor next to me, stroking my paw.

"It's OK Beatrix. If you need to go, you go. I'm not going to put you through any more operations," she whispered, her tears dropping on my leg.

I was still too drugged up to talk to Mum, but I put my paw on her hand to try and tell her I was OK.

"Oh no," wailed Mum, still on the phone with Chlöe. "She's saying goodbye to me."

Then she was on the phone with that Salena person. She was crying too. Is it National Yorkshire Girls' Crying Day? I just wanted to go back to sleep.

"Jim, you need to hurry home if you want to see her before she goes," said Mum on the phone.

Heck, she thinks I'm dying, and she's worrying Dad now.

And for some considerable time, Mum lay beside me, stroking me and telling me how much she loved me, until I heard the back door opening. Dad and Uncle Danny were back.

Oh, what's that smell? I wondered.

Mum sat up, wiping her eyes.

"What are you crying for?" asked Dad.

"She's dying," sobbed Mum.

But I was up on my feet in seconds.

"Do you want some fish and chips Beatrix?" asked Dad with a little laugh.

Walking into the kitchen, I looked back at Mum, who was still on her knees.

"I'm not dead yet Mum."

Chapter 28

A New Lease of Life

September 2022

It didn't take me long to feel like my old self - even though I had the shame of wearing the plastic cone for a long time.

My dog friends in the park sympathised with me, making me feel like a movie star. They played around me, never coming too close to hurt me, but the humans, well, it was like the plastic cone was too much for them. All the humans we bumped into (not literally) on our short walks would ask Dad about my operation and tell me how brave I'd been. I didn't even need to do the head tilt thing to get treats. It was as though the cone was a sympathy medal. Mind you; I'd rather go without treats and not have to wear the cone.

Mum and Dad were so attentive to me. They couldn't do enough.

"Do you want a drink? Do you want a biscuit? Here, lie down on this clean rug." It went on and on.

Then the day finally came for the cone to come off. The vet lady smiled and hugged me, saying she couldn't believe how well I'd recovered.

"Don't let her run up the hills just yet," she told Mum and Dad. "Give it ten days for the internal stitches to heal fully."

For ten long days, our walks remained gentle, with me on the lead, although we could now go beyond the park.

"When can you come to play with us again?" asked my friend, Hamish, the golden retriever.

"Soon, then we'll be able to run around together again. You'll still never catch me," I said, winking at Hamish.

At last, the day came when I could be free once more.

"Let's go around the farm road," said Mum. "You can walk and run as fast as you like, but there are no walls or fences to jump over."

It was great to feel fit and healthy once more. I didn't feel tired, sick, or bloated anymore.

Mum and Dad bought me a new purple coat to help keep my tummy dry and clean.

"Look at you!" exclaimed Mum, as I stood on my window box feeling like a model. "You have a tiny waist again."

Over the next few weeks, our walks became longer, and Dad even allowed me to play with the ball in the park. I needed to get my fitness back as I felt tired after just a little game.

One Sunday, we took a lovely walk around Mugdock Country Park. I love it there; there are so many trees, branches, paths, and a fabulous loch to swim in.

"I'll run on in front of you with my stick," I shouted to Mum and Dad. "I'll wait in the water for you to catch up."

"Not today, Beatrix," called Mum.

I stopped running.

"What? Why? The vet lady said I was OK. Please let me go in the water," I cried.

"No!" said a very stern Dad. "You need to wait a few more weeks before you're well enough to go jumping about in the water. You don't want to overstrain yourself."

My disappointment soon vanished when I saw Mum and Dad take a seat on a bench, and Mum took off her rucksack. I might not be able to play in the water, but we can always have a picnic as compensation; I smiled as Mum passed me a piece of cooked ham.

Chapter 29

Dad Gets Covid

October 2022

"Take a couple of paracetamol tablets," Mum said to Dad.

Did I see her roll her eyes? To be fair, he was coughing and moaning about his sore head and throat. For two days, it went on. Dad moaning, and Mum telling him to take some tablets.

"Positive! Are you sure?" exclaimed Mum.

Dad had apparently caught that Covid thing. I don't know how he caught it because I never saw it running around the house.

I've heard a lot about that pesky virus over the last couple of years, and it was Covid that forced Mum and Dad to close their tearoom. Mind you, life with Mum and Dad at home is much better than them going out to work and leaving me alone. OK, that might be a bit dramatic as I've already told you I had a great dog walker, Trisha, when they left me home alone.

Dad took himself up the stairs, and I didn't see him for what seemed like days. Mum was doing all the walks with me, even the late-at-night ones. When we met any humans, she told them to stay away from us.

"Jim's got Covid. I'm negative but stay away just in case," Mum kept telling people.

She was even making her own cups of tea. Things must be bad as Dad always likes to make Mum's tea for her. Or so Mum tells him. Alarmingly, she was taking drinks and food on a plate upstairs to Dad, but she was wearing one of those face masks. This was getting serious.

"Is Dad OK?" I asked Mum as we settled down to our supper.

"Yes, he's been poorly, but he's on the mend now. Don't worry," said Mum, munching a toasted currant teacake. It looked really nice, but I know I'm not allowed currants. I think that's why Mum eats so many currant teacakes because she doesn't have to share them with me.

A few days later, Dad, looking as white as a ghost, slithered his way down the stairs. Mum was sitting at one end of the room and Dad at the other.

"I think you should go away in Evie this weekend to Blair Atholl," Dad said to Mum in the most pathetic voice I've ever heard him use. His voice was croaky and, oh my, that cough. I slid myself across the room to sit next to Mum, away from him and that Covid thing.

"You're still negative Debra," said Dad, "and you don't want to catch this and pass it on to the vulnerable people you work with."

"I'll decide in a couple of days," answered Mum, but I noticed a definite twinkle in her eyes.

"Right, the fridge is full of meals for you, and there are plenty of snacks. You don't need to do anything. Just rest and get better. We'll see you in a few days," said Mum. I noticed that our bags were already packed by the back door. Mum does love to go on adventures whenever she can.

I felt torn. Could I really leave Dad all alone? But he wasn't going to play in the park with me, was he? Mum's going on an adventure and has already told me I'll be able to play in the river this time. And we're not really leaving Dad alone. He has that Covid thing to keep him company.

"See you soon Dad," I called, jumping into the campervan.

Once at the campsite, we followed the usual routine, Mum getting everything set up as I kept an eye on the proceedings. But this time, she had this new tent thing.

"It says one person can put this up in twenty minutes," gasped Mum from under a massive piece of canvas. There were ropes everywhere, and it didn't seem much like a tent to me. I had a little giggle to myself, watching her struggle.

"That's it," cried Mum. "If even my dog is laughing at me, this tent is going back in the bag."

Oh no. Now I felt a bit guilty. I didn't mean to make Mum sad. I also wondered why all the humans in the campsite watching Mum didn't help her.

"Right. We're going to the pub for tea tonight," announced Mum, wiping away her tears.

The pub's a lovely place. We've been there a few times before. Usually, it's quite cosy, but tonight it was so busy. And it was full of dogs. Dogs on humans' laps, under the tables or the chairs. Mum found a table for us in the corner, away from the rabble. I lay quietly under the table, popping up for the odd chip that Mum offered me.

I was glad when we left because all the dogs were barking and yelping at each other. Why can't they all be like Border Collies? We only talk when we have something important to say. Even the humans were noisy - laughing, shouting, and singing. I'm glad those humans don't belong to me; my mum is so quiet and lovely to be with. She's never noisy like that.

Back at Evie, it was lovely and cosy; the lights were on, curtains were drawn, and the heating was warming the van up nicely. Perfect.

"Is it supper time Mum?" I asked.

The following morning during breakfast, Mum announced, "I'm going to beat that awning today."

And to her credit, it wasn't long before she'd built a canvas room attached to the side of Evie. She didn't need the other humans in the campsite to help her.

"Well done. I knew you could do it," I said, nuzzling her leg. "Shall we have a cup of tea and a biscuit to celebrate?" I asked.

True to her word, once we'd enjoyed our victory biscuits, Mum took me for a long walk around the woods and along the riverbank, letting me paddle in one of the deep, clear pools.

"Thank you, Mum," I shouted to her as I chased the sticks, feeling the cold, clear water on my skin.

A few days later, we returned home, and I was pleased to see that Dad appeared to be much better. He still had that horrid cough, and I was alarmed to see Mum hug him.

"It's OK. Dad's negative now," said Mum, smiling down at me.

Mum never did catch Covid from Dad.

Chapter 30

Minnie Comes Back

Half-Term, October 2022

"Right, I'm off. We'll see you later," announced Mum, picking up the car keys.

I looked around. Dad still had his slippers on, and my lead remained on its hook in the hallway.

"Where are you going, and why can't I go with you?" I asked.

"I'm heading to Gretna services to meet Chlöe, Neill, and the children. Minnie is coming to stay with us for a few days," Mum replied.

"What? Here? With us?" I moaned.

"Yes," laughed Mum. "See you later this afternoon."

We had Minnie with us for four whole days and nights. If I'm honest, she's turning into a bit of a cutie for a little human. She likes to play with my toys, share her food, and even tickles my ears. I wouldn't say we were best friends, but we're certainly no longer enemies.

But I could sense something about her. And I was right. Before too long, she was doing that sick thing and lying on the couch.

"She's got a really high temperature," gasped Mum. "What if it's Covid?"

Heck, that Covid is a nightmare, I thought to myself. I glanced at my little human niece, looking helpless and defenceless on the couch. She looked so sad and tiny. I knew that I had to take care of her. Lying beside the sofa next to her, I was on guard. I wasn't going to let that Covid get her.

Thankfully, after a day or two, she was a bit better, and we had a good time together, playing with my squeaky toys and sharing cooked ham and cheese.

We took Minnie for a walk through the wood close to our house and I showed her all the sticks I play with. I showed her how to jump in the little beck, but she didn't seem to like that. I did remember not to pull her over when she was holding my lead though. I can still remember the stern looks from Mum and Chlöe when we were on holiday at Primrose Valley, and I made Minnie fall over.

I wasn't at all surprised to find that Mum did some baking with Minnie. They made lots of things, including something called scary fingers for Minnie to take to her Halloween party when she went back home. They looked pretty frightening to me, but I was very brave and ate one, just to make sure they were safe for everyone else to eat.

Before too long, Mum and Minnie were back in the car and on their way down to Halifax.

"I think I quite like being a dog Auntie," I said to Dad as we shared a piece of toast. "But it's nice to have the house all quiet and peaceful again."

Chapter 31

Another Trip Up the Campsies

November 2022

Walks had been getting longer, and I was certainly feeling stronger.

"I think we'll go up the Campsie Fells," said Mum. "Let's blow the cobwebs away from both of us."

As we set off up the hill from the car park above Clachan of Campsie, Mum took my lead off me.

"Off you go; just take your time," said Mum.

I set off running. Looking back, I could see Mum smiling at me. We really are like two peas in a pod, both loving to be free on the hills.

I know the route well up the Campsies, and there's no risk of Mum getting lost with me to keep her safe and in such clear weather.

The wind was howling and nearly pushing us off the path. An hour or so later, we reached the little stile where Mum always sits for her lunch.

I watched, smiling, as she struggled with her back bag until she finally managed to tie it onto the fence, so it didn't blow away in the strong wind.

"Don't let the picnic blow away," I said, concerned.

And there we sat in silence, listening to the wind howling around us, Mum having her flask of tea and sharing our picnic food.

"It's like old times, Beatrix," she whispered. "I'm so glad you're on the road to recovery. I was frightened when you were so ill after your operation."

"I know Mum. I know."

The way back down the hills was scary. I don't know how it happens, but we always seem to have an adventure wherever we go. I was a bit tired, and Mum was shattered too, but what a day. The wind was blowing in all directions. I watched in horror at one point when it actually blew Mum off her feet. But she was quickly back up on her feet again, laughing.

"Wow, we'd better get home before this gets any worse," said Mum.

I kept a close eye on her all the way back after that. She even had to sit down a couple of times before we reached the shelter of the car park because the wind was pushing her so hard.

"What a fabulous day," said Mum to Dad as he handed her a cup of tea at home. "Beatrix had an absolute ball. It was amazing to see her running free on the hills once more. I wish you could have been there to see it."

Chapter 32

One Last Swim in Coniston Water

November 2022

"Take care and phone when you get there," Dad said to Mum, giving her a hug. "Have fun Beatrix."

We were off again in Evie, the campervan. This time it was down to the Lake District. Dad said Mum was mad as it would be freezing in the campervan in November. "It's a metal box on wheels," he grumbled. We didn't listen to him.

Like a pro, Mum got Evie set up in the campsite and had the extra canvas room up in no time. "Go Mum," I said, proud of her for doing it herself.

The next few days were bliss. We walked through fields, along tracks and down to Coniston Water. I love this lake, and Mum let me play for what seemed like hours in the water, chasing sticks.

My human brother Benjamin came along to join us with his dog Zeb. A perfect little holiday, meals in pubs, snacking in the canvas room, walks in the woods, and more swimming in Coniston Water. I even had a whole sausage in the Bluebird Cafe. What a life.

But even though I was having a good time, I was exhausted. I was so glad when we finally got back to Evie that evening. Benjamin and Zeb went home again, so it was just Mum and me.

"Time for a last walk before we go to sleep," Mum said, picking up my lead.

"Oh, must I? I feel absolutely shattered."

"Yes," laughed Mum. "Just five minutes, then we can settle down for the night."

The two little steps down from the campervan are usually no problem for me to jump up and down, but tonight they were like a mountain. Mum had to give me a little push back up into the van.

The following morning, I knew things were not good. It was like time had turned back to August when I was ill. Surely not, I thought to myself.

Mum got up. "Come on. Let's go for a walk."

"No, I can't," I sobbed.

Mum looked at me.

"What's wrong," she asked, kneeling beside me. Looking deep into my eyes, she asked, "Are you poorly?"

But I was too tired to talk to her.

"Just come out for the toilet, then you can get back in the van," she said.

It was a struggle, but I managed a bit of a wee, and then got myself as comfortable as possible under the table.

I could hear Mum talking to Dad on the phone.

"She's not well. I'm coming home. I need to get her home; I'm scared."

I noticed that Mum was crying on the phone to Dad. I was frightened myself, but I didn't want to tell Mum.

Mum started to take the canvas room down.

"You should probably dry that tent first," I said to her.

"It doesn't matter. I just want to get us home," Mum said, throwing everything into the back of the van.

Then we were on our way. I was comfortable enough under the table, but I knew all was not well.

"That's us at Gretna services. We'll be home in an hour or so. Could you get us an appointment at the vet, please?" I heard Mum asking Dad on the phone.

"Do you want to get out to go to the toilet?" Mum asked me.

"No, I'll stay here if you don't mind," I answered quietly.

Mum sat down on the floor in the van next to me. I could see tears in her eyes.

"Right, let's get home as quickly as we can."

The van stopped, and the side door opened. Dad was waiting for us in the garden at home. I was so pleased to see him. The rest in the van had helped a little, and I jumped down from Evie to greet him.

"She's OK," laughed Dad. "There's nothing wrong with her. She was just missing me."

Mum and I knew differently.

Then I was in the back of the car and on the now familiar route to the vet place. Once we were inside the vet place, Mum and Dad were quiet.

It was too much for me. I was exhausted, and my legs gave way under me. A nice vet lady took me into the room, took blood from my paw, and felt my tummy.

"Beatrix's red blood cells are too low. Even without her spleen, her body should have been making red blood cells by now. She's very ill and needs a more specialised scan to see what's going on," the vet lady told Mum and Dad. "I've organised this for tomorrow," she continued.

Mum and Dad took me home. They were so sad, but we had a peaceful evening. Mum and Dad sat on the floor next to me. I remember feeling my dog mum's all-encompassing love for me when I was a puppy. That night, I could feel that same powerful love from Mum and Dad surrounding me. I hoped they could feel my love for them too.

"I'm sorry we put you through the operation in August if it's all been a waste of time," sobbed Mum.

"Oh, Mum. Please don't think that. I have had an amazing few months since then. Just think of the fun, the laughs, the walks, the swims, and the snacks. I've had the time of my life," I said, snuggling up to her.

The following day we travelled to a new vet place. Mum and Dad left me there while the lovely vet people took pictures of the inside of my body.

When Mum and Dad returned, they took me outside for a walk, but I didn't have the strength and sat down.

"Is it time, Beatrix?" Mum asked gently, kneeling beside me.

"Yes, Mum."

Dad knelt beside me too, and we all cuddled. We were all crying.

We all went back inside the vet place, where I felt very peaceful. Then a mist started to appear. I looked at Mum and Dad, tears flowing.

"It's OK. I can feel your love. It will go with me, and I will carry it forever," I whispered to my amazing human parents.

As I glanced over at Mum and Dad's slumped shoulders, I could see a bright light, and through the mist, I could see a wooden bridge.

I heard a gentle, familiar voice calling me, "Beinn Fhada. I'm waiting for you."

"Mummy, I'm coming," I cried out as I ran over the rainbow bridge.

Chapter 33

A New Puppy

1 February 2023

Flicking through photos of Beatrix on her phone, Debra thought she could hear a gentle humming, and a bright light shone through the front room window.

With a thud, a little black and white Border Collie, carrying a large stick in her mouth, landed at Debra's feet.

"Well, hello, little one. You look like a very special Border Collie," Debra said, gently rubbing the puppy's ears.

The puppy noticed the human lady was smiling at her and the puppy knew that she had reached her new, safe home.

The End

Author Notes

(Because sometimes Beatrix didn't know)

Covid 19 – At the time of the national lockdown due to the Coronavirus pandemic in March 2020, I was the girl living the dream of running my tearoom in Falkirk, Central Scotland, with my husband, Jim. It was a tiny tearoom with only sixteen seats, too small to be dog friendly, but we had a fabulous dog walker, Trisha from Campsie K9, who took Beatrix out each day when we were working.

When the tearoom was forced to close permanently due to the social distancing restrictions of Covid 19 rules, I found myself at home, not knowing what to do with myself. I felt lonely without the hustle and bustle of the tearoom, and the joy of sitting with friends and family, sharing tea and cake. Beatrix was also forced to adapt to a different life as she could no longer go out with Trisha and her dog friends.

During the lockdown, I used the time productively to finish my first book, The Magical Tearoom on the Hill, which included stories about adventures and mishaps I'd had with Beatrix.

Once that book had been published, Beatrix began talking to me about all the stories I'd written about her, but telling them from her viewpoint, which was often very different from my memories. That's when Beatrix had the idea of writing her own book, and she asked if I'd type it up for her if she told the stories in her own words.

I didn't hesitate. Writing this book for Beatrix has made me see the world differently through the eyes of a clever, sensitive, loving, energetic, intuitive, and bossy dog.

Beinn Fhada - is the name Beatrix was given at birth when she was registered with the Kennel Club.

Beinn Fhada (or long hill) is also the name of one of the 282 Scottish Munros. This is not known as one of the most majestic mountains, but it stands proud and provides a challenging climb. The only roadside view of Beinn Fhada is at Morvich, near the head of Loch Duich, heading up to the Northwest Coast of Scotland.

A Munro is a Scottish mountain with an elevation of more than 3,000 feet (914 metres). They're called Munros after London-born Sir Hugh Munro, a keen mountaineer who loved exploring and who charted Scotland's highest peaks in the late 1800s.

At the time of writing, I still have to climb Beinn Fhada.

Beatrix Potter - I fell in love with the Lake District as a teenager, and still dream of one day living somewhere in the Lakes, with a view of Langdale Pikes, to walk and cycle the same hills and fells, that Beatrix Potter held so close to her own heart.

I've always been in awe of Beatrix Potter. I still love to read the Peter Rabbit tales to anyone and everyone. Although we don't have a television at home, we have a projector and screen, and during the dark, chilly winter nights, I can often be found tucked up under a hand-crocheted blanket on the sofa, watching the original Tales of Peter Rabbit on DVD. The world is forever indebted to this lady, not just for her fabulous books, but also her foresight in protecting many of the hills and properties in the Lake District. When she died in 1943, Beatrix Potter (or Mrs Heelis) left four thousand acres of land and fourteen farms to the National Trust to ensure that the Lake District is still as beautiful for us now as when Beatrix Potter lived there.

Sally the Rottweiler – was a gentle giant. At first, I was terrified of her, but I soon realised there was nothing to fear. Sadly, Sally passed over the rainbow bridge in 2021, but her human mum was pleased to hear Beatrix would include Sally in her book.

Ben Lawers - features in many stories in this book. It's one of my favourite mountains, despite the catastrophes that have occurred up there with Beatrix and myself.

Ben Lawers is the tenth highest of the Scottish Munros, standing at 3,984 ft (1,214 m). To put it in perspective, Ben Nevis, Britain's highest mountain, is 4412 ft (1,345 m).

Being a high Munro is not why this is one of my go-to mountains. I love this range of mountains because of the remoteness you feel, even though you're only a short distance from civilisation. Our preferred route up the hill takes you first up the smaller Munro of Beinn Ghlas. There have been many times when we've not reached the summit of Ben Lawers due to weather or other reasons. Beatrix would always be disappointed not to reach the top but understood that sometimes the bravest thing to do is to turn around. The mountains will always be there for another day.

Two-Second Rule – This rule is aimed at stopping drivers from tailgating. You know what I mean - when the driver behind you drives so close to you that the only thing you can see in your rear-view mirror is the whites of their eyes.

To use the two-second rule, you should allow the vehicle in front of you to pass a fixed object, such as a lamp post or road sign, and then count to two. If you reach that same fixed object before you can count to two, you're driving too closely to the vehicle in front. Of course, the faster you drive, or if the weather conditions are poor, you should increase that gap even further. You want to be able to stop in time if the vehicle in front of you stops suddenly. Interestingly, I was chatting with one of my proof-readers who had worked for many years on the railways. He told me that the railway used to have a four-second rule for when they were working on the train lines – from the moment you hear the train coming down the track, you have four seconds before the train hits you!

Map Reading - I love them and can happily spend hours with a map on the floor, planning my route and imagining where I've been and where I might yet go.
Beatrix had her own built-in navigation system, so she didn't need to read the maps. Still, she read them patiently with me as I told her the names of the mountains and how high they were. I'm sure that in her mind, she thought she didn't need to know all this stuff, so she humoured me, and was probably just pretending to love the maps as much as I do.

Asdel - The story of the six little kittens takes place in this village in Northern Denmark I had visited years ago with my friend Katrine. I was entranced by this snow-covered village where I consumed copious amounts of food and drink that I didn't recognise, but I still managed to communicate with everyone there, even though I couldn't speak a word of Danish and they couldn't speak English.

Hygge - Beatrix says she understands the feeling of hygge at home with us. In Denmark, this is pronounced 'hooga' and translates simply into English as 'cosiness'. With long, dark, cold nights through the winter, things like having candles flickering, the log fire burning and snuggling under a blanket on the sofa drinking hot chocolate could give a feeling of 'hygge'. Beatrix always felt safe, warm, and loved at home, and that's why she says she knows the feeling of 'hygge'.

Gertrude – In chapter 23, Beatrix rescues a girl from drowning in Grasmere in the Lake District. Readers might have wondered how I chose the name of the drowning girl. I liked the idea of one amazing person being rescued by an equally fantastic dog.

In 1926, Gertrude Ederle became the first woman to swim across the English Channel from Dover to Cap Griz-Nez.

And that's why I chose the name, Gertrude.

Acknowledgements

It's easy to think a writer's job is solitary, and that we do the whole book thing ourselves. In one way or another, it involved many people in getting the words from my head into the book form you have before you.

The fabulous drawings were created by Jess from The Ricketty Desk. Thank you, they are perfect.

A huge thank you to everyone in Masterclass 2022/23 who gave me so much support to get this book over the line. Special thanks to Erika, Charmaine, Elaine, Jan, Judith, Lis, Mark, Pen, and Sam.

Thank you to everyone who listened, read, re-read, or re-listened to the stories and gave me unending support and feedback. Special thanks to Karen Lilley, Stephen, Teresa, Jim, Ruth, and Eddie.

To Rakesh, what can I say? Thank you for all the emergency phone calls and late-night meetings, fixing my computer and rescuing my work on more than one occasion, and then organising and setting up a new computer system for me.

To John, gone but never forgotten.

To Stephen, for your enthusiasm for my writing and for being somebody who cared. It made such a difference.

For Katrine, for taking me to Denmark all those years ago and encouraging the real me to emerge. Thank you.

For everyone who loved Beatrix nearly as much as I did, even though many of you only met her on social media. Thank you.

To the amazing team at Pets at Home in Bishopbriggs for the ongoing support, care, love, and treatment you gave Beatrix over her ten years with us. Thank you just doesn't seem enough.

To Kim and Sinclair for continuing to believe in me and supporting me along my new path in life.

To my family and friends, who have allowed Beatrix to include them in her tales, I love you all.

Jim, I told you Beatrix would be a great name for our new bundle of fun all those years ago. Thank you for being the linchpin of our lives and supporting our adventures together, even though we stressed you on so many occasions. And for all the picnics and tea! You are still the wind beneath my wings.

And of course, last but not least, to each and every one of you who have bought this book. You have ensured that Beatrix will be remembered for many years to come.

Bonus Section from Debra's first book,

The Magical Tearoom on the Hill

Recipes, Tales, and Adventures

The Girl Who Would Be Hannah

Today's hike was to go up Ben Ledi of the Trossachs, the hill you see when driving to Callander. Standing at 879 meters, it's a Corbett rather than a Munro, but still a good hike to the top. I knew I'd have a good day when I found my lost Maltesers from last week's walk in the bottom of my rucksack. That was the morning's first snack sorted.

It should be a forty-minute drive from my house to the car park just past Callander. Do you know how many people work at Prudential just off the A9? Well, after this morning's rush hour drive and long wait along the A9, I can hazard a good guess.

All that was forgotten once I'd parked the car by the Strathyre Lodges off the A85. Beatrix looked excitedly out of the car, recognising the scenery.

We were soon strolling along the track, me munching my newly found Maltesers and Beatrix finding herself a new stick.

I was chuckling at the weather warnings for temperatures of minus ten degrees, along with snow and ice this week. Looking up at the fells, there did seem to be some snow on the tops, but nothing to shout about. It was so mild, and before I got much further, I stopped to take off my gloves and neck warmer and tuck them safely away in my rucksack for later if needed.

After a bit of a pull up the forest, the climb eases as you meander your way up Stank Glen. It's so peaceful up through this glen that you can practically feel all of life's stresses and anxieties falling off you as you stroll along.

Before long, the climbing started again, and the snow level was reached. It was time to put on my crampons and an extra layer of clothing under my jacket as the wind started biting a little. The photo I never managed to get today as I was busy getting my crampons on was of Beatrix finding the bones of a dead sheep and running around it with its leg in her mouth. I'm glad that ITV News was not following me today as this would have made for a strange film – Yorkshire Lass, who would be Hannah Hauxwell, chasing her Border Collie to stop it from eating a dead sheep's leg. Fortunately, I had one of my Fab Slices with me, and Beatrix is quite partial to my baking, so I bribed her away from the leg.

I've walked up Ben Ledi many times in the past and was looking forward to reaching the top slopes to be rewarded with a good view of the many Munros you can usually see and imagining they would all be dusted with snow today. The forces of nature had other ideas for me though. Clouds were heading my way, but I thought nothing of it.

However, thick, freezing clouds quickly descended on us, enveloping us in a coldness I'd never experienced before. It reminded me of a scene from the film, The Day After Tomorrow. Beatrix was starting to look like a polar bear, my purple jacket was turning white, and ice had suddenly formed on my walking poles. I knew the summit couldn't be far away and decided to continue upwards, following in the footsteps of previous walkers, with my adrenaline just shy of turning into fear.

Turning around wasn't an option, as the route back was now so ill-defined in the clouds. I thought that if I could reach the top, I'd be out of the clouds, and once at the summit trig point, I'd be able to get my bearings and start the relatively straightforward descent.

Thankfully, like some miracle, in the distance I could just make out the summit trig point and made a bit of a spurt for this before it disappeared into the clouds again.

Sitting behind the stone pillar, out of the wind, I grabbed a quick cup of tea and a sandwich and gave Beatrix the lovely ham Mr M had packed for her. She did, of course, have half of my tuna butty too. Have you ever tried to resist a Border Collie's begging eyes – especially an ice-covered Border Collie's begging eyes? It's impossible.

Sitting there, I realised I could only see just past the end of my arm and had absolutely no idea which was the correct route off the mountain. Beatrix told me to take a deep breath, get out the map and compass and work out the direction. I did, but as I stood up, my plastic mat blew away. I asked Beatrix if she'd get it for me, but she just laughed.

I worked out the direction of travel required, but I was so unsure about my decision and had a bit of a panic. I got my phone out of my pocket – a full signal. I can't even get a signal in my front room, and here I am in white-out conditions on a mountain in the Trossachs with a full signal. Usually, I'd ring Mr M and chat with him, but thinking he'd have a major panic and have the mountain rescue called out for me, I did the next best thing and phoned my friend Crafty Sal. Salena's phone rang and rang but no answer. Salena's friendship membership was cancelled there and then.

Suddenly, out of the clouds appeared two icy figures, walking from precisely the same direction I had planned to go. Chatting with the two men about which way they'd come from; it was clear they had indeed come up the route I needed. The next time my compass reading skills are required, I'll have more faith in myself.

We set off again with Beatrix taking the lead, calling her back when she was getting too far in front for me to see her. Even in my anxious state, I was able to find the funny side of watching my ice dog slide herself down the hill as though she was on a sledge, run back up to me and then do it all again, having a roll in the snow for good measure. And there was me worrying that I would kill Beatrix with the cold.

We were soon able to descend from the summit at a fair rate, and the clouds began to open out a little, giving glimpses of the route ahead. Before long, we found ourselves out of the clouds and below the snow level. Stopping to take off my crampons, I took the opportunity to enjoy a break with my now lukewarm tea and the rest of my lunch.

Sitting there looking down on Loch Lubnaig in all its glory, I sighed with relief at surviving another one of my adventures and started to contemplate which bits I'd share with Mr M.

A couple of hours later, I was home, showered, changed, and being pampered by Mr M. If only he knew!

You might ask, why did our Fab Slice that I enjoyed on the hill become Charlotte's Fab Slice? Making these many years ago, long before we opened the tearoom, it was an adaptation of a recipe for something called energy bars. I found the bars way too sweet and sticky, so I put in less honey, sugar, and butter.

These became one of our favourite snacks for our cycle trips, with a big stash made for our five-week cycle tour of Scotland. They lasted a good couple of weeks but only thanks to me being very strict with Mr M, as he would have had these eaten within the first few days.

When we later opened the tearoom, I was sure these would be one of the most popular bakes. When the customers didn't seem interested in these delights, I couldn't understand it, and I discussed my problem with a few people. It transpired that the name was putting people off, as it sounded like something too healthy.

As a trial, I changed the name to Fruit and Nut Slice, and would you believe it, they sold like hotcakes? It's incredible that the name we give a cake or bake in the tearoom can hugely affect whether it's popular or not.

Not long after we started our Craft, Chat and Cake sessions in the tearoom, in popped this smiling, chatty young lady, Charlotte, who quickly became part of our tearoom family. If there was an award for the friendliest, happiest, most helpful person, Charlotte would win hands down. Charlotte is incredibly talented and crafty, and we are often in awe of her creations at the Craft, Chat and Cake Sessions. Embroidery, sewing, and drawing – all free-hand – are just some of her talents. She does lead us into temptation though, by showing us new things every time she comes along, leading to her nickname being The Temptress.

Charlotte likes nothing better than to have a pot of weak tea to accompany her crafting, chatting and cake. I could list hundreds of cakes that Charlotte loves, but the fruit and nut slices were one of her favourites, and when they were drizzled with chocolate, she described them as fab. That's it! Fab Slice for the name, and of course, Charlotte's Fab Slice.

They still sell like hotcakes in the tearoom, and it's not the first time I've hidden a couple away for myself for my walking or cycling trips.

Charlotte's Fab Slice

(gf/ df/ egg free)

Makes 28 squares

My recipe is for a large 16" x 12" tray bake.

Remember to adjust your quantities depending on your tin size if your tin is smaller.

Ingredients

350g Stork block
350g runny honey or golden syrup
525g gluten-free porridge oats
350g soft light brown sugar
2 pinches salt
175g dried apricots, chopped
175g dried dates, chopped
175g raisins
175g cherries, rinsed and chopped
100g chopped nuts
100g sunflower seeds
100g pumpkin seeds
175g desiccated coconut

1 x 16" x 12" traybake tin

Method

1 Preheat oven to 180c/160c fan oven.
2 Grease and line a tray bake tin with parchment paper.
3 Put the Stork and honey/golden syrup into a pan and heat gently on the hob until melted.
4 Once everything has melted, bring the mixture to a boil, and cook for a further two minutes, stirring continuously. Remove the pan from the heat and leave it to cool.
5 Put the remaining ingredients in a large bowl and mix well to combine.
6 Add the cooled honey/golden syrup mixture and mix until everything is well combined.
7 Tip the mixture into the prepared baking tray and spread with a spatula to level the surface.
8 Bake in the preheated oven for 20-30 minutes until golden brown.
9 Remove from the oven, mark into squares, and leave to cool in the tin.
10 Once cool, cut into squares.
11 For a special treat, drizzle some melted chocolate over your fab slices and leave to set before cutting.
12 Enjoy with a hot cup of tea and think of Debra and Mr M cycling over the Applecross Bealach na Ba Pass in the North of Scotland to earn an extra Fab Slice.

THIS IS NOT JUST A RECIPE BOOK; IT IS MOTHER MURPHY'S BOOK, WHERE GLUTEN-FREE AND DAIRY-FREE RECIPES, TALES AND ADVENTURES COME TOGETHER TO CREATE MAGIC.

Everyone needs a special space to feel loved and nurtured, where you can relax and let go of your worries and troubles. Debra Murphy fulfilled her dream and created Mother Murphy's Tearoom as a place where people could find solace and healing, where gluten-free and dairy-free are the norm and not the exception.

This little tearoom became a welcoming haven for the community, with lots of laughter and a few tears shared over tea and cake. Friendships developed as people connected, told their stories, and helped each other to solve problems and feel better. It was a magical tearoom.

Now you can enjoy the warm, cosy feeling and get to know Debra, Mr M, Beatrix and all the lovely people in the tearoom family.

The Magical Tearoom on the Hill is a book to curl up with a cup of tea and a slice of cake (that you can even bake yourself). With a fabulous mix of stories to warm your heart and delicious gluten-free and dairy-free recipes to create beautiful cakes and bakes, you too, can create your own magical space.

The
Magical Tearoom
on the Hill
Recipes, Tales and Adventures
Debra Murphy

Milton Keynes UK
Ingram Content Group UK Ltd.
UKHW041859071124
450904UK00003B/146

9 781838 283087